Making scorin

"You have to be the sexiest sports reporter I've ever met. I would really like to kiss you. Would that be okay with you?"

Olivia should have turned away, but she couldn't find the willpower. Hatch's kiss was soft and gentle, a mere brush of lips, a touch of flesh. Then it was over, but she wanted more. A lot more. She could feel this spinning out of control, and she was powerless to stop it.

"If you invite me in, I'm not going to turn you down."

She was crazy to do this. She hadn't recovered from the burns left by her relationship with Daniel. Why on earth was she looking to jump into the fire again? She'd never in a million years considered herself open to some kind of a second chance at a true relationship. But idiot that she was, she didn't even hesitate, just nodded, and ushered him inside.

She didn't do this. Never had, even before she met Daniel. She was never sexually impulsive, certainly not where something important was concerned. But now she didn't seem able to help herself. She tried to remind herself not to screw up her situation, but her long months of need coalesced in the center of her body. She was about to do something stupid.

She nodded. "Yes. Please come in."

Numbers Game

by

Desiree Holt & Liz Crowe

Numbers Game

Contact Information: info@thewildrosepress.com

Cover Art by *Diana Carlile*

The Wild Rose Press, Inc.
PO Box 708
Adams Basin, NY 14410-0708

Visit us at www.thewildrosepress.com

Publishing History
First Edition, 2021
Print ISBN 978-1-5092-3644-2
Digital ISBN 978-1-5092-3645-9
Published in the United States of America

Dedication

This book is dedicated to the Brothers Harbaugh.
John—Head Coach, Baltimore Ravens
Jim—Head Coach, University of Michigan (Desiree's
Alma Mater)

Author Acknowledgments

Desiree Holt

To Liz Crowe for putting up with my crazy calendar and crazier deadlines as we worked to create this work from our hearts.

And to my team, without whom none of this would ever happen—Maria Connor, Margie Hager, Steven Horwitz, and of course, the fabulous Diana Carlile whose patience and editorial talent are what make stories into great books. You all rock.

~*~

Liz Crowe

I would like to thank Desiree Holt for even considering this crazy idea of writing a football-based romance together, not to mention helping find NUMBERS GAME a wonderful publishing home. And many thanks to Diana Carlile at The Wild Rose Press, Inc. for humoring us both.

Chapter One

Olivia Grant took a deep breath and let it out, hoping to steady her sudden attack of the jitters.

Okay, Olivia, this is make it or break it. Don't blow your big chance.

Because, after all, how many chances did someone get?

Starting over when she was almost forty wasn't the easiest thing in life, especially after Daniel. She'd been lucky to get the job with the local network television station. It had taken all the remnants of her nearly-destroyed self-confidence to apply for it. It had taken another dose to approach the brass about this project.

She had one goal—to revive her career and her reputation. Nothing else was important and she wouldn't allow anything to get in the way. But what if she couldn't pull it off? If she blew this, where would she turn next?

That made today's appointment even more important. The moment she heard that Duncan "Hatch" Hatcher, sexy football hero of local Lakeview University and pro football, was returning to Lakeview University to revive their flagging football program, the idea for the documentary popped into her head. This wasn't the first documentary she'd produced, but it was for sure the most important. She couldn't afford an attack of nerves right now. If she failed, Daniel would be proven right, and she refused to let that happen.

I'm calm. I'm calm.

But when she looked in the mirror, the lie was all over her face.

Go ahead and tell yourself that all you want. You can't get away from the fact your nerves are doing a jitterbug.

Well, maybe because I'm getting past my sell-by date, and if this doesn't revive my career, it might kill it. I'm certainly not the twenty-something, hotshot female sports reporter whose career is on the rise.

A career nearly destroyed by the biggest bastard in the world.

Both her ill-fated marriage to Daniel Forrest and the subsequent messy divorce had derailed her career. With his insufferable ego and his conviction that he could do anything to anyone and get away with it, he'd done his best to obliterate all she'd done as a serious sports journalist. His arrogant obsession with controlling everything about her, from the way she walked and talked to her on-air content and how she presented it, made her life a nightmare. He just about killed her career that first time around. Thank god she'd found the strength to leave at last.

If she'd never married him, who knew where she'd be by now?

One of the first things she'd done after the divorce was legally take back her own last name.

"Good riddance," Daniel had snapped when he called her about it. "I don't need people associating us together anymore."

Then why don't you leave me alone, she'd wanted to ask.

Yeah. So. Time to focus.

Hatch might be the hottest guy on earth, but she had no time for that. None. Zero. Zip.

So just shut up, Olivia, and get on with it.

Yes, get on with it. She wasn't getting anywhere staring in the mirror, talking to herself.

Ding ding ding!

Her cell phone buzzed across the top of her dresser, vibrating with the ring of an incoming call. She looked at the readout. Of course, Lee Ann would be calling right now. Right this very minute. But no way could she ignore the call. The woman had been there through every step of the nasty divorce, the collapse of Olivia's career, and the painful process of rebuilding it. Olivia was sure, without Lee Ann, she'd never have gotten her life together again.

Sighing, she pressed Accept.

"I'm put together and getting ready to wow him," she said, skipping a greeting. "All is good."

"Just making sure. You can do this, Liv. Don't let that bastard's attitude take this away from you."

She heard the concern in Lee Ann's voice. Her best friend had been her strength and support through some seriously tough times. She was the only one who knew all the nasty details of Daniel Forrest's campaign to ruin her and prevent her from ever succeeding again. Lies, lies, and more lies. But people paid attention to a man in the industry with his position and money. Without Lee Ann, she'd probably be writing cut lines for some small county newspaper's practically defunct website.

"You can rest assured I'm set to go." She checked her watch. "And I'd better head out or I'll be late."

3

"I saw those clips of your subject on television. He's still a damn fine-looking specimen," Lee Ann teased. "Plus—bonus—I hear he's divorced now." She paused. "Like you."

Olivia gritted her teeth. "His looks are only important in the way he photographs. This is business, not pleasure. And important business at that. If I drop the ball here, I'm done. You know that. And Daniel will have won again."

Lee Ann sighed. "If you say so. Anyway, I just wanted to tell you good luck, and I want lots of details. Oh." She laughed softly. "And text me a shot of Hatch if you can. I'm not too old to appreciate hot male flesh."

"Uh huh. I'm hanging up now. Call you later."

She really needed this to go well today. She was getting herself back on track but was acutely aware there wouldn't be many more chances like this. *No blowing this one.*

She took one last, quick look at herself, turning to catch a rear view. Okay, good to go. Slacks and a classy sweater, not too casual for her and not too dressy for her meeting. New, shorter haircut that had her dark blonde curls falling smoothly into place. Just a touch of makeup.

Not bad, Olivia Grant.

Thank heaven, at thirty-seven, she still had the complexion of a younger woman.

It was all about age. There'd always be someone younger, more energetic, more determined. But she had experience and knowledge, and she wasn't bad-looking. If only she was more petite or her butt was—

Oh, shut up, Olivia. You're not auditioning for a

4

centerfold. As long as you brush your teeth and comb your hair, you'll be fine.

After all, hadn't she been eating healthy and exercising regularly for her entire natural life?

Damn those male sportscasters and reporters who rode their careers well into their sixties while women seemed to have a short shelf life.

Okay. Enough.

Purse, keys, phone, messenger bag. Check, check, check, check. Then she was in her car and headed out to the highway.

"I'll be happy to meet with you," Coach Duncan "Hatch" Hatcher had said when she called him. "As long as you're prepared. I didn't get here in time for early spring practice, so this next month before the first game will be intense. I have a lot of work to do shaping the team. My time will be limited, but I promise I'll give you what I can. Scott and I both think this will be great for Lakeview."

She'd make it work. She had to.

The hero had come home, back to work his magic with the school where he got started. He was a legend in both college and professional football, a fact enhanced by his incredible good looks. Looks that had only gotten better with age. A newly crowned king couldn't have been given a better reception. Or had heavier expectations draped over his broad shoulders.

Sort of like where she was.

At forty-two, he was stepping into an awfully bright spotlight, and she wanted to help him maximize the opportunity by telling his story. Not to mention establishing herself again as a legit producer.

Just don't screw this up.

She'd been repeating this mantra silently for the past week, ever since she got the go ahead for the project. Channel Five would run the finished video in primetime with the agreement that, if a major sports network was flashed out by it, they'd pick it up.

She'd done her homework. She was prepped. She'd watched old videos of games he both played and coached and surfed through every article on him that she could find. She thought it odd there was a noticeable lack of information about his marriage except for the wedding and nothing about the divorce. That tickled her curiosity, but she'd vowed to stay away from personal stuff. She was still recovering from the unwanted publicity surrounding hers. She wasn't about to do anything to cause Hatch to back out of this.

Otherwise, she was as ready as she could possibly be, so there was no reason for her attack of nerves. Damn Daniel Forrest anyway for making her doubt herself and feel so conflicted. It took every bit of willpower not to pull to the side of the road and throw up, or scream. Or both.

Cruising through the campus was good medicine for her. So many memories of her years as a student athlete here came dancing back to remind her how much fun she'd had. Students were everywhere, their energy electrifying the air. Olivia loved the excitement and vitality of campus life. How fitting that this would be the place where she began the next phase of her life.

She drove slowly around to the far side of campus where the field was located, pulled into the parking area, and eased into an empty slot. The stadium was brand new since she'd been a student here. A billboard with a field of red and a black jaguar leaping across the words Jaguar Nation crowned the structure. And now the most vaunted Jaguar had come home.

She sat a moment, waiting for her nerves to settle. Then, taking a deep breath and letting it out nice and slow, she climbed out of her SUV, grabbed her messenger bag, and slipped the strap over her head. *Go time.*

As she crossed the pavement, the sound of a whistle blowing and of voices shouting filled the fresh spring air. At the gate used by media and other authorized visitors, she flashed her credentials at the guard and stepped out onto the rich turf of Jaguar Stadium. Big Red, as it was called, after one of the school colors. When she found herself on the sidelines, nervous excitement sizzled through her veins.

Spring practice was in full-out mode. She could sense the energy pulsing from the field. Hatch and several of his coaches stood on the sidelines, watching in silence. He had his whistle clamped between his teeth, something she'd seen in pictures of him at games he'd coached.

As she headed toward him, the shrill sound of that whistle pierced the air, followed by shouts of, "Do it again. And do it right this time. Remember the diagrams," from various assistants.

Some of the assistant coaches glanced at her as she eased her way along the sidelines, but she just smiled and nodded. She'd cleared this with Scott Durbin, the athletic director, just as she told Hatch she would, so she moved with confidence. She found a spot where she had a good view but didn't get in anyone's way and just took a moment to watch the man himself.

Okay, it was official. He *was* still a damn fine

specimen, as Lee Ann had reminded her earlier. Age had only improved his model-worthy looks, and maturity gave him a new, rich kind of sexiness. His trademark khakis showcased long legs and a really nice ass—*Yes, ass, Olivia. You're old enough to use that word.*—while his black Jaguars T-shirt outlined broad shoulders and set off the musculature of his arms. Quarterback arms, still in shape after all this time. A black Jaguars cap sat atop his neatly trimmed dark brown hair. He'd look fantastic in the documentary.

A faint zing rippled through her, one she hadn't felt in forever. Damn it, why did her libido choose this minute to show up after being in cold storage for so long? The thing she really couldn't afford was some kind of physical attraction to her subject. *Discipline*, she reminded herself. *Hold it together, girl. There is way too much at stake.*

At that moment, Hatch blew his whistle and motioned to the players on the field. They jogged over to where he stood. Both the quarterbacks coach and the offensive line coach joined him so Olivia dug her small camera out of her messenger bag and shot some pictures. Everyone else might use cell phones today, but she still liked the feel and the quality of a real camera. At the television station, the younger staff members thought it was cute to tease her about being a dinosaur. Well, this dinosaur still had teeth and she planned to use them.

As Hatch and his coaches talked with the team, she walked slowly along the sidelines, snapping shot after shot while keeping out of everyone's way. She'd take a lot more before she sat down with her cameraman to plot out the actual video. These would give her a good sense of the team dynamics and help her formulate the message she wanted to send.

At one point, Hatch turned around to take something from the student behind him and spotted her standing there. He smiled, and a feeling hit her like warm sunshine, spreading through her body.

When he turned his attention back to practice, Olivia, fascinated, watched him interact with the players, kept snapping away with her camera. She wasn't aware how much time had passed as Hatch worked his magic with the players. Then suddenly, he was high-fiving all of them, shaking hands with the coaches, and they all jogged off the field into the locker room. All except Hatch, who headed straight for her, smiling.

"Hello," he said, his voice rough, as if he'd been asleep. He stuck out his hand as he approached her. "Olivia Grant, right? I'm not sure why anyone wants to do a documentary about me, but if it will help the school and the team, I'm all for it. Why don't you come on into my office? You can tell me exactly what you're looking for in the visuals and how much of my time you think you'll need."

She nodded, his welcoming attitude relaxing her slightly, taking the edge off her nerves. This might go well after all.

"As I said when I called, the A.D. assured me he'd spoken to you about clearing some time for me. And that I'd be able to come to the practices."

"He did." They came to an open door with the words *Coach Hatcher* on it. "Let's go in and sit down."

Olivia looked around, taking in the space where he spent so much of his time. There were pictures on the wall of him scoring his final winning touchdown for Lakeview his senior year, the game that sent the team to its first of several post-season bowl games. Of him with his coach and the president of the university. Others cataloguing his career in pro football, both as player and coach. The newest was one of him with this team, taken the day he was introduced to them.

"I'm sorry I don't have more time today," he told her, "but I'll give you what I can. Then, if you can let me know what you're looking for from me, we can work out a schedule."

She nodded. "Understood. I'm grateful for any time you can make available. A lot of this will be video of the team interspersed with clips of my interviews with you. Will that work?"

He grinned. "We'll make it work. Have a seat and fire away."

"Is it okay if I record this? My memory isn't what it used to be."

Good going, Olivia. Make yourself sound old and decrepit.

"Sure. No problem."

She opened the recording app on her phone and placed it on his desk. Here came Chapter One in her campaign to redeem herself both personally and professionally. She'd better not blow it.

"My first question is more to satisfy my own curiosity. How old were you when you started calling yourself Hatch?"

He chuckled. "Ever since I discovered I'd been named after my two grandfathers—Duncan and Jerome—and decided they made me sound too old."

"I'm sure a lot of people have asked you this. What

10

made you choose to come back to Lakeview rather than accept one of the other, more lucrative offers you had?"

He was silent for a long moment, staring at all the pictures before he answered her.

"Lakeview's had some tough years recently. The shine is off the apple, so to speak, compared with how it was ten years ago. Scott, along with the president of the athletic association and two major donors, convinced me I could be the one to bring it back. I'm definitely going to give it my best shot. I guess you could say it's an emotional thing."

"How do you feel about this team? You arrived after signing season, none of the players, including the newest ones, are your recruits."

He rubbed his jaw, pausing, as if carefully choosing his words. "I've been able to assess the team in practice, and we have a lot of young talent out there to work with. Luckily, they're enthusiastic and feel they have something to prove. Feel free to come to as many practices as you like. I'll set it up with security."

"Thank you. I appreciate that." She checked off a few more questions before turning off the recorder. "That's it for the moment. I have more, but you said that you have limited time today. I'm sure there'll be additional questions as we go along. If you can give me some idea of when you'd be available, I can put together a schedule for you."

He flashed her that amazing grin once more. "I can work with that. Now, how about telling me the way you see this documentary laying out."

"I want a double hook. I think it will capture a wider audience and really spike people's interest."

He raised one eyebrow, a gesture that gave her an

utterly inappropriate thrill. "Like what?"

"The desire of the university to restore its football program to its former glory paired with the journey of Duncan Hatcher from player to coach and what that journey has meant. Personally as well as professionally."

Again, he was silent for a long moment. Then he picked up a pen from the desk surface and began flipping it back and forth between his fingers. The muscles in her stomach tensed as she got the feeling there was something hidden beneath the surface here. Something that would screw things up. Oh, please, no.

"Please don't take this the wrong way, but I'd like for you to leave my personal life out of this as much as possible. I still believe the constant lack of privacy and the pressures of my…situation played a big part in breaking up my marriage."

Olivia studied his face. There was something closed off about his expression when he referenced his ex-wife. She had a feeling there was a lot more to the story than privacy issues and pressure, but she wasn't here to get into that aspect of things. And if she didn't respect his boundaries, he'd kill the documentary in a hot minute.

Still, her reporter's nose was twitching, and she made a mental note to do some research on his personal life, even if just for herself.

"What about your parents or either of your siblings? Are they off limits, also? Your brother is a well-known coach, and your sister is married to—"

"Minimal exposure for them, and I get to approve whatever it is before you air anything." His face was flushed. "Sorry. I didn't mean to interrupt you or be rude. But it's something I'm firm on, okay?"

She cleared her throat. "That's not a problem. I'm not here to produce an exposé, only a story that will garner interest for the football program and show how an icon can make a big difference."

At that he laughed, again treating her to that slight tremor of something she shouldn't feel. "I don't know if I'd call myself an icon, but if I can do anything to promote this team, I'm all for it."

"You said you only had a little time today, but I prepared a list of questions. I can go over them with you and then email them to you if you like."

"Sure. Let's have it."

Olivia reached into her messenger bag, pulled out her tablet, and opened the document with her notes. She explained how she had outlined the script and what visuals she'd need to best carry the message. And the kind of questions she'd be asking him.

Hatch nodded as she spoke, making notes on his own tablet. "Why don't you email them to me anyway? Maybe I'll think of something else to add." He wrote something on the back of a business card and handed it to her. "Use my personal email and my number."

Her eyes widened as she took the card from him. "Your personal number?"

He shrugged. "I like to think I'm a good judge of people. My senses tell me I can trust you."

"Thank you. I promise not to betray that trust." She leaned back in her chair. "I'd like to come to as many practices as possible, and of course, the games will be an important component."

He pulled over a scratch pad and wrote something on it. "I'll have the department office get you the credentials you'll need to be a sideline reporter for the games. I watched you today. You're savvy enough to know how to stay out of the way and still get what you need."

"Thank you. I appreciate it."

She had to tamp down the thrill of excitement that tickled her yet again.

"When do you plan to release this?"

"I'm hoping to have it ready to go at the end of the regular season, before the bowl games, since I'm sure the Jaguars will get a great invite this season. We can always add that bit after the fact."

Hatch nodded. "Scott says the video is self-funded. Is that right?"

Olivia nodded. "That's correct. It will run on Channel Five, but I also plan on shopping it to major sports networks."

He grinned. "Looking for a foot in the door, right?"

"I am." She lifted her chin and stiffened her back. "I hope you aren't one of those men who think women can't produce good sports material."

He smiled, then laughed, surprising her. "My mother and my sister would tan my hide if they thought I felt that way. No, I've seen damn good video and some excellent reporting by women in the industry. I just want to know where you're going with this. It will help me make sure you get what you're looking for."

"Thank you. And thanks for making time for me tomorrow. I know your schedule's very tight right now."

"Then you'll understand if I have to cut out any time."

She nodded. "I will."

"So." He leaned back in his chair. "Tomorrow?"

"Sure. Thanks for making the time."

"You're welcome." He paused and seemed to be studying her through narrowed eyes. "Listen. They've got me doing a bunch of charity events that you might want to get some shots of. I'm sure the folks sponsoring them wouldn't mind. The first one is a 10k race on Sunday."

Olivia swallowed her smile.

"Actually, I'm running in it myself, although I'm sure I won't be anywhere close to your time."

His eyes lit up. "Yeah? You are? I bet you'll do better than you think."

"We'll see. But I can have my cameraman there to get some action shots. And Hatch? Thanks again for agreeing to do this."

An undecipherable expression flitted across his face, there one minute and gone the next. "I'm totally on board. Scott and I agree it will be a great way to give the program a shot in the arm. Let people know things are moving forward here. Help the program."

He rose, signaling their meeting was over. "See you then."

She gathered her messenger bag, practically dancing her way out of the office. She felt like pumping her fist and shouting, *Yes! Yes! Yes! Take that, Daniel.*

Her good mood lasted until she reached her car and found Bert Hoekstra leaning against it, hands shoved into his pants pockets. He had been a thorn in her side almost from the first day she'd begun reporting sports on television. The freelance reporter had a well-deserved reputation for being a slimeball and muckraker who was now denied access to almost every team in the Division I College Sports. He wasn't interested in anything except digging up the deepest secrets of players and sports personnel, and his enemies would fill Jaguar Stadium.

He'd certainly done a number on her about her divorce and how it affected her job. She couldn't let him screw this up, even though his influence was mostly limited to his podcast and the accompanying, always negative, twitter feed, both his and those of his rabid minions.

"I think you're standing in my way," she told him. "Move."

"Now, is that any way to talk to a fellow reporter?" Even his smile seemed slimy. "You seem to have everyone's ear here. I thought maybe you could get me into one of the practices and possibly a game."

"Sorry. I'm not in charge of credentials."

She punched the button to unlock her car and yanked the door open, forcing him to move. She thought of a million things she'd love to say to him, none of which would do her any good. Instead, she cranked the engine and backed out of her space, pulling out of the parking lot with a little more force than necessary. When she looked in her rearview mirror, Bert still stood there, watching her.

With a deliberate effort, she focused on mentally reviewing today's meeting with Hatch and the documentary. This was her ticket to re-establish herself and, hopefully, open some important doors. No way was she letting a jerk like Bert Hoekstra screw it up. Or that asshole, Daniel. He'd done enough to ruin her life already.

But a nauseating thought hit her as she left campus.

Could Hoekstra be working with Daniel on this to once again destroy her career? She drew in a deep breath and let it out slowly. She was not going to let him ruin her life. Not again.

****

Hatch sat down at his desk again, eyes focused on the doorway, brain still processing the meeting with Olivia Grant. The sensation gave him a bizarre, full-body shiver. Something he'd been missing these last few years, in the relentless spotlight of pro football and the fallout disaster of his divorce.

When Scott Durbin set up this arrangement, he hadn't bothered to warn him how gorgeous Olivia Grant was. He wouldn't have refused to help with the project, but at least he'd have been prepared. He had one thing on his mind these days—rebuilding his career as a football giant and, this time, without the stupid mistakes that had nearly destroyed him. But at this moment, he felt sideswiped by her. Overwhelmed, maybe, was a better word. And he needed to maintain his focus on the task at hand.

He was damn lucky to have this chance. His addiction to gambling that started with friendly poker games had grown until he could never resist the lure of anything to do with numbers and odds. And the lure of online gaming only made it a hundred times worse. He was lucky he had a fat salary, or he'd have ended up broke. But it had cost him his marriage and his job as a pro coach. He was grateful that everyone had agreed to keep a lid on the real story as long as he agreed to walk away from the job—not to mention his marriage—and deal with his addiction.

Lakeview was his best—okay, his only—shot to

rebuild his life, which at forty-two wasn't the easiest thing in the world. He was grateful he was in a profession where his age was considered a virtue since it implied experience. He'd do well to remember that the only numbers he could focus on from here on out were those used to call the different plays. He also had to make sure Olivia Grant never uncovered the truth about how he'd derailed his entire life. If that happened, he'd have to find a hole to crawl into.

He thought about his first day back on campus when he stood in the center of the football field emblazoned with the red and white artsy rendering of a jaguar. He'd completed a full, three-hundred-sixty-five degree turn, taking in the seating, expanded in recent years thanks to booster enthusiasm during a spate of victorious years about a decade after he graduated. Those, however, had been followed by a longer streak of ignominious defeats.

He could still recall the smells, the sights, the sound, and the bone-shattering cold of one particular game day. He smiled and picked up the football he always kept on his desk, hit with the long-embedded muscle memory of throwing. He gripped it, pressing his fingertips into the laces the way he had for so many years. He didn't throw much anymore due to his doctor's nagging about his shoulder. But he held onto it now, knowing that the feel of it was always good for helping him focus.

He thought about the end zone, recalling it as his ultimate goal for so damn many years of his life. A goal he'd been so focused on it had dominated and ruined his marriage. He was pretty sure he and Alex could have worked through the gambling thing if he had been

18

a better husband to her and less consumed with success on the field.

"You don't give a rip about anything but that damn game," his ex-wife used to say, half-kidding at first…until she wasn't. *"If it doesn't involve turf, pads, helmets, X's and O's, you don't want to hear about it."*

He'd wanted to remind her this was the man she'd married, but in the aftermath of the divorce, he realized what a selfish bastard he'd been. It was sort of hard not to care, given that it had been his one and only mission for so many years. To start at a Division One school. To play professionally. To coach a pro team—albeit for a fairly brief, super shiny, moment. His shoulders slumped at the ghostly memory of her angry voice.

She'd been right, of course. His priorities had been skewed in favor of his career success, at the sacrifice of other parts of his life. He was self-aware enough to understand and accept that.

Of course, that other reason for the failure of his marriage and the brevity of his seemingly stellar career as a coach was one he was grateful had never leaked. One he'd managed to keep so secret, sometimes even he forgot about it. Until he'd open up his laptop and read the daily mantra he had plastered on the opening screen.

"One bet might as well be one hundred."

He shook his head. *Let it go, Hatcher. You have way too much work to do and an image to re-establish to be mooning around out here.*

His saving grace was his love for this damn game. He'd made it his job to understand football the way an engineer builds a bridge or a car. This job at Lakeview would be tough. It was major change without a doubt, but after the year he'd just had, he was more than ready.

"So, Coach, how did it go?"

He looked up to see Scott Durbin, his new boss, standing in the doorway. "Hey, Scott. I think it went well."

"You ready for this craziness?"

He grinned. "Born that way."

He wasn't sure he meant it. But it sounded good. He was nervous as hell, truth be told. After a solid two weeks of media hype, press conferences, podcasts, photo ops, grip and grins, random fundraisers, and all the usual hullabaloo that went along with being the newly named, returning hero-style head coach of his alma mater, he was ready to coach some damn ball. Bring on the x's and o's.

Which was one reason for his rare case of nerves. When he'd been a coach in the pros before everything had gone to hell in a handbasket, he hadn't felt this level of power over the lives of so many young men—kids, really, all of them. It was a heady, terrifying sensation. But he'd made it clear to each and every one of them what he would do for them, as long as they held up their end of the bargain.

"Well, guess I'd better let you get to it then," Scott said.

He winced at the memory of how goofy he must have sounded to the lovely woman he was going to be having a fair bit of contact with this season. Olivia Grant was, without a doubt, beautiful, not to mention sexy as hell. She was a natural reporter, putting him at ease, even in the face of his high-school-ish reaction to her at first. But dear Lord, the crap he'd said? That shit about her being "better than she thought" at the race?

And "looking for a foot in the door"? He'd sounded about as slick as the grandpas he'd been named for.

He groaned and pressed his forehead to the leather blotter on his new desk. After his divorce, he'd made a point not to notice women, something that was a bit of a self-imposed penalty. But there was no not noticing Olivia. Her soft, dark blonde hair that kept dropping over one of her deep green eyes as she'd look down at her notes, then back up at him. That smile, and those full, barely lip-sticked lips. And there was no denying she had a body that would be hard to shake out of his brain. Scott had told him she used to play soccer here, a few years behind him as an undergrad. How he'd not known her... Granted, he hadn't been a big partier then, kept mostly to himself and his close group of friends and, as always, focused on the game.

But damn. He'd missed out on something then, without a doubt. He felt his face flush red and his entire body begin to react in ways that didn't really serve him well as a fully grown man, with plenty of experience under his belt, so to speak.

Thankfully, she'd left before he could embarrass himself any more.

Home. Shower. Beer. Stare at a string of old movies on the giant television screen. Anything to get the lovely Olivia Grant and all her many attributes out of his head. She was, after all, the media. And everyone knew how he felt about the media.

It was get a grip time—on all parts of himself.

This was his chance at redemption. The opportunity was a godsend, considering the sorry state he'd left his life in on the west coast, and he didn't intend to do anything to screw it up. He couldn't afford to get distracted by a single thing. But how the hell was he going to do that when Olivia Grant might prove to be the biggest distraction of all?

Chapter Two

Why hadn't a man like Duncan Hatcher come into her life years ago? Why now, when she had to focus exclusively on her video?

Olivia stood at her kitchen counter sipping from her mug of coffee and wondering at the timing of things in her life. Why now, when her one purpose was to redeem her reputation and hit the big time, had a man like Hatch been placed temptingly in her path? She had to remind herself that while she might be attracted to him, that didn't mean it went both ways. It probably didn't.

Her sleep last night had been restless, every scene from yesterday replayed over and over in her mind. Had she asked the right questions? Been professional enough? Been well prepared? Lord knew, she'd studied everything she could get her hands on about Duncan Hatcher way in advance.

As if that wasn't bad enough, her dreams had been interspersed with images of Coach Duncan Hatcher at football practice, the hard muscles of his body visible in khaki pants and a Jaguars shirt. When he strode down the sidelines or jogged out to the field, she could almost see the flex of his thigh muscles and his...

Oh, god! She had to stop thinking like this. She had no room in her life for it, at least right now. Maybe never. Would she ever be ready to take chance on a relationship again?

Every minute of yesterday's meeting remained etched in her brain like an engraving. Age hadn't lessened his sex appeal one little bit. If anything, maturity had enriched it. And damn, there was plenty of it. Okay, she could admire him from a distance and think about him when she was alone. That was it. Period. He had agreed to do this documentary, and she had to be the total professional about it.

Of course. Yes. She could. Really.

She finished scrolling through the notes on her tablet for today's session with Hatch, focusing on what was important. Then she rinsed out her coffee mug and popped into the bathroom for one last check of her makeup and outfit. Like yesterday, feminine but not over the top. Basic but not too plain. Her personal appearance had to convey just the right message to him and be professional enough to settle her nerves. Daniel had certainly chipped away at her confidence about the way she dressed.

Despite herself, though, she couldn't help wondering what kind of women appealed to Hatch. All her background info on him was what she called "flat." She had a file jammed with all his football stats, both as a player and a coach, as well as a list of community activities he'd lent his support to. But it was all one-dimensional. Nothing about his personal life. Almost as if he didn't have one.

She was still curious as to why none of her research turned up more than scant information on his marriage, his divorce, and his ex-wife. There were plenty of photos of Alexandra Hatcher. She was tall with midnight black hair that framed a sculpted face, and she had a body Olivia would kill for. In the few shots of them together, there hadn't been any evidence of animosity or trouble in paradise. Absolutely nothing about the reason for the divorce, and that was a puzzle. Reporters, no matter what field they covered, were always gossip-hungry. She filed that mystery away in a corner of her mind for further research, although it had more to do with her personal curiosity than the documentary.

This was about Hatch the coach. Period.

On the drive to the campus, she replayed her last conversation with him. Had he sounded a little weird earlier when she they discussed today's session, or was it just her imagination? She had one hour with him, and she planned to make the most of it, show him she wasn't into wasting his time.

Today, they'd also begin collecting B roll—video clips that would show him in all his activities as coach. Drew, her cameraman, had an outline of what she wanted to accomplish today and was meeting her at eleven at the athletic offices. The day was gorgeous, sunny with a slight breeze, and low humidity. Perfect day for shooting video.

When she pulled into a parking space, she was pleased to see Drew already there, standing by his van.

"I want to go in and let the coach know we're here," she told him. "Come on. I'll introduce you, tell him what we're looking for today before we actually start shooting."

"Good." He reached into the van for his camera bag. "I can check the light and angles in his office."

She took out her tablet and reviewed with him one last time what they were looking for today—shots of

Hatch in his office and of the campus itself. And, if Hatch agreed, of practice this afternoon. In his office, she wanted shots of her talking to him, asking him some questions, letting him tell her what his goals were with this team.

"Got it." He gave her a nod.

Of course he got it. He'd been doing this for a long time, which was why she'd begged hard to use him for this. Her boss had agreed, with the unspoken caveat that he expected the finished product to blow his socks off.

Olivia was sure she hadn't been this nervous since her first year out of college.

Stop it! You're a professional.

She needed to keep reminding herself of that. And that she wasn't here to let her mouth water over her subject. Her future was riding on this documentary, not on Hatch's hot ass.

She drew in a deep breath and headed into the building, Drew right on her heels. Hatch was at his desk, one of his assistant coaches next to him. He was reading over Hatch's shoulder and nodding his head. Olivia wasn't sure if she should interrupt so she just tapped lightly on the door jamb.

"Yes?" Hatch looked up, frowning. When he saw her, he gave her a slightly distracted smile before glancing down at his desk. "Is it noon already?"

"Yes." She nodded. "Sorry. I promise we'll be quick about this."

"No, don't worry. I set aside plenty of time."

The tension eased from her body, and she felt herself relax. "Great. Thanks." She gestured at Drew. "This is my cameraman, Drew Maguire. While you and I chat for a minute, he'll check lights and camera

26

angles. I wanted to go over with you exactly what I want to cover today." She managed a smile. "Make the best use of our time here."

"Can you just give me a second? Then I'm all yours."

"Of course."

All hers? If only.

She stood out of the way while Drew did his thing and Hatch finished up his business with his assistant coach.

Hatch made a note, then put down his pen. "All set. Thanks for being so patient."

"No, I'm the one thanking you for giving me the time. I know these are especially busy days for you, taking over the program and designing what it will be going forward."

"Let's hope I get the job done. Now. What's on your list for today?"

She pulled her tablet from her messenger bag and brought up the file she wanted. As she leaned over to point things out to him, the scent of his soap, or maybe his shampoo, drifted across her nostrils and—

Oh, god! What was the matter with her? Gritting her teeth, she forced herself to focus on what she was doing.

"The first thing I want to do," she explained, "is get some sound bytes of you here in the office. Maybe with your work spread out on the desk. I'd like you to tell us what it's like being back at your alma mater where you were such a hero, what's changed and what's the same, and why you chose to come here rather than accept any of the other offers you had. That's the first thing people will want to know."

Did he actually tense up, or did she imagine it? Was there something, as some had speculated, that no one but Hatch himself knew? Well, if there was, as long as it didn't have a negative impact on his coaching or damage the documentary, what did it matter, anyway?

He looked at her and flashed his trademark panty-melting grin.

And by the way, who said her panties couldn't melt at her age?

"Sure." He winked. "I can do that. I think I've answered that question at least ten times a day since the announcement was made, anyway."

"Good. That's good." She tucked her hair behind one ear, a nervous habit she was trying to break. "Then I'd like a little clip of you talking about your plans for the coming year and what you've gotten so far from spring practice. All good so far?"

He nodded and seemed to relax. "No problem."

"If there's anything specific you want me to address, just tell me and we'll work it in. The important thing is that the viewers get a full picture of you and the new look for Jaguar football." She took a step away from the desk so she could put some distance between them. "Normally, I'd want to sit down with you before any of this, talk to you about everything, get a real feel for you and your environment. But you're not an unknown quantity, and for me, neither is the university. Besides, you said your time was limited this week, so I'll take whatever I can get and work around it."

"I appreciate it."

There was that grin again, with its way-too-sexy dimples.

Oh, god. Her will power was really being tested.

She hadn't been attracted to a man since her marriage to Daniel fell apart.

She cleared her throat. "If you could check your calendar and see when you might have time for it, that would be great."

"Sure." He looked at her for a long moment, as if trying to make up his mind about something before clearing his throat. If she didn't know better, she'd swear he was nervous. She smiled, to put him at ease. The last thing she needed was for him not to feel comfortable around her, for any reason.

"How about dinner?"

Of all the things in the known universe that she though he'd say, asking her out on what was, of course, a working date wasn't one of them. She attempted not to let her jaw dangle open for too long.

Dinner. That was harmless. Right?

"That sounds great. What time and where?"

"Eight o'clock, and I'll let you know where once I figure that part out. So what's the prize?"

"Prize?" She stared at him.

He nodded. "Gotta have a prize for the 10K. I figure you're probably just as competitive as I am."

"Winner buys dinner?" It slipped out before she could shut her stupid mouth. A professional dinner, right? To discuss the documentary.

He chuckled. "I think you got that wrong. It's supposed to be the loser who pays, isn't it?"

"Oh, I don't mind buying. It will be my pleasure to rub it in."

He studied her for a long moment. "Okay, then. You're on. As long as you think you can manage going to a...working dinner after a 10k." The slight hesitation before he said the word "working" made her bite back a wide grin.

They locked down the details, then got into what she'd really come for.

Drew was a dream to work with, always getting the best angles without being intrusive about it. The sound bytes turned out great. Hatch was a natural, relaxed, and warm and sometimes even funny. Of course, she'd seen that side of him at the press conference and hoped it would translate into this video.

When they were finished, she shook hands with him. "Thanks for taking the time for this. I feel good about the way it's going even in the early stages."

"When we have dinner, let's map out the full schedule of what you need."

"That's terrific. Thanks so much. See you Sunday."

After Hatch went back into his office, Olivia and Drew spent time outside getting B roll of the athletic complex and the team practicing.

"I think we can wrap this portion of it," she told Drew an hour later. "How about getting some shots of the campus before you leave. Then I'll meet you back at the studio. We can look over what we've got and outline what comes next."

"Sounds good to me. See you in a bit."

Drew jogged to his van, but Olivia stayed behind, soaking up the environment. Today had gone very well. Not only had she gotten some great footage, the man had actually suggested they go out. To dinner. So they could work out the scheduling details of the next few weeks, but still. She could almost smell the success of this project. It was the most important thing in her life right now, and she would not allow herself to fail.

As she looked out over the field, she thought about Hatch, a complex man if she ever met one. A mature man with little trace of the carefree college hero. She hoped she wasn't making a mistake having dinner with him. Business, she reminded herself.

But there was that pesky, unexpected hint of sexual attraction that she needed to kill, much as she might not want to. This documentary was too important career-wise to screw things up. And she might be finished with Daniel marriage-wise and career-wise, but he'd still be keeping an eye on her. His ego wouldn't let him do otherwise.

Probably waiting for me to fail so he can rub my face in it. It still makes me sick that I didn't fight harder, but he had all the power, damn it.

Stop. I can do it. I'm not an immature co-ed anymore.

She was so busy having an internal conversation that she tripped over a stone in her way. Drew, even carrying all his gear, managed to reach out a hand and steady her.

"Watch out! Can't have you face planting and ending up in the hospital before we really get started."

"Thanks," she said, giving him a sincere smile of appreciation. The list of requests for him was always long, so he got to pick and choose, with the station manager's approval, of course. He grinned back at her as she regained her equilibrium. "This really is going to be special, isn't it?"

"You know it is," he said. "'Special' is too weak a word for it, in my opinion."

"I'm sure *Liv* believes she's very special." The grating sound of Bert Hoekstra's voice made her jerk her head to see him walking across the parking space toward her. Great. She'd been so lost in her own head she'd nearly broken a leg and totally missed noticing the guy was in the parking lot again.

"Why, Bert." She curved her lips in a patronizing smile. "How irritating it is to see you again."

The look he gave her made her skin itch. "You should be a lot nicer to me, *Liv*." He stressed the nickname again. "You never know what information I might have for you that you need for this hot project of yours."

Drew had stopped beside her, his equipment still hefted to one shoulder, every line in his body tense. She had worked with him a lot, and she knew his protective instincts were in full battle mode.

"You want me to get rid of him?" Drew asked.

Bert sneered at the cameraman. "Lay one hand on me, and I'll call campus security first and the television station next."

"We're good, Drew. Go on. Put your gear away." She turned to Bert. "I can't imagine what you could possibly have to tell me that I would have the least bit of interest in."

"You never know. For instance, have you done any digging into Mr. Wonderful's marriage?"

She shrugged, making the gesture as casual as possible. "I'm here to discuss his professional career, not his personal life. That's not what this project is about."

"They may be tied to each other. You ought to check before you end up with egg on your face."

Olivia ground her teeth. "I'm not a dirt digger like you, Bert. Besides, I'm not looking to do an exposé.

Not the kind of grubby stuff you do."

He shrugged. "Sticks and stones. I'm just sayin', things are never as they seem. I'd hate to steal your thunder after all the work you're putting into this. Be careful, *Liv,* that your career doesn't take another nosedive."

Then he climbed into his car, cranked the engine, and backed out of the space.

Damn!

Did he really know something, or was he just yanking her chain as others had tried to do when she was getting too close to a subject they wanted to avoid. What could a man like Hatch possibly have to conceal?

Chapter Three

The chilly morning air bit into Hatch's face with the precise amount of sting required to focus him. He needed the assistance, considering he'd spent the wee hours of the day staring out into the darkness and attempting to forget the vividness of the dream that had jolted him awake and kept him that way.

The sensation of running at five a.m. around the large lake just outside Avon, Michigan, brought back a headful of memories. He'd grown up here, safely ensconced in his upper-middle class home complete with a stay-at-home mom and a business-man dad. His life had contained few speedbumps, other than the ones that involved his intense—some would say epic-level— ongoing competition with his older brother.

Their father had encouraged it. Their mother had enabled it. Until recently, he and his brother texted each other when they felt they'd achieved something the other would find enviable. The life-long one-upmanship contest had gone beyond friendly more than a few times. He recalled those moments with the sort of mental clarity that hurt.

When he had received the prestigious Kressler Trophy for college quarterbacks, Jack managed to take the shine off that moment by nearly killing himself in an auto accident. When Hatch had married a woman who could easily pass for a lingerie model his second year as a pro, Jack broke the news that he and his doctor wife were splitting up, which had managed to ruin Hatch's good news. They'd had one of their typical passive-aggressive back and forth texting sessions over it, and when the time came for his and Alex's over-the-top, Hawaiian destination wedding, Jack hadn't even bothered to show up.

Of course, the fact that he'd been passed over for the best man designation might have had something to do with that. But seriously, what man took a powder for his only brother's wedding?

They'd spoken sporadically at best, ever since. When Hatch's life had crumbled underneath him a few years ago, he wanted to reach out to his brother, seek his advice, or at least get a few you'll-be-fine-style comments. But he hadn't. And that had somehow solidified their estrangement.

Hatch slowed during his second lap around the five-mile diameter path he'd been running on since he was twelve years old. He'd known every bump, hill, and crevice in it at one time, but since he'd been gone, the city had paved over it to accommodate bicycles, which made the run a lot easier, if about a half-mile longer. He wasn't gassed or even breathing that hard, but thoughts of his brother had put a hitch in his pace that was pissing him off.

He came to a full stop at the crest of the hill overlooking the entire span of the lake, his breath visible around his face. His life had been a series of forward motion successes, fueled by his own dogged determination to do nothing but succeed. He'd been the first one up, the first one working out, the last one to leave every practice, ever striving for the pinnacle. And he'd by-god surmounted it. He'd had it all—the career he'd dreamed about after college, even if it meant bouncing around between teams as a "small" quarterback with a penchant for running his own plays, the hot-as-shit wife, the huge house, vacations, clothes, cars. The works.

And he'd collected it all up in his arms and tossed it out the open window at the highest floor possible. Period.

Dumb. Really, really dumb.

He leaned forward and rested his hands on his thighs, letting sweat drip onto the asphalt between his feet. He had loved his ex-wife, in as much as he could love anything that wasn't directly related to the game of football. They'd been happy, anyway, and he'd fucked it six ways to Sunday out his own stupidity. But he'd let it, and her, go, resolved to never hurt anyone else like he'd hurt her.

"Shit," he spat out as he shoved thoughts of his many failures out of his head. "Focus, Hatcher. You've got work to do."

He resumed his run, willing his mind blank and free of remorse, memories, or anything else that would distract him. He'd planned on a three-lap course today, counting on the fifteen miles to bring him to the Zen state he'd been residing in since he agreed to take the coaching job. Or at least the state he'd inhabited between that moment and the one where he'd clapped eyes on Olivia Grant.

Hatch set his jaw and went faster, pushing himself to his newly established limit as a non-pro player and semi-sedentary older man. God knew he'd worked harder than this in his life, many times over, but for now, the fifteen-mile, fast-paced run was what he was counting on to help him out of his Olivia-induced fog.

The time they'd spent together so far had been pleasant. She had a clear idea of what she expected from the documentary and a well-thought-out plan to implement it. He'd been impressed by her focus and intensity—not to mention her legs—during the hours they'd logged discussing the project so far. It had taken every ounce of his willpower not to reach across the desk and tuck an errant strand of her blonde curls behind her ear every time it dropped over her eye.

When she'd looked at him, pinned him really, with those shocking green eyes, it took him several seconds to gather his wits and say something he hoped made sense. He'd even caught himself winking at her at one point. *Winking.* That was so far outside the realm of his normal behavior he knew something about her was making him crazy.

After deciding that four laps around the lake would be necessary to drive Olivia's compelling green eyes—and her perfect rear view—out of his brain, he finished up with a light jog to cool down and get his pounding heartbeat back to normal. As he slowed, other thoughts filled his mind, mainly the challenge he now faced as head coach of a program that had been allowed to run to seed. Everything from the weight equipment to the players themselves looked sloppy and second-rate. And that pissed him off.

He was ready to fire a couple of assistants as he'd been told he could do but didn't look forward to that process. A gaggle of rich boosters were already after him with their emails and text messages full of suggestions and ideas and, of course, invitations to their lakefront homes, their golf clubs. It was, in short, a massive task. One he relished, but also one he dreaded.

He climbed behind the wheel of his classic SUV, one of the few things he'd kept after the great pre-divorce sell-off, and drained over half a water bottle in a couple of long gulps. It was only late spring but it was going to be a warm day, even though the breeze off Lake Michigan always provided relief to Avon and to the football stadium, which sat perched on a hill, not far from the body of water separating Michigan from Wisconsin.

"Call Rob," he said as he screeched out onto the still-deserted road and the sound of the ringing phone filled the vehicle's interior. He figured he might as well cut one of these cords now. Waiting around didn't do anyone any favors. He gritted his teeth while the ringing sound filled the vehicle's interior.

"Hello?" The about-to-get-canned assistant D-line coach answered on the second ring.

"Hey, Rob," Hatch said as he turned onto the main road into town. "We need to talk."

****

"Well, that sucked." Hatch sat on his small back patio that evening, water bottle in hand.

"Yeah, but it all had to be done, and we all know it." Scott Durbin tossed another log on the bonfire in the pit, then sipped his beer, keeping his back to Hatch.

"All in a day's work, boss."

Hatch glanced at the other men on and around his patio. George Hawkins was one of the three previous staff members he planned to keep and even to promote. The other two were tossing a ball back and forth beyond the fire pit in the waning light. He held up his water by way of response. George reached over and touched his beer bottle to the plastic. They both drank. The silence in the wake of the firing he'd done earlier felt heavy, like a thick blanket on his shoulders.

He observed the game of catch a few more minutes, his mind awash with the protestations and other negative responses he'd gotten from his former staff. With a loud sigh, he rose and stretched his arms up over his head. His legs ached, and his head was starting to pound from stress and too little food.

"Where's that damn pizza?" He wandered inside, taking in the surroundings of his new home, knowing that the frugal, some would say miserly way, he lived was the topic of plenty of athletic department buzz. As he approached the front door of the rented bungalow he'd chosen because it put him within walking or biking distance of his new office, the bell rang.

He thanked the delivery guy, handed him a tip, and was shutting the door when the guy spoke, "Hey, aren't you the new coach? Hatcher, right?"

"That's right," Hatch said, holding the four heavy boxes of food in one hand. He wasn't in the mood for this but knew from direct experience that pissing off a fan could turn around and bite you in the ass. "You go to Lakeview?"

He'd done a quick appraisal of the kid and decided he could be college age. Then again, he could be in high school.

"Not yet," the young man said. "But I want to. And I want to play ball there."

"That's great," Hatch said, trying to sound enthusiastic. "Be sure and stay in touch with the assistant coaches."

He knew the drill. If he even so much as said a single thing to this young man about playing for him, he'd be in violation of multiple recruiting rules. He smiled, hoping the kid would get the hint and get off his front porch. But he lingered, his eyes bright, his smile wide.

Hatch did yet another assessment of him. Tall? Check. Wide shoulders? Check. Huge hands? Check. "Hang on a second."

He dropped the pizza boxes on the kitchen counter and headed outside. "George, would you talk to the kid at the door? He's apparently a football player and…"

"Got it, Coach." George jumped up and headed inside.

"Food's here," Hatch said.

He flopped into his chair, not hungry, not thirsty, not anything but exhausted and also somehow enervated at the same time. His phone buzzed down in his jeans pocket, so he pulled it out. When he saw the name of the message sender, he got the oddest sensation, as if an army of ants were marching across his skull and down his back. He shivered.

"You all right, Hatch?" Scott had a couple of slices of pepperoni on a plate and was sitting down at the table with a fresh beer.

"Yeah," he said, opening the screen so he could read Olivia's message. He by-passed the ice-choked cooler well stocked with local beer and grabbed another water. He sipped while gazing down at her words.

Coach, I was wondering if we might be able to interview you on film this coming week. I know we said that wouldn't happen for another week, but I'm ahead of schedule on editing, and thought I might get a jump on the footage of you.

He sighed and leaned back in the chair. This whole documentary thing was beginning to feel like a giant mistake. There was no time for it, much less inclination. Plus, the woman in charge was simply too tempting and he had to focus.

Sorry, can't.

The response was almost immediate.

I know I'm getting ahead of our schedule, but it will shorten the length of time you're bothered by me. I promise. I'm batting my eyelashes at you right now if that helps...

Hatch groaned and tossed the phone on the tabletop.

Scott snagged it and glanced at the text exchange. "Hey, if she's being a pain, I can rein her in for you."

"No, she's not a pain. I'll handle it."

But the mental image of Olivia, she of the firm, fit legs, the perfect ass, the lush lips, and compelling eyes, batting her lashes at him for anything, much less so he'd get more one-on-one time with her was making him weak in the knees. And way too hot below his belt. He waited a few seconds, then got up for food, grabbing his phone from Scott on the way.

Ok. But I really only have about two spare hours this coming week. And it has to be before Friday, sorry.

Her reaction was almost as fast as before, which made him wince at being such a jerk about the whole thing. Even if it were pure self-preservation on his part.

Ok. No problem. I get it. See you at the race!

"Are you still in here sexting with that hot as fuck reporter?"

Hatch glanced up at George, annoyed at the

interruption at the same moment he had to acknowledge that the concept of Olivia sweating alongside him, in shorts and a sports bra at the 10k made him have to mentally run stats tables of his last year as a pro quarterback to keep from popping a teenager-worthy woody right in his grown-up kitchen.

"None of your business. Here." He tossed one of the full boxes at George's chest and tapped out his quick reply.

Yeah, I'll see you there. And you should know, I never lose when I'm betting on myself.

He sighed, staring at that last comment, realizing how very close to home it hit. He had lost plenty of bets. But that was in the past. He tucked the phone back in his pocket, grabbed more beer, and headed outside. "Okay, I didn't invite you assholes over here just to eat my food and drink my beer. We have work to do."

The men all pulled out their laptops and notebooks. Hatch passed around the beer and an opener. "That's better," he said, taking his seat and flipping open his comp book. He kept physical, hand-written notes and always had. It was how his mind worked best.

Later that night as he was about to turn out the light, he plugged in his phone and noticed that Olivia had sent one last message.

Well, you've obviously never bumped up against me. I don't lose, either. See you at the race!

With a loud groan, he fell back on his pillows, wanting more than anything not to be fixated on "bumping up" against Olivia Grant but knowing full well that, thanks to that last message, he'd be wide awake again by three a.m.

Chapter Four

It was a good thing there was still a little chill in the air, because only minutes into the race Olivia had worked up a good sweat. She paused at the water station to hydrate before blending back into the line of runners. Clearly, she had a rampant case of stupidity. What did she think she was going to accomplish by proving to Hatch she could compete with him? If she didn't quit all her self-questioning and get rid of her insecurities, the video would end up in the trash instead of on national television.

Besides, running on a treadmill, no matter how fast she set it, wasn't quite the same as pounding the pavement for real. She was grateful, however, that she'd at least had that much exercise to get herself in shape. Daniel would probably have taken a look at her and told her that her ass was still too fat and her thighs needed work. But Daniel wasn't a factor in her life anymore. Besides, his own ass left a lot to be desired and his thighs weren't all that great.

So shut the hell up, Daniel. Get out of my head.

And that right there was a good reason why she didn't need a man in her life. Nor did she even know if she wanted one. Apparently, she wasn't good at making choices.

Tossing her empty water bottle, she slid back into the race, setting her pace again. There had been so much commotion around Hatch at the beginning, she'd managed to slip into line without him seeing her. She figured that was good since her body had begun to flag. Then she'd stopped for water, and— Oh, hell. She'd damn well come in with a respectable time.

Putting on a final burst of energy, she managed to hit the finish line in time to see him receiving congratulations from everyone. Of course. From the moment he stepped down from his SUV, he'd been corralled by a handler, surrounded by fans, photographed, the works. Now, he was on a platform set up just so people could take selfies with him. As she stood there, catching her breath and listening to people congratulate her and others, she heard a young voice call out to Hatch.

"Coach! Coach! Hey, Coach."

She saw Hatch turn his head toward a voice coming from the crowd of people pressing toward the platform. In the next moment, he held out a hand to the next person eager to snap a pic with him, then peered down at the crowd, trying to find the source of the voice.

"Coach! Hey, over here!"

"Excuse me a second?" He looked at the woman holding out her smart phone. "Be right back."

His minder, a purse-lipped, librarian-type, frowned and glanced at her computer tablet. "Coach, I don't think—"

"Just one minute. I promise."

When he turned back to the crowd, he smiled, waved, and followed the sound of the voice until he reached a trio of people, the parents, Olivia figured, of the young boy sitting in what looked like a custom wheelchair.

"Coach!" The boy's face lit up as Hatch approached him. "You found me!"

Hatch shook the parents' hands, then knelt before the kid so he could be on his eye level. Olivia knew from reading background on him that he'd always preferred interacting with his youngest fans. Something the press always managed to comment on.

"I like to make kids feel like they've achieved a goal," he always said. "Even if that goal is to get a photo with me or an autograph on one of my jerseys."

"Hey there." He grinned at the boy. "I'm Hatch. And you are?"

The boy and his parents were decked out in Lakeview University gear. Olivia saw the boy was gripping a full-sized football in his arms.

"I'm Hunter," he said. "Pleased to meet you."

Hatch grinned at the kid and held out his hand. "That's a nice-looking ball you've got there. May I see it?"

Hunter held it out to him. Olivia was close enough to see Hatch's eyes narrow just slightly as he noticed the boy's atrophied arms, thin legs, and small feet encased in a pair of Lakeview Jaguars-labeled Adidas, not unlike the ones the Jaguars got from the shoe company, along with their other piles of on- and off-the-field gear.

"So, Hunter." Hatch tossed the ball up a few times. "I'm wondering. Have you ever been to a football practice before?"

"No…" The boy's smile widened as he glanced up at his parents. "I've never seen a practice."

The crowd watched the scene with avid interest

while cameras and cell phones clicked away. She was struck with the sudden revelation that Hatch actually enjoyed doing this. It wasn't just for the promo ops. He'd interact even if no one was around except him, the boy, and his parents. This was a situation she'd seen all too rarely during her years covering sports. Something turned over in her heart, and she had to swallow past a lump in her throat.

Don't get all fluttery. He's just doing his thing. It's not for your benefit or anyone else's but that kid's.

"Would you like to?" Hatch asked. "See a practice?"

It wasn't enough that he was sexy. Now he had to go and be a super nice guy on top of everything else.

"Yes!" The kid gave a bright yelp of pleasure. "Yes, I would like it very much. Can I? Mom?"

"You don't have to do that," the woman said, her hand on the boy's shoulder. "But thank you."

Hatch tossed the ball up in the air once more, then backed away from the group. "Hey Hunter, slant pass, you ready?"

The kid nodded and held out his arms. Hatch lobbed it to him softly. She was pleased when it found its target and Hunter had it wrapped in his arms again. More cameras clicked and flashes flashed. Olivia hoped Drew was getting all of this. What a great bite for the video.

Hatch shook the parents' hands again. "Give my office a call on Monday. Tell them you're Hunter's parents, and we'll get you some passes for a few practices. Now, let's get some photos." He knelt by Hunter's chair so his mother could snap some pictures.

By the time Hatch made his way back to the

platform, Olivia was nearly in tears, so choked up she couldn't have said a word if someone spoke to her. This was a side of Hatch that few people ever saw. She was sure it was, because he didn't do it for the publicity. He had a genuine love of kids. Which made her wonder why he and his wife never had children. It wasn't the kind of thing one just asked someone, but maybe she could find a way to work it into a conversation.

She didn't know why she hung around as long as she did, except that watching Hatch fascinated her. After all the selfies, he stood in his sweaty running gear, towel around his neck, Jaguars cap on his head, patiently answering questions from the media, doing television sound bytes, and posing for what seemed to her like a gazillion photos. It was obvious he had a full publicity schedule, obligations that he'd accepted as part of who he was and what he did, and he did them with a casual grace that drew people to him.

She'd been focusing on his accomplishments as a player and a coach and had overlooked what really made up the man. Again, she wondered how his marriage had disintegrated to the point of divorce. Who would walk away from a man like this, one who combined sexual attraction, magnetic personality, and unbelievable athletic skills? If she started digging, what would she find?

If it was negative, she'd just pretend she hadn't seen it. If she could. But what could possibly be so bad?

She sighed. It was past time for her to leave, and she had no idea why she was still there. She spent another fifteen minutes talking to people she knew and was headed toward the parking lot when someone took her arm and tugged her around.

"Running out on me?"

She looked up into Hatch's sweating, smiling face, saw the dimple flash in his chin and humor gleam in eyes that reminded her of deep pools of melted chocolate. She wanted to rip of his damp T-shirt and run her hands over his ripped, sweaty chest.

Oh, my god!

She grinned. "I didn't want to tear you away from your adoring public."

He laughed. "Most of that is just for show. I thought maybe you didn't want me to remind you that you lost the bet."

"Actually, I was giving you an out. Winner buys, remember?"

The grin left his face, and heat flared in his eyes, sudden and sharp and unexpected, and then it was gone. But not before it made all her lady parts go on high alert. Maybe this wasn't such a good idea after all. Her and her big mouth.

"I never go back on my word." He reached out his fingertips toward her cheek, then dropped his hand, as if it had caught fire. "I still have some stuff to take care of, but I'd like to have that dinner tonight."

"I'll have to check my schedule." Why was she so off balance?

He lifted an eyebrow. "Are you that busy?"

"Oh, well." *Flustered much, Olivia?* "I mean, not me. I don't want to take you away from obligations."

"I've had plenty of those since I got here. I think I'd like a little fun. So how about it? Is eight o'clock too late for you?"

She stared. "Tonight? Won't you be tired?"

He grinned again. "In case you haven't noticed,

I'm in excellent physical shape."

Oh, she'd noticed all right. It was hard not to. "Eight is fine."

"Good. Text me your address. See you later. We can talk about all those pesky little details you said you wanted to know."

"Wait." When he stopped, she asked, "What kind of place? Jeans? Ball gown?"

He laughed. "Something in between. See you at eight."

Then he jogged back to where his minder waited, staring pointedly at her watch.

****

At six thirty, Olivia poured herself a glass of wine to settle her unexpected nerves and began to get ready. She took extra care, smoothing scented lotion over every inch of her skin and dabbing the companion scent behind her ears, her knees, and inside her elbows. She pulled a tissue wrapped package out of her drawer and removed the scandalous lingerie she'd bought on a dare and never worn—a bra with lace that cupped her breasts and a thong that wasn't much more than a triangle and some dental floss.

She stopped with it still in her hands. What was she doing? This wasn't a date. Was it? Well, was it?

It doesn't matter. I can still feel feminine and elegant, even at a business dinner. Right?

When her townhouse bell rang promptly at eight, she took in a deep breath and let it out slowly. Then she took one last look in the hall mirror, hoping she'd chosen the right outfit, let out a breath, and went to open the door.

She'd chosen a sleeveless navy dress of soft

material with a draped collar, the one Daniel always said accentuated her worst features. Apparently, Hatch didn't agree as he stared at her, mouth slightly open. Maybe gaped would have been a better word. Then his mouth curved in his trademark grin, and the look in his eyes told her it had all been worth the effort.

"You do something in between very well."

"Um, thanks." She grabbed her purse from the table by the door. "I'm all set."

She hadn't given any thought to what kind of vehicle he drove and was slightly dismayed to see the four-by-four SUV in her driveway. He opened the passenger door for her, but then she just stood there, figuring the logistics. Hello, big step up, meet straight skirt.

"My bad," he said. "I didn't think about climbing up to the seat. My social skills are still pretty rusty."

Okay, that was an interesting little piece of news. She stood there for a moment, trying to figure out the best way to handle this. Then his hands closed around her waist, and he lifted her in one smooth motion into the cab and onto the seat.

She smiled at him. "No problem. And thanks for the lift."

As he closed the door and jogged to the driver's side, she could still feel the warmth of his fingers pressing into her waist and the light touch of his body behind her. She wondered if she was playing with fire. Six months ago, she'd been clawing the pieces of her life together again, trying to relaunch her professional situation and rebuild her reputation. The last thing on her mind was being attracted to a man. How was she going to get through dinner if all she could think about was having him touch her again and wondering what he'd look like without any clothes on at all?

"I made a reservation at La Plaza," he told her, breaking the silence. "I hope that's okay."

Her eyebrows headed to her hairline. "I understand you have to take out a loan just to order appetizers there. There's no need to spend that kind of money on dinner. Really."

"I promise it won't break the bank." He said it casually, but there was an edge to his voice. "Anyway, it's owned by a Lakeview alum who's been after me to try it out. I'm looking forward to it."

"It's gotten great reviews."

"Good." He slanted a look at her. "Hope it lives up to its publicity."

Olivia felt trapped in the sudden silence, as if they'd already run out of words. But then they were at the restaurant and Hatch was lifting her out of the cab the same way he'd helped her into it. The waiter escorted them to a table in a little alcove, pulled out Olivia's chair for her, and with a flourish swept her napkin into her lap.

"Good evening." He bowed slightly. "Welcome to La Plaza. May I bring you a drink?"

Hatch looked at her and she nodded. He ordered a Rusty Nail, and she ordered a vodka martini. Then they settled down to study the menu. Everything looked mouthwatering and unique, basic foods but prepared with a flourish.

Olivia looked around. The thick rugs on top of dark hardwood, the heavy velvet drapes swagged at the windows, and the soft music floating out from hidden speakers all created the sort of intimate atmosphere she loved. The whole thing accentuated the illusion of privacy their little alcove gave them.

The waiter returned with their drinks, and Hatch lifted his, touching his glass to the rim of hers. "To a great evening. Best bet I ever won."

"I could say it's the best bet I ever lost." Olivia sipped her drink. "This place is fabulous."

Out of nowhere came the thought that this was exactly the kind of place Daniel relished. Not for the food but for the expensive, exclusive reputation. She couldn't help thinking how much this was a place he would love, except he'd want a table in the middle of the room. A place where everyone could see him bringing someone for a very expensive dinner and hear him ordering the most expensive wine on the menu and giving orders to the chef, as if he knew what he was doing.

An involuntary shudder ran over her body as memories of a marriage that never should have happened taunted her. Would she never be able to get past that?

"Cold?" Hatch asked.

"No." She shook her head. "I'm fine. Really."

This was neither the time nor place to tell him her sad, dreary story. She hoped to use tonight to learn more about Hatch, the person.

"Good. Okay, then. Know what you want yet?"

They placed their orders, and she sat back, determined to relax and enjoy herself.

"I have to admit you ran a good race today," he told her. "I guess your soccer legs are still in great shape."

At the mention of a part of her body Daniel had

often disparaged, she tensed. God, he'd never let up about her legs.

Hatch frowned. "Did I say something wrong? You've got great legs. I figured it was okay to tell you on a sort of athlete to athlete level. But I probably overstepped. I'm sorry."

Relax. "No, it's fine. I'm sorry for acting so weird." She took a breath. "So. How does it feel to be back at Lakeview after all these years?"

He chuckled. "It feels great, despite the giant weight everyone's put on my shoulders. But the kids are terrific and Scott's behind me one hundred percent. I'm really looking forward to the season." He paused while the waiter set their appetizers in front of them. "But can we put a pin in that for a while so you can tell me a little about yourself?"

"This isn't supposed to be about me," she reminded him. "Besides, my life isn't half as exciting as yours."

"Outside of football, my life is really pretty boring. Anyway, I'm not sure I'm in the mood to discuss business tonight, and that's what the documentary is, right? Business?"

"Yes." She'd do well to remember that.

There was a tightness to his face when he said it, an edge to his words that made her wonder. Did she need to dig deeper into his personal life? No. She knew what it was like to have her personal life on everyone's front page. And he'd asked to keep it out of the story. But it sure made her damn curious.

"So is mine," she told him.

She wasn't about to spill the story of her own unpleasant history. This project, if successful, was meant to put all of that behind her.

Then he smiled, and every one of her pulse points made themselves known. She was glad that the dress she wore was dark because she could feel how tight her nipples were, poking hard against the fabric. No, no, no. This wasn't the time in her life for a very appealing man to, well, appeal to her. She took a big gulp of her drink, nearly choking herself.

"You okay?" Hatch's face settled into an expression of concern. "I didn't mean to upset you. I just want to know more about you." He studied her. "You fascinate me."

Oh, great. "I do?"

"Uh huh. Beautiful smart woman choosing to do a documentary about me. How can you not?" He held up a hand as she opened her mouth. "I asked Scott about you. You aren't the only one who approached him about this."

"I'm not?" Her fingers tightened around her glass. Of course others had had this idea. So why had they agreed to let her do it?

"Uh uh. So I wanted to know who the real person was in charge of production, not just the face on the request. You had to expect that. This whole hero's homecoming thing drives me nuts, but everyone wants to make a nickel on it. The fact that you're the one who got approval piqued my interest."

"And what did he tell you?" *Yes, Scott, what did you spill?*

Hatch moved his empty appetizer plate to the side. "Just the basics. You started reporting on sports in college even as a busy athlete yourself. Got a job as a sideline reporter at a small station after you graduated and worked your way up from there. You've got good industry creds and are well-respected, despite the fact that your ex-husband is obviously an asshole who tried to blow up your career when you divorced."

She stared at him her mouth open. "Scott told you all of that?"

He nodded. "Even the part about the asshole husband. One of these days, maybe you'll tell me about him, but not tonight. Tonight, I want to hear all about you and what your goals are now that you're getting your feet wet again."

Olivia relaxed. Maybe this would be okay after all. They could be friends, and she could send her misbehaving hormones back into cold storage. Giving in to the unspoken questions hovering over the table would be a disaster. She breathed a little easier.

Maybe it was just that she'd locked up her libido for so long or that Daniel had permanently doused her needs in cold water. Whatever the reason, as she and Hatch ate and chatted the self-contained professional began to drift away, leaving in its place a woman so fascinated by the man across from her, she sometimes forgot to eat.

She caught herself watching his lips move and his Adam's apple when he swallowed. Or the vague scent of something that could be a mild cologne or maybe soap that drifted across the table. Whatever it was made her want to climb into his lap and lick the side of his neck. Open his shirt and run her hands over his chest. Make him strip so she could see just how fine his ass was, how tight the muscles. And how thick and long his—

She jerked herself back to reality. She hadn't had thoughts like these in months. No, years! Really. Her libido had been in cold storage for so long and what an inappropriate time for it to defrost. She had one goal here, and she'd better keep that in mind or she'd be dead in the water.

"Are you okay?" Hatch reached across the table and placed his hand over hers, his eyes full of genuine concern.

She stared down at their hands, mesmerized by them. "Uh, yes. I'm fine. Thanks."

She managed to get through the rest of the meal without looking and acting like an idiot, although she wasn't sure how. The electricity she'd felt from the moment she walked into Duncan Jerome Hatcher's office had only grown in intensity, a very bad thing in a professional situation.

But holy god, the man was hot. Age had only refined his sexiness and mouthwatering masculinity. It had been a lot of years since she wanted to get naked with a man and try every possible kind of sex with him. Many, many years.

And he wasn't helping. Much as he tried to hide it, there was blatant interest, something she hadn't experienced in a long time. She wondered if he'd try to act on it? God, she hoped not. All she could see that way was trouble.

"So, uh, Olivia, does that sound good to you?"

She blinked. Had he been talking to her and she zoned out as her unexpected conflict tumbled in her mind? "What? I'm sorry."

He studied her face, probably wondering if she'd gone suddenly nuts on him.

"I asked if you wanted to split dessert. They have an incredible chocolate cake with their homemade ice cream that's more than one person can eat." The look he gave her was part playful, part heat. "In fact, that's what they call it. Chocolate Decadence."

"Um, sure. That sounds really good."

When the waiter placed the dish on the table between them, Hatch took one of the two spoons, scooped up some cake and ice cream and held it out to her. She closed her mouth over the spoon and dragged the sweet confection into her mouth. It certainly lived up to its name.

"Good?" He cocked an eyebrow.

"Yum." She licked her lips.

He fed both of them alternating bites, his eyes never leaving her mouth the entire time. When he unexpectedly reached across and dusted a fingertip over her lower lip, she wasn't sure if she should close her lips around it or leap up from the table.

"There was a little chocolate there." His voice was low and husky.

Every move after that, to her, seemed to have some kind of sexual connotation. The air between them vibrated with the electricity sparking back and forth. By the time he paid the check and they left the restaurant, every pulse in her body pounded, her breasts ached, and her teeny tiny thong was soaked. She wanted to hurry home and take a cold shower before she did something really stupid.

In the truck, he turned on the radio and found a station playing oldies rock music that he tuned low. They rode in a silence that was more electric than uncomfortable, especially when he reached over and took her hand in his, giving it a gentle squeeze.

When they reached her townhouse, he again lifted

her from the cab and walked her to the door, holding her hand. When she had the door open, he turned her to face him and studied her face for a long time. She waited, wondering if she had the willpower not to cross that line from professional to personal and how much damage she'd do if she did.

"You have to be the sexiest sports reporter I've ever met. I would really like to kiss you. Would that be okay with you?"

She should have turned away, but she couldn't find the willpower. The kiss was soft and gentle, a mere brush of lips, a touch of flesh. Then it was over, but she wanted more. A lot more. She could feel this spinning out of control, and she was powerless to stop it.

"If you invite me in, I'm not going to turn you down."

She was crazy to do this. She hadn't recovered from the burns left by her relationship with Daniel. Why on earth was she looking to jump into the fire again? She'd never in a million years considered herself open to some kind of a second chance at a true relationship. But idiot that she was, she didn't even hesitate, just nodded, and ushered him inside.

She didn't do this. Never had, even before she met Daniel. She was never sexually impulsive, certainly not where something important was concerned. But now she didn't seem able to help herself. She tried to remind herself not to screw up her situation, but her long months of need coalesced in the center of her body. She was about to do something stupid.

She nodded. "Yes. Please come in."

Chapter Five

Hatch must have talked himself in, and then out of, his hope that Olivia would ask him into her place a thousand and a half times during the ride home from the restaurant. When he'd chosen La Plaza, it was a bit of a show-off move. Something he'd never felt a need to do before. Hell, they probably could have gone out for bar-b-que and beer. Or should have, more like. Taking the woman, who was about to do some kind of a full-on video story of his life, out to an obnoxiously expensive dinner was stupid and tacky and...somehow absolutely necessary.

She looked like a million damn bucks in that sexy blue dress. Legs that went on for days, strong legs, he recalled earlier from the race. Full high breasts. Gorgeous smile, and bright green eyes. Jesus. He had it bad. And now, he had it even worse.

Which only made his inner conflict over the whole thing worse. He had no reason to expect that life would hand him a second chance at anything, much less love, on what seemed to be a gorgeous, sexy, fascinating silver platter named Olivia Grant. He doubted he deserved it. But here it was. Here she was. And he was all out of self-control.

When he reached over and took her hand in the truck, it had felt like the most natural thing in the world. In fact, he'd go out on a limb and claim that he'd never felt more comfortable in the company of a woman in his life. Sure, he'd loved his wife and had pursued her with relentless focus. But a lot of her appeal had been her ability to keep him at arm's length. To pretend that she didn't give a shit about him—a superstar, handsome, rich young football player. He realized that now, in hindsight.

He was grateful to her for one thing. Everything else aside, she'd kept his secret after the divorce. He'd always be grateful for that. But he realized that his attitude during those years may have left him with no idea how to form a real relationship. He just hoped to hell it wasn't too late to learn.

As Olivia preceded him up the short walk to the front door of her townhouse, keeping her palm in his, giving him a perfect view of her perfect ass in that perfect dress, he'd circled back around to the "please invite me in" space. So, he'd asked her permission and then had kissed her. She'd tasted exactly the way he'd imagined she would. Chocolate, a hint of wine, a touch of mint. And a whole hell of a lot of amazing woman.

He managed to choke out his polite request to come inside, his entire body itching, burning, aching from the top of his head to the tip of his toes. With plenty of sensation in between. He cupped her cheek in one hand. Her huge green eyes were wide. Her lips slightly parted. She nodded, unlocked her door, and tugged him in behind her.

Something came over him, something that drove out all thoughts or plans of being subtle, going slow, making her want him as bad as he wanted her. The fact that she grabbed him and pulled him against her warm body, her back pressed to the hastily shut door didn't help.

"Hatch," she whispered, her lips centimeters from his. "I don't…know if…"

"Me neither," he admitted. He slid one hand into her hair, relishing its silky smoothness. "I don't know anything right now. Other than this."

He pressed his lips to hers, going slow, even as everything in him was clamoring for him to go fast, faster. She shifted and put her arms around his neck, opening her mouth to his tongue with the sweetest noise, made somewhere down in her throat. It almost made him come, that noise. But he clamped down on his libido, reminded himself that he was a grown ass man, not a horny teenager, as their tongues tangled a few minutes.

When she broke the kiss and leaned her head back against the door, a soft light from a nearby room hit her neck, highlighting its length, drawing first his gaze and then his lips. He nibbled his way up to her jaw, then back down to where her neck met her shoulder. It was one of his favorite places on a woman, that juncture. He pulled her closer, wishing he could eat up that damn sound she was making as he licked, sucked, and took small nips of her flesh.

Her hands tangled in his hair. Her breasts were jammed against his chest. He could smell her—the luscious odor of turned on female, now overriding her light perfume. His cock was so hard it hurt like hell. His need to get her naked and be inside her was blinding him, deafening him to everything but that god damned…sound she made.

He forced himself to stop, to take a step away from her. Hands jammed in his pockets, breathing like he'd just run a marathon, he stared at her, willing something logical to hit his brain. This was…crazy. He'd only known of her existence for, what? A week? And she had a job. One that could turn her life back onto a positive track. The last thing she needed was to get mixed up with him. He screwed up everything he touched and had plenty to keep him occupied. For one, trying not to destroy his second chance at a career in football.

Olivia stayed leaning against the door, as if frozen there. Her hair was messy where he'd had his fingers threaded in it. Her color, what he could see of it thanks to the light thrown from the other room was high. Her lips were slightly swollen and full. But her eyes, those green emeralds that had struck him the moment he met her, were shining and full of intent. Intent he knew would be matched in his own gaze.

"We really shouldn't do this." His voice sounded gravelly, as if he hadn't used it for a while. "Should we? Olivia?" He loved the way her name rolled around in his mouth, slipped off his tongue. He held out his hand.

She hesitated long enough to give him a wriggle of worry.

"No, Hatch. We shouldn't."

But then she slid into his arms and kissed him with an intensity that almost blew the top of his damn head off. Her hands were on his chest, tugging his shirt out of his trousers, even as she kept her lips on his.

"Whoa, whoa, hang on a second," he insisted. "Holy shit. Olivia. Wait." She had his pants unzipped and her hand wrapped around his eager cock before he realized he had to stop her or he would come, right now, in her hand, like that aforementioned horny teenaged boy.

Her turned-on scent was even more intense, rolling around in his head, making him dizzy with need. He had to get this under control, though, or he was going to embarrass himself in a big way. He swallowed hard, took a deep breath, smiled at her— Dear Jesus but she was so beautiful.

He zipped up his trousers and took another deep breath.

"I hope one of us still has a functioning brain here," she breathed.

"I'm trying. Believe me." He took her hands and kissed them, then turned them over and pressed his lips to first one, then the other of her palms. He needed to slow this the hell down. He *wanted* to slow this the hell down. He pulled her into his arms again, counted to twenty, during which time he convinced himself that he should kiss her, then turn around and leave.

He'd never really been into random hook-ups. He didn't want her to get the wrong impression. Because all of a sudden, all he wanted was for Olivia Grant to have a good impression of him as a nice guy, a good man, a solid human being. Not some sorry-ass, has-been, lucky-to-be-here horn dog who started pawing at her the minute her door was closed.

He thumbed her chin and lifted it so she had to meet his gaze. Then words tumbled out of his mouth that were essentially the polar opposite of what he'd been thinking. "I want this. You want this. We're grownups. As a matter of fact, we're more grown up than a lot of people, you know?"

She nodded. A tear formed in the corner of her left

eye. He touched it before it could make its way down her flushed cheek.

"One thing you should know about me. I don't make women cry."

"Oh no?" She swiped at her face and wrenched herself out of his embrace. "Jesus. I'm a mess."

She headed into what he assumed was her kitchen, leaving him standing, his arms still out, as if he were still holding her, boner tenting his dress trousers, his ears ringing with lust. He sucked in another breath and counted to ten, then followed her.

She filled a glass with water, drained it, and refilled it. "Water?" She kept her back to him. He tried hard not to fixate on how much he wanted to press his fingertips into her full hips.

"Sure," he said. "Thanks."

She filled another glass, turned, and handed it to him without meeting his eyes. He drank it, trying to regroup and figure out what he'd said to mess all this up. He'd only spoken the truth. He didn't make women cry. Even when she'd told him she wanted a divorce, Alexandra hadn't cried. No matter that she claimed to still love him, but that she couldn't put up with his problem anymore on top of his laser focus on his career instead of her. That she was glad they didn't have kids to screw up with a divorce.

Shit. Nothing like a quick trip down ex-wife memory lane to soften the old erection, especially when no one could ever know the real reason for their split. He sighed and leaned back against the kitchen counter, waiting her out. She glared at him a few seconds, her eyes bright with unshed tears. Finally, she plunked the empty glass down and brushed past him, heading into the other room, he presumed. He finished his water, put his glass next to hers, and turned.

She was in the doorway, her jaw set, her eyes now dry. "I want to have sex with you, Hatch. Which makes me feel a hundred types of shitty. And stupid."

He tucked his hand in his pockets, a flicker of hope stirring back to life. "Well, that makes two of us. And I don't feel shitty at all." He meant that. He'd worked his way through guilt, worry, and well past shitty. He wanted her now. Plain and simple. He wanted to make her feel, to sigh, to cry out his name and latch onto his shoulders or his ass or the bedsheet.

He moved into the space that separated them, keeping his hands in his pockets. He inhaled, pulling the scent of her light perfume, her skin, *her*...into his lungs.

"Here's the deal, Olivia. You are an amazing, gorgeous, incredible woman. Any man who says otherwise is lying." He took a deep breath and summoned his better self. "I don't want to have sex with you. I want to make love to you. Maybe I have since the minute we met. I want to go slow, to undress you one piece of clothing at a time. To lay you down on your bed and slide off your shoes, rub your feet, kiss my way up the inside of one leg and back down the other."

He heard her breathing hitch, saw her eyes darken. A light sheen of sweat had broken out on her neck. He resisted the urge to lick it off, going with words for the time being, since it seemed to be working. He was a hard as granite again, that much was true. He kept a few inches of air between them, loving how her face and body reacted to what he was saying.

"I'm going to lick my way up your stomach, suck each of your nipples. Something tells me you'll like that. Would you, Olivia? Would you like it if I sucked your nipples?"

She nodded and lifted one hand, as if to touch him. He took a step back. "No. Not yet. I'm not done telling you what I want to do."

She dropped her hand to her side and moved backward until her legs hit the couch and she sat. He remained standing, grooving on this a little, enjoying how much she seemed to be getting off from the sound of his voice talking dirty.

"I'll put my hand between your legs," he said, watching as she spread her knees and put her arms up over her head, which made her back arch and her tits push upward in a way that rendered him momentarily speechless. "I want to put my entire hand over your pussy, Olivia. To hold it, feel it pulsing under my palm while I suck your delicious nipple."

"So help me, Duncan Jerome, if you don't shut the hell up and get over here, I'm going to shove you out a window."

He grinned. She held out her hand. He took it and yanked her to her feet. She yelped when he picked her all the way up, like some kind of ersatz Rhett Butler. Damn, he was screwed. He knew himself well enough to accept that. He shoved aside all his inner misgivings about this, about what she'd think of him tomorrow, about anything but his desire to make her come, a lot.

"What are you doing?" she demanded.

"I'm making sure you don't push me out a window. Okay, where in the hell is the bedroom?"

He stumbled down the hall that she'd pointed at,

trying not to bonk her head against the doorjamb in his haste. Once in the room, he set her down, hoping his eagerness didn't reveal the sort of breathless rookie level he felt he'd regressed to. His mouth dried out when she turned around so her back was to him. He slid the long, metal zipper from the top of the dress to the bottom. It fell to the floor, leaving her exposed—and how.

"Nice touch, this. Thongs are my favorite."

"Gee, I wonder why," she said. "They're as uncomfortable as hell if you must know."

"Thanks for the reality check," he said. "Wait. Don't turn yet."

He put his hands on her shoulders, slid her bra straps down, unhooked it and watched it join the dress on the floor in front of her. He reached around and cupped her breasts, running both thumbs across her nipples. She arched her back again, pressing her sweet ass against his crotch while he kissed her neck and shoulders and teased both of her firm nipples.

"Jesus," he muttered when she flipped around quickly before he could protest. She was even more exquisite than he imagined when he'd been ogling her in those running shorts and sports bra earlier that day.

She put her arms around his neck and smiled. "I'm sorry I lost it earlier."

"It's okay. This is a little...unexpected," he admitted. He cradled her face in his hands. "Unexpected. But very..." He kissed one cheek. "Very." He kissed the other one. "Nice."

He licked her lower lip, then her upper one, then slid his tongue into her mouth. She kissed like a pro, he'd admit, even as he started mentally reciting his own career stats, his go-to distraction whenever he got this worked up.

After a few moments spent letting his mind wander on purpose, he realized he'd lost his focus on what he was doing, which was crazy. He had a beautiful, sexy woman in his arms. One who'd had a moment, granted. A moment that had nearly derailed their pleasant progress. The sensation of the warm length of her body pressed along his brought him back from his brief, odd reverie about whether or not her ex-husband laid angry hands on her. He'd deal with that later. Because he was the sort of man who needed to know that sort of detail.

He broke the kiss and led her to the bed. "I wasn't making all that up. Have a seat. I have some things I'm dying to do. But be sure and let me know if you like it."

She lifted an eyebrow as if daring him.

He took that dare. And was ready to run with it.

He knelt in front of her, slid off her shoes, gave each foot a brief massage, then licked his way up the inside of one leg. Pausing at the thong, eager to rip it off, he made himself fulfill what he'd claimed he'd do. She was writhing on the bed, her hands gripping the duvet cover by the time he'd reached her delicious— and amazingly sensitive—nipples and was propped over her, still fully dressed, quite literally within seconds of blowing in his underwear.

He dropped over onto his side and tugged her thong down, smiling when she kicked it off her foot onto the floor. He pressed his whole hand over her sex, groaning at the glorious sensation of it warm and soft under his palm. She angled her hips, eager for him.

"Do you like this?" he kept asking. "How about this? And this?"

She sighed and moaned. "Yes," she said every time. "More of that," she'd say. Or, "No, not that. But yes, that....oh my god yes, more of that!"

He slid a finger inside her and pressed his thumb to the firm bit of flesh above her entrance, rubbing slow, then fast. And faster. He lowered his lips to her nipple as he stroked and teased, keeping one finger deep inside her, his thumb working a little magic on the outside.

"Hatch!" she shouted, shoving her hips up, eager, encouraging him while he sucked her nipple one more time. "Yes!"

He felt her spasm. Warmth flooded his hand. He lifted his head so he could watch her face, loving the way her lips parted and her skin flushed red as she climaxed.

Once she came down off orgasm mountain with shivers and sighs, he put his fingers to his lips, tasting her. When she opened her eyes, and turned her head to look at him, he grinned.

"So...be honest," he said. "I can take it. Have I lost my touch?"

She made something resembling a growling sound, rolled, and pinned him beneath her. The heat against his crotch made his whole body tense. She smiled down at him. Her hair hung loose, curtaining them from the world.

"You haven't lost your touch, mister. And you know it. I hate false modesty. You know what else I hate? All these damn clothes you're wearing."

She got up, unbuckled his belt, unzipped him, and tugged everything down and off. With a wicked grin she took his perfectly nice shirt in both hands and ripped it, sending buttons flying through the air.

"Damn, woman." He had to gnaw the inside of his cheek to regain control of himself. Again.

She tugged his undershirt up and off, then pushed him back down and straddled him. "Hang on a minute," she panted.

She reached over his head for something in a bedside table drawer, putting her luscious nipples at mouth level. He took advantage of that a few seconds. She moved down his thighs and rolled the condom down his aching flesh.

"Hatch," she said, breathless again as she eased up his body, flicking her tongue over his nipples, making his hips jerk under her. She bit his shoulder, his neck, covered his lips with hers until, with a shift of her hips, he was exactly where he'd wanted to be for the last, oh, three hours or so.

"Holy shit." He groaned as she sat up, one hand propped on his chest, the other on his thigh behind her. She started rolling her hips, clenching and unclenching him. "You don't have to...I'm not gonna...oh...dear God."

Dropping over him again so he could suck that sweet, strawberry of a nipple into his mouth, she ground down on his pubic bone, gaining external friction even as he was buried so deep inside her he never wanted to escape the warm, velvet grip of her body on his.

"Come," she whispered into his ear. "Come with me, Hatch. Please."

Well, that tore it. With a loud only mildly embarrassing yell of relief, he did exactly that, letting the rhythmic pulse of her second orgasm send him into the abyss. Their bodies rocked together, his sweaty face buried in her neck, his mind a pleasant blank.

That killer wicked grin never faded. "So, be honest. I can take it. Did I lose my touch?" she asked before she flicked one of his nipples, then rose up and off him with a loud sigh of satisfaction. "And if you say yes, I'm shoving you out that same window."

He chuckled and grabbed her hand, threading his fingers in hers, then putting her hand to his lips. "That was amazing, Olivia. You're amazing." That was all he could conjure. Lame. But he'd do better next time.

Next time?

Oh, yes please and thank you very much.

"Yes, well…" She rolled onto her side and stared at him, her hand playing with the light hairs on his chest. "You're not too bad yourself. Duncan Jerome."

He groaned. "If you're trying to keep me from a second round, it's working." Her hand made its way downward. He sucked in a breath.

"Liar, liar," she whispered, leaning over to take his earlobe in her teeth. She tugged the condom off and dropped on the floor behind her. "I think it's my turn to show you what I can do." Her hand kept moving. Her gaze never left his.

"Oh, I don't doubt your skills," he said. "But, you know, I'm all about constant quality testing. So…do your worst, madam."

She took that to heart. By the time they finished, she'd utilized two more from her condom stash and Hatch had never in his life felt better with a woman sleeping in his arms.

****

Hatch woke with a jolt from what could only be termed a nightmare. He was breathing heavy. Sweat coated his skin. A newly familiar voice echoed in his dreaming brain.

He rolled away from Olivia's sleeping form after kissing her shoulder a few times to ensure he was, indeed, awake. His right arm tingled as feeling returned to it. He smiled to himself recalling that, regardless of that one minor inconvenience, he always loved sleeping with his body curled around a woman's. But this woman…

The nightmare returned with such clarity, it was as if he'd fallen back asleep and was experiencing it all over again. He sat on the side of Olivia's bed, rubbing his hand over his face, his eyes clenched shut. He must have made a noise.

"What time is it," Olivia mumbled.

He got up, needing some space to process the way his pulse was racing and his mind wouldn't let go of a single thought—that Olivia's ex-husband had hurt her in some way, other than the obvious number he'd done on her self-esteem. He had done all he could to ruin her career after she'd resigned from the sports department of his station and presented him with divorce papers. Was he also physically abusive?

Hatch shook his head to clear it of that thought before he did or said something stupid and ruined their afterglow. "Uh, not sure. My phone is somewhere on the other side of the room I think."

"Very funny," she said.

His eyes had adjusted enough to the gloom that he could see her and watch when the sheet slid down, exposing one full breast. Olivia Grant was something special. That much he knew already. He'd known it a few days ago, after he'd experienced his first, sexy dream about her.

She wasn't the twenty-something, groomed, coiffed, and starved down to a bone rack type that plenty of men his age and life station seemed to chase. Her sort of gorgeous was more refined, less brittle, more sure of itself. The fact that she'd been a D-1 athlete meant she'd spent more time worrying about her speed and agility or how much weight she could squat than whether or not she could wear a size zero, something his ex-wife had fretted about with near terminal obsession. But did that mean he could take a chance again? Or rather, would he be subjecting her to something broken in him? Should he warn her about it before they went any deeper into this...whatever it was?

She stretched like a spoiled house cat, which sent that sheet even further down her body, exposing both breasts. Her body was perfect. He actually preferred hips and breasts that contrasted with a woman's waist. He liked a woman to have some flesh on her ass. All the better to grip it, after all. While he'd admit that she was probably the oldest woman he'd ever been with—it was only because the one woman he'd been with the longest had been six years his junior. Since his divorce, he'd had plenty of opportunity. All of which he'd passed on in a fit of remorse over ruining a perfectly satisfactory marriage with his one, stupid weakness.

Hatch felt his body stir back to life as he stared at Olivia. Which shocked the absolute hell out of him. He was a forty-two year old man. Forty-two year old men did not go three rounds, sleep a few hours, and come roaring back.

She smiled up at him, eyes blinking as she woke

fully, her dark blonde hair a messy halo around her face.

He frowned as her voice, raised in fear and pain, filled his brain. *"No! Stop...please, Daniel, don't do this."*

"I need to pee," he muttered.

"You know where to go for that," she said, rolling onto her side.

That damn sheet kept up its conspiracy to make him hard again, slipping down her body so he could see the sweet, heart shape of her ass. He sighed and headed for the bathroom.

Mission accomplished, he washed his hands, splashed water on his hot face, and stared at himself in the mirror, which served to remind him that he was no spring chicken himself, nor was he some kind of a perfect male specimen. Something he'd been fooled into thinking for a few years.

"No...please stop, Daniel."

Hatch dropped his head, willing the sound of Olivia's terrified voice out of his head. He had no idea why he was obsessing over this. Or rather, he did know why it was happening. What he couldn't square was why his all-of-a-sudden jealous brain was formulating some kind of a scenario involving abuse. He clenched his jaw and stared at himself a few more seconds, taking in his weather-roughened face, his bed head, the small red marks on his neck she'd gifted him during one of their enthusiastic tumbles earlier.

He grinned. If she had been abused, it definitely hadn't affected her libido. The woman was the sort of insatiable that any man would appreciate. Not to mention multi-orgasmic. As well as stellar at blow jobs.

A total unicorn, Hatcher. Enjoy it and stop with all the BS about her former spouse.

"Hey."

He flinched at the sound of her voice.

Pull it together, man. You don't have to save her from anyone, unless it's you, of course.

He frowned at that core reality before turning to face her. She was wrapped in the sheet. She had her hair tugged up in a utilitarian ponytail, her expression pensive, her body language tense. "You okay? I mean...we...um, probably shouldn't...I mean. Maybe you should go home now." She glanced at the phone in her hand. "It's almost three a.m."

Shoving everything but the glorious sight of her out of his rattled brain, he took one step forward and scooped her into his arms. "You really want me to go? Now?" She smelled of sex, of him, and that made him even hornier.

She let the sheet drop. "No, not really. I was only being pragmatic. You know. About your super obvious vehicle parked at my place all night kind of a thing?"

He sighed into her neck. "You're probably right."

She pulled away, completely comfortable in her nakedness in front of him.

"Christ, Olivia. You are so..." He reached for her. She stepped back.

"I know I'm right." Her voice was soft. "But I don't want you to go." Her gaze dropped down his torso to the obvious, that he wasn't terribly keen on leaving either. "Impressive," she said, her voice dipping lower. "I mean...you know."

He chuckled and yanked her back to him, grinding his fully revived erection against her. "Oh, I know. But

I'm not about to question it."

When she looked up at him, her eyes shining in the harsh bathroom light, something in him shifted. He actually felt it in his chest, or maybe his brain. He opened his mouth to say something that he probably shouldn't say, at least not at this juncture. As if sensing this, she wrapped her arms around his neck and kissed him, hard, her small tongue shoving its way into his mouth, as if to jam the words back into his brain.

It worked.

"Olivia," he whispered her name over and over as he made love to her a fourth time, at nearly three in the morning, forcing himself not to fall asleep afterward so he could sneak out and head home at four.

He cranked all the windows down and let the early morning air hit his face, cooling it, but not his brain, which was now roiling in a way he knew was going to be a problem. After losing Alexandra and his former life as a famous, rising star in the world of pro football coaching, he'd decided that he didn't need anyone in his life at that level ever again. He couldn't allow it. He was weak in ways he couldn't explain or justify to anyone. His gambling was almost worse than an alcohol or drug problem. He could drop thousands of bucks one minute, and then function, unimpaired, the next. It was insidious and horrific, and he'd let it ruin him.

As he waited at an empty intersection for the red light to change, he knew he couldn't do that to Olivia. While he had it under control now, it could come roaring back any moment. He ran his fingers under his nose, smiling at the ghostly scent of her lingering on his skin. He'd never felt so conflicted about a woman in his entire life and wasn't at all comfortable with the sensation.

By the time he'd made it home, he had a plan. Something he probably shouldn't do. But he'd heard the rumors about her ex. Now he wanted to know objective facts. And he knew just the man to get them.

Thinking he'd sleep a while, he lay on his back in his austere bedroom long enough to give up on that, then watched the sun rise over the lake instead, coffee in hand, body sated, his mind a wash of confusion, emotion, and resolve.

Chapter Six

Olivia opened her eyes and blinked at the sunlight filtering in through the shutters. A pleasant lassitude gripped her, and her body ached in places that had long been neglected. She touched her nipples that still tingled, remembering Hatch's mouth on them, and between her legs her sex clenched with the memory of his body against hers, inside her.

Four times.

Four times he'd driven her to intense, exquisite orgasms. And each time he made sure to wring every drop of pleasure from her that he could. He was such a contrast to Daniel, for whom sex had been an exercise in gratification—his. He had an obsessive need for praise, as if he was the king of the bedroom but had to be constantly reminded of that fact. It had taken her too long to recognize that this was all part of his narcissistic personality, the need to rule in every area of life, especially hers. She wondered what he'd think if he knew she considered his performance less than memorable. Especially after he stopped trying to satisfy her or demand compliments after each and every move.

Don't think of him, or anyone else. Focus on Hatch. Enjoy the afterglow. Fall into it. When was the last time you felt this good?

Maybe never.

She wanted to be angry with herself. After all, she

had a goal here and she'd really be fucked if it all fell apart. But sweet lord, that was the best sex she'd ever had.

Hatch was, without a doubt, an expert lover, intense and dedicated, focusing on her needs and her desires. She'd never felt so cherished in her life. Or had such intense, exquisite, erotic sex. There wasn't a part of her body left untouched by his mouth and his hands.

An unexpected hum slipped from her mouth as she recalled every single moment of the night. When she had been a student at Lakeview with an Atlas-sized crush on the big football hero, never did she ever think this would happen.

The question now was, where did they go from here? Would he ask her out again? Would he want to go to bed with her again? How did he feel after last night? Her screwed up psyche had ruined her ability to sense those things, and she really, really wanted to go out with him again. But how would that fit in with everything else?

Okay, after the period in her life known as The Disaster, she now had a hot job, a hot project, and a sexy guy who found her attractive. The most important thing on that list was the video. It was her ticket to reclaiming her reputation and her position in sports broadcasting.

I'm a professional. I can keep the two parts of my life separate. She just hoped, when she went to the football field again, she didn't lose it and act like some simpering teenager.

Gah!

She *was* acting like a teenager. Crap. She needed to get over that. She'd go right on with her project, take her cue from Hatch, and whatever happened, happened. But there was something so magnetic about him, something she'd never found in another man, certainly not Daniel. Was she compromising her professional integrity? Not if they both behaved like adults and kept their personal business to themselves.

She rolled over in bed and covered her eyes with her forearm. She needed to pull herself together and get on with her workday. She had video to review, a story to finish for tonight's sports segment, and a meeting with her videographer to plan what they would shoot tomorrow.

But she took a moment to bury her face in the pillow Hatch had used and inhale his scent, something fresh and outdoorsy that made all her pheromones and hormones and any other -ones start to do a tap dance up and down her nerves. She could have lain there another ten minutes, maybe rubbing her face into the soft linen, except her damn phone rang.

She flopped onto her back and reached for it without checking the screen. She wished she'd used common sense and looked first.

"Well." Daniel's harsh voice cut into her euphoria. "I hear you made quite a spectacle of yourself last night."

For a split second, she was confused at the sound of her ex-husband's voice. It was as if she'd conjured him, somehow, with the incessant mental comparisons she kept making—not in his favor—to her experience the night before. Then, for a brief moment she wondered if he'd had someone spying on her, caught Hatch walking into the townhouse with her. Then her brain settled. That was ridiculous. He wouldn't spend the money on that.

She inhaled, a deep settling breath, and let it out. "Good morning to you, too, Daniel. I have no idea what you're talking about."

"You weren't showing yourself off last night at La Plaza? And with a cheesy, washed-up football coach on top of it?"

Don't let him bait you. He's too good at that.

"I was having a business dinner. Not that it's any of your business."

"Everything you do is my business," he snapped. "People in this city, in this industry know we were married. We'll always be connected in their minds. If you misbehave, it reflects badly on me. I can't have that."

Well, his ego certainly hasn't shrunk at all.

Deep breath. Deep, deep breath.

"Then I'd say that's their problem. And yours. Because we certainly aren't connected in mine. We're divorced, remember? We're officially done. Finished."

"I wouldn't cut all those cords too fast." There was a nasty edge to his voice. "Like I said, people still tend to link us together."

"That's their problem," she said again. "I have my own life, and you have yours. Stay out of mine."

"I hear you're working on a big project. Too bad for you if it got torpedoed."

A chill wriggled through her, followed by a surge of anger so great she was afraid it would consume her. She forced herself to take a deep, calming breath.

"What I do is no longer any business of yours," she pointed out. "And my work speaks for itself."

"Just keep telling yourself that. But if you think

you're going to sleep your way into that coach's good graces to help your little video, think again. You'd need a hell of a lot more talent than you have."

"Maybe if I'd had a better teacher, it might have helped." She'd told herself not to antagonize him, but the words were out of her mouth before she could stop them.

"And maybe if you'd been a better student, you'd be a lot better in bed today. And on the air. Don't think I'm going to let a piece of shit in any way connected to me to be shown."

She had to grit her teeth to keep from blowing up. "I don't work for you anymore. And if you try to meddle in my business, well, two can play that game."

"Be careful, Olivia. You never know what will come back to bite you in that fat ass of yours."

Fat ass? Fat ass? She should have told him it was better than a skinny dick. But no, she was too mature for that.

"Goodbye, Daniel."

She broke the connection and flopped back on the pillows, her pulse racing. Would she never be rid of this man? He'd fought the divorce, although she had no idea why, since he'd made it plain he didn't want her. He'd also done his best to make sure she didn't get another shot in the industry. When she'd gotten the initial go ahead for her documentary, it must have shocked him to find out not everyone worshiped at the altar of the great Daniel Forrest. Still, he continued to wield enormous power and she could find herself out of business again if he decided to play games.

Hell!

She needed to get him out of her head. She'd

promised to meet Drew at the student union and flesh out the rest of the shooting schedule. Then she'd call Hatch and see when he could fit her into his schedule again. She still needed to set up a lengthy one-on-one interview that could be interspersed with the other footage. Would he still be as amenable? Had she ruined it with her behavior last night? Would he decide he didn't want to complicate his life by mixing business and pleasure? Or was she letting Daniel get under her skin, yet again?

It would appear so.

Get up, Olivia. Fix a cup of coffee, and get your shit together.

But just as she swung her legs over the side of the bed her cell rang again. This time she checked the screen and blew a sigh of relief when she saw the name. Lee Ann. Damn! Now she felt guilty. She'd been so busy with Hatch and everything that was leading to that she hadn't called her best friend in days.

"Hi, Lee Ann. If you're calling to harass me for not calling you lately, consider me thoroughly chastised. I am so very sorry." She headed for the kitchen, talking as she went, zeroing in on her single serving coffee maker.

Lee Ann laughed. "No, I'm calling because it looks like you're keeping things from your best friend."

Olivia frowned. "I have no idea what you're talking about."

She smiled at the hiss of the coffee maker and the sound of the water dripping into the mug. The incredible aroma was already teasing her nostrils and waking up her pleasantly overworked body.

"Oh, come on, Liv. It looks like things are working

out just fine between you and the uber sexy football coach. At least, that's how it looked to everyone who saw you being so cozy at La Plaza last night."

"Jesus Christ! Was the whole world there? How did you know?"

Lee Ann laughed. "Right now, that place is the new hot spot in town. Jenny and Kyle Fitzpatrick were there with some friends, and they saw you. She said you were looking very intimate with the guy who's everyone's new dream fantasy. So how was it?"

Oh, my god!

"How was what? The food is excellent and the service unequaled. Great dinner spot."

"Uh huh." Humor still edged her voice. "Coach Duncan Jerome Hatcher hasn't been seen out with a woman since he got back in town. In fact, if the media is to be believed, not since his divorce. So, I'm asking again. How did it happen and how was it?"

How was it? Her nipples tingled, and a heavy pulse throbbed between her legs as inappropriate memories flashed through her brain. Her body clenched with the memory of the unbelievable orgasms he'd coaxed from her, and she swore she could feel the heat of his body pressed against her. She took a swallow of the hot coffee, almost welcoming the burn on her tongue as it cut into her illicit thoughts.

"I'm doing that documentary on him," she answered. "You know. I told you all about it. We needed a quiet place to go over some of the details, and his office is just too busy."

"Uh huh." Lee Ann laughed. "And the only place you could find was a romantic restaurant, right?"

"It was just—"

"It's okay, Liv." Her friend's voice softened. "You need to do that once in a while, even if it really is just dinner." She paused. "Although you sure could use some of the other, too. Man, that guy is sex on a stick."

And wasn't that just the damn truth. She needed to rally every bit of her self-discipline if she was to finish this in a professional manner.

"So, this is none of my business," Lee Ann went on, "but while you guys were being so *friendly* with each other, did he happen to mention anything about his marriage and why it ended the way it did? I mean, so sudden and quiet. There was plenty of speculation, as I'm sure you know, but not one single fact emerged. Give it up, lady."

Olivia took another sip of coffee.

"There's nothing to give up. He made it plain from the beginning that subject is off limits. This focuses only on his life as a player and coach and what brought him back to Lakeview."

"But aren't you curious?"

"Of course, but I also respect his boundaries. This isn't a scandal piece, you know."

"Aha!" Lee Ann pounced. "So there is a scandal."

"No. At least not that I know of. And anyway, if I want to pitch this nationally, I need to focus only on his career."

"When will you see him again?"

Olivia glanced at the clock on the stove. "As a matter of fact, I have to call him and see if I can shoot some more video tomorrow and also make plans for another one-on-one. I'm telling you, the guy is fascinating. He vibrates with energy, and football is his drug of choice."

"Sounds like you're interested in him as more than a subject of a documentary."

"Absolutely not." And she'd better not be, despite last night. She let out a deep breath. "Daniel called just before you did."

"That asshole!" The words exploded from Lee Ann. "What in the hell did he want?"

Despite the situation, Olivia had to chuckle. Her friend seldom swore, except when Daniel's name came up. "Apparently the entire world saw me at La Plaza last night. He wanted to tell me that I was ruining my reputation by going out with my subject. That, according to his friends, the two of us looked very cozy. And that I'd better watch my step, because everything I did reflected back on him. Oh, and he could screw up my project any time he wanted to."

"I'll say it again. What an asshole. Liv, I hope you're smart enough to know there's really nothing he can do, right?"

Olivia sighed.

"Yeah, I guess so. But he's still in a powerful enough position with the network to make trouble if he was so inclined."

"I know he says that, but Daniel's just flapping his jaw. He likes to yank your chain. You've got this, Liv. Go do it."

After she disconnected, Olivia stood for a moment staring out the window. Would she never be free of Daniel Forrest? Marrying him had been the biggest mistake of her life. Being young and foolish and starry-eyed wasn't enough of an excuse. She also had a brain, and she should have used it. Well, she'd use it now and push him out of her mind. What she did was none of his business anymore. If he thought it was, well, she could fight just as dirty.

One thing was for sure, though. If she and Hatch had another meal in public, it better not be at a restaurant like La Plaza. Someplace innocuous, less glamorous, and less in the public eye.

Fixing another cup of coffee, she took a sip to settle her brain, then punched the button to call Hatch. Her hand shook only a little as she waited for him to answer.

"Good morning." His deep voice rumbled through the connections, setting off her hormones again. Was he happy she'd called? Irritated?

For god's sake, Olivia. Quit acting like a deflowered virgin after prom night.

"Good morning. I, uh, wanted to thank you for a nice evening last night." She wondered if he'd think she was talking about dinner or the sex?

"Me, too." Pause. "Probably the best night I've had in a long time."

"Yes. Um, ditto on that."

"We still didn't get started on the personal interview part of this process."

"So, you're still good to go with the whole thing?"

There was a second of dead air when she thought her heart would stop.

"More than good," he said at last. "Olivia, I hope last night was as great for you as it was for me. I haven't spent time with a woman in what seems like ages, and I enjoyed every minute of it." Another pause. "Every minute. I hope you did, too."

"Yes. I did."

"Since we sort of wiped out the run and breakfast

this morning, I guess you're calling about shooting some more video?"

"Right. I'd like to come out tomorrow afternoon if that works for you. We're going to shoot some more B roll of the university to show people the setting. Plus, we still need to set a convenient time for the one-on-one interview."

"Practice is at two tomorrow so come on down. You said you wanted to talk to a couple of my coaches so you can go ahead and set that up." Another pause. "And if you're up for it, I thought you might like to come over to my place after you're finished. We could talk. I'll grill a couple of steaks. Would that work for you?"

"That would be nice. Yes. I'd like that. And thank you." And she'd better stick to business.

"My pleasure. See you tomorrow afternoon."

After she hung up, she stood still for a moment, holding the phone and letting everything roll around in her brain. She knew how unprofessional this whole thing was, but she couldn't seem to make herself care. Plus, Hatch had as much to lose if they fucked this up as she did. But, at least this time, they wouldn't be under a microscope for the world to see.

She kept turning the relationship—if that's what it was—over in her head while she worked on changes in the outline for the documentary. She was eager to interview the coaches and get their take on Hatch. The excitement of redeeming herself rushed through her veins. She'd do well to focus on that.

But first she wanted to review what Drew had already shot. She called him about the next day and also to see if he had time and could book an editing room.

"There's one free this afternoon after two," he told her. "I'll block it off."

"Good. See you soon."

No sooner had she finished with Drew than her phone rang again. What the hell? Didn't people know it was Sunday?

"I hear you're adding a personal note to the documentary you're doing." Bert Hoekstra's irritating nasal tone zipped across the connection.

Damn. She'd have to figure out a way to handle him. This was getting to be too much of a pain.

"If you're referring to the dinner I had with Coach Hatcher last night, it was all about the doc and getting a bit of personal information from him."

"Uh huh. Sure. And how personal did it get?"

"Bert, you're disgusting," she snapped. "I have a job to do, and I'm doing it."

"Did he give you any details about why he hauled his ass back to Lakeview from the big time?"

"You already asked me that once." She blew out a breath. "I guess you'll just have to watch the video to find out."

"Or maybe I'll keep doing some digging myself. You never know what you'll find."

"Nothing," she said and hoped she was right.

"What did the great and powerful Daniel Forrest think about your so-called not-a-date dinner?

What? The? Hell?

"This must be a pretty damn boring town," she said between gritted teeth. "It seems no one has anything to do except comment about who I have dinner with."

Even his chuckle had a nasty sound to it.

"Just checking out my facts, Liv. Always on the

hunt for my next big story."

"Well, you won't find it with me. Stay out of my hair and out of my way, Bert. I mean it."

She disconnected the call, but a tiny feeling of unease dusted over her. What the hell was he talking about? There was nothing for him to find where Hatch was concerned.

Only something was tingling her reporter's antennae, and that something was making her feel pretty damn nervous.

The feeling didn't leave her as she drove to the studio, and she forced herself to put Hoekstra out of her mind and concentrate on the upcoming task. What would the raw footage show? Had she given Drew the right directions? Had she gotten enough footage to capture Hatch in all facets of his coaching persona on the field? Did she have the right variety for a great B roll, which could set the tone for the entire video?

Drew was already set up in a viewing room when she arrived at the studio. It had been quite a while since she'd done a major project like this. Of course she'd been grateful for the studio gig. She was grateful for anything as she rebuilt a career Daniel had destroyed. The thought that if it was good, the video would go national made butterflies dance in her stomach. This was her chance, her shot to basically give the proverbial finger as well as re-establish herself. Everything had to be just right.

She could do this. She would not let her nerves get the best of her or let Dan's anger and disdain diminish this opportunity. Settling herself in the seat next to Drew, she nodded.

"I'm going to take notes as we go along." As she

always did when reviewing tape, she took her pen and notebook from her messenger bag and set them on the little counter in front of her. She was old enough that, at times, she still felt more comfortable taking notes the old-fashioned way.

"Good deal. And any time you need me to stop or rewind, just tell me."

"Let's do it." Her voice was tight.

"Okay, kiddo. Here we go."

He pressed a button, and the tape began to roll across the screen in front of her. She watched, mesmerized, as frames of the team on the field going through drills and executing plays filled the screen. Hatch stood in his normal pose, bent over, hands on knees, as he took in the action with a visceral intensity. Drew had even zoomed in a few times on his face, set in lines of concentration. In his signature khakis and a university sweatshirt, the shot captured an iconic image of him doing what he loved.

"Stop right there and back it up," she told Drew.

"How far?"

"Just until you have the closeup of him like that. Yes, that's it. Freeze it."

Drew tapped the keyboard, and the image froze on the screen.

"Oh, Drew, you really caught the essence of him. Of who he is." A tiny thrill ran through her as she studied the screen. This was what it was all about, showing the viewers who the man really was. Showing his love for what he did. "Can you print that for me? I'm going to talk to the boss about using it in the promo we set up."

"Hatch has been out of the public eye for a while

so this is sure to draw people's attention," Drew said.

"Good. That's what I want." *He sure drew mine.* "Okay, let's keep going."

The video of the team practicing and executing actual plays was right on target. The excitement of the game fairly leaped off the screen. She hoped it would grab viewers the same way.

They went through all the footage once, a lengthy project, from start to finish. Olivia managed to keep from chewing her nails or tapping the arm of the chair. She was just so damn nervous. As the video rolled, whenever she saw something she really liked, she had Drew pause it so she could write down the numbers of the location on the roll. After they'd viewed every inch of what he'd shot, they went back to the beginning.

She breathed a little sigh of relief. Drew was good, which was why she'd asked for him and been thrilled when her request was granted.

"Okay." She looked at him. "I'd like to go through it one more time, but just hitting the specific places I've marked. Can we do that?"

He grinned. "We can do anything you want. You're the boss."

"The boss." She gave a tiny laugh. "Not exactly, but at least I'm in charge of this project."

And no one is second guessing me and telling me why my ideas suck.

When they were finished and she'd told Drew which parts to extract for the final tape, she sat back in her chair, smiling. "You do some good work, my man. You really caught the essence of the man.

Chapter Seven

The air struck the quarterback's exposed skin like a million tiny needles. Steam rose from the scrum of sweating, breathless players surrounding him. The odor of frozen turf—something entirely different from the odor of the near melting version they'd suffer through in early season games—filled his lungs. The roar of the crowd almost overwhelmed the sound of his voice yelling the crucial information about the next play to his teammates.

The quarterback jammed his hands into the warming sleeve at his waist for a few seconds, seeking quick relief from the exquisite agony in his reddened, swollen fingers. He willed the timeout clock to slow, to give him a few more seconds to think, to plan, to pull this crucial game out of his ass.

He took a moment to look up at the stands. Thanks to his lack of a right eye contact lens from a brutal sack in the first quarter, all he saw was an undulating blob of red and white. When he exhaled, the cloud of his own breath around his head blurred everything even more.

"Break!" he shouted before trotting backward toward his spot under his center, willing his offensive line to understand that this was their last shot at victory. They'd been porous in the face of their rivals' defensive freight train, and he'd taken more than one enthusiastic slam to the turf. He'd lost a contact lens in the first quarter and shaken off the trainer's concern about concussion in the second.

A hit in the third had left him lying on his back, his breath shoved out of his lungs, wondering if this was what it felt like to die. But right after that, his defense had stopped their opponent's seemingly inexorable march to the goal line. Which had given him an opportunity to heave a serious Hail Mary and a Half up into the air at the start of the fourth. A tricky, two-point extra points drive he'd called on the fly, and at the risk of his coach stroking out on the sidelines, had tied the game.

And now, with twenty-two seconds to go, he was determined to end their losing streak to this particular challenging rival and to earn a spot in a major bowl game for his team.

"Forty-nine! Forty-nine! Forty-nine!" He hollered out the secret code for the double-pass play he'd insisted would work. He'd spent a lot of minutes studying how closely the opposing defense had their number on other plays. Their best shot right now, as he watched the other team line up against his, would be to toss the ball backward, rugby style, to his favorite receiver, then dart around the edge while the other team scrambled to figure out what was going on. He'd position himself as close to the goal line as possible and catch the damn thing himself.

This wasn't some kind of a hero move. The quarterback wasn't into that kind of thing. He was notorious for not going out after victories to celebrate the way his teammates preferred to do. He kept a low profile for a young man who'd already won college football's top VIP trophy as a junior, and was now predicted by all the sports talking heads to go second or third in the draft.

"That kid'll be playing on Sunday, mark my words," was a phrase he'd been hearing about himself since his sophomore year at this mid-major, Division one Michigan school. His father had already vetted a half-dozen sports agents. His older brother, who'd also played college ball at a small school and had made a name for himself until suffering a career ending injury before joining management of another team, would even admit, under duress, that his little brother might be better than he at the game. Which was saying something, since the two of them had competed at absolutely everything from an early age.

But now, all the quarterback wanted was to silence the doubters and to beat this damn team, historic rivals in their conference, at this, the last game of the regular season. He wanted the victory so badly he could taste it in the back of his throat, could feel it on the ends of his fingers. He visualized the win once more in his head, even as the offensive line shifted to the right after the quick snap, exactly as they'd practiced for the upcoming play.

The quarterback took two steps back, spotted his target in the corner of his eye, turned, and tossed the football to him. The corresponding curses and grunts from the defense gave him hope that they might pull this off.

"Go! Go! Go!" his receiver called. Tank, as Theodore Eugene Pasternak was more conveniently known, was one player the quarterback trusted implicitly. They'd been playing together since their junior football days and had been fast friends from first grade. They'd concocted this play their freshman year on a whim, when they'd both been trying to gain muscle mass and playing time.

The quarterback juked to the left to avoid a random defenseman who seemed to have figured out what they were doing, turned, and saw the ball sail up and toward him. For a split second, it seemed to hang, suspended by invisible forces. At the same moment, the crowd went almost completely silent, waiting and watching for their star quarterback to save the day.

He made a quick shift to his right, reached up, and felt the ball dancing on the ends of his fingertips for a few more terrifying and somehow longer than normal seconds. With a loud grunt of effort, he hauled the ball to his chest, cradling it like a newborn baby so he could turn and take the two steps required across the white line to win the game.

The hits came from both sides. The next thing he knew, the quarterback was staring up at the unforgiving, ice cold blue sky. Faces ringed his vision, each one more freaked out looking than the next. Tank broke through, shoving everyone else aside including their coach, grabbed him, hauled him to his feet, and lifted him with both arms. "We won, you obnoxious bastard! We fucking won!"

The quarterback's vision blurred and things went strangely gray and purple around the edges until his friend put him down and let the trainers take over, all of them shooting eye daggers at Tank as he ran around the sidelines, screaming his lungs out with the student section. The quarterback watched his friend celebrate a few more seconds before he passed out cold.

****

Hatch blinked after jolting wide awake, clearing his mind from the crystal-clear dream memory of that game. It took him two cups of strong coffee and a slice of buttered toast to realize what was making him feel so…happy. He'd not slept so hard in, well, years most likely. It was great. But it also made him groggy and fuzzy well past eight-thirty—an hour he'd usually glance at the clock on his phone or laptop and realize that he could actually reach out to one of his coaches or staff now that it wasn't some ungodly number like five or six.

By the time he'd stumbled into the shower, belly full and nerves attempting to respond to the caffeine he'd dumped onto them, it was nine a.m. If he didn't get his ass in gear, he'd miss his own coaches' meeting. As in, the one he'd called for every Sunday morning until the end of the season.

But as the water heated up, he stood, frozen, the vivid memories of the night before making his face flush and his body break out in goose bumps. He stared at the generic white tile surround of the shower, not seeing it at all. Seeing instead Olivia's full lips, her wide green eyes, the messy state of her hair. Oh, and her tits of course. And her ass. And more. He sighed, and shut his eyes tight, as if to drive the vision of her away so he could concentrate.

He had to take things in hand in the shower. Another shock to him, since he'd had several monster orgasms mere hours before. Once he was cleansed of all hint of Olivia on his skin, he pulled on a freshly ironed pair of khakis and tugged a Jaguars branded polo down over his torso.

Time to focus. He had some changes in mind for

the defense and wanted to talk to those guys before the meeting to see what they thought.

The team, man. Focus on the team. Your job, remember? The one you're damn lucky to have, regardless of how the school has been spinning it as being their luck to have you back. Get your mind out from between Olivia's thighs and on the day ahead.

At the mere thought of "Olivia's thighs" his stupid, overworked dick got hard. He groaned and got busy preparing his morning protein shake and pouring coffee into the extra-large stainless steel cup. He was still half hard when he got behind the wheel of his truck.

"Jesus, Duncan Jerome. You're not some kid. You're a grown-ass man. Act like one." He glanced at his reflection in the rearview mirror, noting the flush on his cheeks with a roll of his own eyes.

****

"Hatch?"

"Yo. Coach!"

"What?" He flinched, realizing he'd been drifting in the middle of the morning status meeting. Luckily, he'd already drained the huge stainless coffee cup that he'd just sent rolling down the middle of the wooden table.

His coaches were all staring up at him, confused by his inattention.

"Sorry." He glanced at the yellow legal pad in front of him, then over at the giant whiteboard where he'd sketched out his thoughts on some defensive strategies that would better fit the young men in those particular positions.

Since these were not his recruits and what he knew about them amounted to their bio files and what he'd seen so far on the field, he felt like he was doing a running start at a blind curve. Scary. But he'd woken with this new concept in mind, and he was pleased to note that both Marc and Alonso, his new hires for the defensive line, agreed that it might just work.

Setting aside the high tech, he tugged his well-worn comp book from under a stack of files and flipped it open. "Okay, where are we with the team today?"

George heaved a long sigh, his typical response Hatch had learned after an initial flash of panic when he'd heard it the first morning in response to this question.

"Well, a couple of them are in a bit of...personal conflict," George began.

The table groaned in unison. They were a room full of overgrown boys who were lucky enough to get paid to coach a sport they'd never been able to let go of. Himself included. They all knew what "personal conflict" meant. He leaned on his elbows and met George's gaze. "Let me guess. Tony and Josh are still at it over..."

"Yeah. Her," George said. "Anyway, last night was a doozy. I dealt with it."

"You should've called me," Hatch said. A flash of anger hit his brain. He'd insisted that his staff deal with all low-level problems, but that he be notified of them immediately. He didn't want plausible deniability. He wanted to know everything, even if he didn't deal with it directly.

"I did, Hatch," George, said, his lips pressed into a firm line. "You check your phone or were you too busy on a...date?"

The briefest of pauses between the last two words

of George's sentence made him snap to attention and realize something he'd forgotten. Avon, Michigan, was a damn small town. Anchored as it was by Lakeview U and tourism, the city revolved around sports, wind conditions on Lake Michigan, and how the fish were biting in the smaller lakes surrounding the immediate area, which had inspired the name of his alma mater.

And he'd taken Olivia to what was easily the nicest restaurant in town. The key words being "in town." Jesus, he was an idiot. And in his idiocy had jeopardized her, professionally and otherwise. He resisted the temptation to slap his forehead.

"Uh, right." He pulled the device from his pocket and noted the four missed calls and string of texts outlining how George and Marc had had to go to the dorms and break up Fight Night, Jaguars-style. Since the team had broken down into two camps, they were going at it so hard, several of them were going to show up to practice with black eyes and fat lips.

"Shit," he muttered under his breath. When he looked up, every set of eyes was on him. None of them accusatory, but all of them curious. He put the phone face down on the table.

"Yes, George, I was out to dinner…and it went…ah…late."

The loud whoops of delight that hit his ears made him lean back. He held up both hands and waited while George collected the dollars tossed at him. Boys. Boys in men's bodies. He bit back the smile and kept his expression stern while George made a show of counting the money before folding it and tucking it into his pocket.

"Do you mind? We have a team to prepare." He

pointed at the whiteboard. The men around the table got back to work with only a few more high fives and smirks.

They finished up and headed toward their various offices and responsibilities, leaving Hatch alone at the head of the table. He flipped his phone around in his palm and stared at the whiteboard, now covered in x's, o's, and arrows. He rose and stood in front of it, pondering the men who'd be in the places of those tiny symbols. Thanks to his near-photographic memory, he could picture their faces and names and even their personalities.

The volatility between the two young men currently coming to blows at regular intervals over a girl was a problem, considering they were his starting quarterback and center. He stared at the two x's that represented Josh Higgins and Tony DeLong. Both of them could easily be drafted in two years, if they bulked up a little and got decent representation. Neither of them were anywhere near ready, emotionally, for that life yet, of course. Not that it mattered. He hadn't been either. Not many guys in their early twenties were prepared for the massive amounts of money thrown at them, along with the extreme stress of going past the glow of being drafted into the gut-wrenching stress of training camp prior to cuts. Not to mention practicing their guts out every week, dressing to play, and watching from the sidelines pretty much every weekend.

He sighed and turned from the board. He'd been lucky to have both his college and high school coaches working with him the summer before the draft, giving him and his parents great advice. Would he be that helpful when it came time to talk with the Tony's and Josh's in his coaching future? Could he provide any decent advice other than "wear a condom every time"?

Probably not. He was, in essence, useless to both of them unless he could get his damn mind off Olivia and back on what mattered right now. His shoulders slumped, and his fingers curled around the phone in his pocket at the exact moment it buzzed with a call. He dragged it out and smiled at the name on the screen.

"Tank, my man," he said as he picked up a few papers that had slipped to the floor during the meeting. "How's it hanging?"

"Low, heavy, and a bit to the left, as you know."

Hatch chuckled and headed toward his desk. "Good to know some things never change." He sat, leaned back in the soft leather chair, and propped his feet up on the desk. He could hear murmured conversations and tapping keyboards in the background.

"No, god damn it," Tank burst out. "Sorry, Hatch, give me a sec."

"Sure thing." He waited while Tank ripped into the staff at his high-tech security and surveillance company.

"Sorry, man. Jesus, these people."

"You handpicked them, remember?"

"I know, I know. They're fuckin' great at what they do, and I pay them well for it. Problem is, they know how great they are. Not unlike a few pro players I could name."

"True that." Hatch let his feet drop to the floor so he could get up and pace.

"I don't know about you, my friend, but I'm as

busy as a cat burying shit right now. I know you get to float around and be the big shot super star coach back in A-town, but…"

He let his question about Tank having an office full of staff on a Sunday afternoon slide. He'd just get sarcasm about having banker's hours in return. "I'm sorry. Listen, I need a favor."

Hatch had the hand not holding the phone to his ear jammed into his pocket and curled into a tight fist. He consciously took a moment to release it and take a deep breath. He was headed into dangerous territory, and he knew it. It was all kinds of not his damn business. But he couldn't let go of it.

After hearing Durbin's quick assessment of Olivia's ex-husband he'd been intrigued/obsessed. But now that he'd been with her, had held her close, kissed her, been so deeply connected with her… He shivered and gritted his teeth against the onrush of erotic memory.

"Okay, who do we need to fuck with? My overpaid staff is at your service."

"We don't need to fuck with anyone. Not this time."

"Fine. Then what is it?" Typical Tank. Right to the chase, no time for chatter, at least not during the workday. He'd be all over the chit-chat over beers or bourbon after hours.

"I want to know something about a guy. And you're the only man to get what I need to know for me."

"What do you want to know? His blood type? What he bought at Amazon yesterday? What kind of porn he prefers? What he posted on social media recently? What streaming series he binged last week?"

"No, no, I mean…I don't know. Shit."

A heavy sigh hit his ears. "What's this about, Hatch? Tell me that, and I can figure out what you need." The background noises had silenced, telling him that Tank had left the pit, as he liked to call it, and shut the door of his huge, glass-enclosed office at the top floor of a renovated building in the newly revived Detroit.

"His name is Daniel Forrest. He's some kind of a—"

Tank's low whistle cut him off. "Dude. Have you found yourself on the wrong side of this particular individual? I mean, I know you're used to dealing with scary motherfuckers lending you betting money and all, but…"

Hatch's face flamed hot. "Yeah, so I need to know…about him."

"Why?"

"Because…I do. That's all." He had his hackles up over Tank's throw-away comment about the mobsters who'd tried to blackmail him, thanks to his gambling weakness. But his friend had been instrumental in helping him dig himself out of that horror show after all. He took a deep breath. "Sorry."

"No worries, Hatch. No worries at all. So, what has you interested in this guy? I mean, I know who he is. And I know he's gotten where he is at the top of the sports television heap by being a giant, intimidating asshole. What else is there?"

"I want to know about his…" Did he really want to go here? Was it the best idea to have his old friend, who happened to be the go-to guy for corporations and the military when it came to digging up intel on individuals, start digging into Olivia's ex-husband's life?

What could he possibly find out that would make him feel better? Nothing. That's what.

"The size of his dick? I'm guessing it's miniscule given how much he overcompensates."

Hatch fell back into his desk chair and leaned over his knees, trying to sort through his thoughts about this. "I want to know about his marriage."

"Which one?"

Hatch sat up fast. "There's more than one?"

"I believe that he's working on locking down wife number three at the moment."

"Oh, wow. I didn't know that."

"Spill it, god damn it. I don't have time for this fuckin' innuendo. Do you owe the guy money?"

Hatch almost hung up on his friend at that. But he knew it was only Tank being Tank. Not Tank trying to needle him over his past transgressions. Their relationship was too long-standing and involved for that. And it simply wasn't in Tank's repertoire. He only liked to needle when it came to football.

"Fine. Okay. Here's the deal." Hatch sucked in a breath. "I guess it's ex-wife number two who is doing this documentary on me right now."

"Oh, man, okay." He could hear Tank tapping notes on his computer. "And do you think it's a hack job, set up by her ex? They're gonna expose your, um…past?"

"No, no, no. Not that." But that thought was going to remain stuck in his head now, and he knew it. "I'm…interested in her."

There was a beat of silence. "You boning her?"

"Not your business."

"Okay. So Hatch is boning ex-wife number two of television asshole number one... Interesting."

"God damn it, Tank."

"What? I need to know the whole story. Just because you don't like to brag about..."

"Stop. Listen. I'm worried about her, that's all. She seems somewhat...I don't know, obsessed with him in a way."

"Obsessed with him."

"You know what I mean."

"I'm afraid I don't. Enlighten me, old friend."

"I like her, all right? Are you happy now? Jesus."

"God, but you're cute when you're chasing tail."

"Will you help me or what? I want to know if that...if her ex-husband, Daniel...abused her. I'm thinking he did."

"And what, pray tell, do you plan to do with that information if I get it for you? How's that going to help?"

"Since when do you give a shit about what people do with the dirt you dig up?"

"Since you're my friend since forever. And I'm unsure that knowing whether or not the target of your adorable affections was knocked around by a guy who seems like the sort of guy who would knock her around is good for your budding relationship. Why not ask her?"

"Because." He ground his teeth together. Since when was Tank so intuitive? "Stop playing at psychotherapy. Can you find this out for me?"

"Sure. Of course."

"Good. Thanks. Bill me at your real rate this time."

"Whatever."

There was a longer beat of silence. Hatch tried to calm down and not let himself get pulled into the hard truth his friend had just laid down. What would he do with the information he had a feeling he already knew? Why not just ask her?

"So...tell me something," Tank said. "One last thing before you go and do your overpaid job coaching a bunch of pimply kids."

"What?" He pressed on his thigh to keep his leg from jittering. Why in the hell was he so nervous? This was crazy, that's why. Utterly stupid and bound to do nothing but cause trouble.

"Does she have as nice a rack as Alexandra? I mean, I know your type. When you commit, you prefer them stacked."

Hatch chuckled, then burst out laughing. One thing he could always count on with Tank. There was no filter on his mouth. And at that, he felt better. "You'll see photos of her soon enough. You figure it out."

"Ah, okay. And you have, indeed, tapped it, right? You're not still playing romance games? I mean, I know your tendencies, my man. And I think you're due a little tapping of..."

Hatch touched the end call button. He grinned all the way through the mid-day meetings with managers, and felt like the smile was pasted to his face by the time he blew the whistle on the afternoon's practice. He glanced over his shoulder and saw her talking with her camera guy. Olivia Grant. The woman he was pretty sure he'd already fallen for. The woman he had no business even thinking about much less fantasizing about how hard he was going to rock her world in a few hours.

"Thanks for everything this afternoon," she told him as her camera guy walked toward the parking lot. "It went really well."

"I want to make this successful as much as you do. It will be great for the program."

"I'm happy to hear that."

"So, um, seven o'clock? You have the address?"

She grinned. "Yes and yes."

"Okay, then—"

"Coach!"

"You have to go. See you later."

He turned and frowned at his star quarterback's hugely swollen nose and cheek. "What is it?"

"I'm gonna take him for an MRI," the QB coach said, walking up to him. "Just to be safe. The idiot."

"Yeah, fine. Listen," he said, squaring up on Tony, who looked appropriately embarrassed by the attention. "Whoever she is, she's not worth tearing up the team right now. Figure your shit out with Josh. I've got two perfectly capable quarterbacks right behind you, and I will use them. You follow me?"

"Yeah."

"What?"

"Yes, coach. Sorry, coach. It won't happen again."

Hatch raised an eyebrow and crossed his arms.

"Coach," Tony said, his eyes flashing once before he dropped his gaze to the turf at their feet.

Hatch slapped the young man's shoulder pads. "Come on. Walk with me. Tell me about it."

They walked together toward the tunnel. Hatch listened. He recalled the feeling of thinking he was so utterly in love with someone he was willing to sacrifice everything over it. But he also knew that it would pass. It would fall out however the young woman wanted it to, no matter how these boneheads acted.

"Go with Coach Vega," he said, pointing toward Alonso, who'd followed behind them, chatting with some of the other players. It was important for team coherence and motivation that every player got a bit of one-on-one contact with coaches. It was something Hatch firmly believed and had ingrained into his staff. "Then you and Josh sit down and talk. Really talk. And at the end of the talk, remember that you're on this team for a reason. You both have potential to play on Sundays someday. But not if you screw it up now, today, this week, over something you really have no control over."

"Got it. Thanks coach." Tony met his gaze again. Hatch was relieved to see that the kid's eyes no longer flashed with hormonally fueled anger.

"You're welcome." He spoke with a few other players, let one of them film him doing horrifically age-inappropriate dances for social media, slapped a few more shoulders, and decided he wanted to go home and shower before Oliva came over.

"Have a good night," George called, waving from across the locker room. "Lover boy."

The entire room erupted in whistles, cat calls, and worse. Hatch shook his head. Boys, every last one of them.

But when he caught sight of himself in the rearview as he pulled out of the parking lot, that shit-eating grin was firmly back in place.

Chapter Eight

The afternoon could not have gone better, as far as Olivia was concerned. She was sure Hatch had prepped both his staff and the players, because everyone was courteous, pleasant, and informative. She got some great sound bytes, and Drew was pleased with the B roll he'd shot. When Hatch introduced her to everyone, he had complimented her work and told them all how excited he was this documentary was happening. He stressed how lucky they were to have someone who did such quality work wanting to do this.

She couldn't remember Daniel ever complimenting her once they were married, unless it was to reflect glory on himself for guiding and directing her. All in all, by the end of the afternoon, she was on a high that had her smiling as she walked out to her car. She could hardly wait for the first game of the season.

The high lasted exactly another five minutes until she rounded the corner to the parking lot and saw Bert Hoekstra once again hanging out at her car. Damn! That man had an uncanny habit of showing up just where and when she didn't need to see him. Like today.

"Are you stalking me?" She elbowed him aside as she unlocked her car door. "Wasn't the phone call enough?"

"Maybe I just missed seeing you in person." He winked.

The gesture made her skin crawl. "Yeah, right."

"Looks like you got a lot of good material today," he said. "Hero worshipping at the feet of Hatch, the football god?"

She shook her head. "Is this all you have to do, Bert? Dog my footsteps and make idiotic remarks?"

"Idiotic, huh? Maybe there's stuff you don't know yet. Or maybe you already do and just plan to overlook it."

"I have no idea what you're talking about. And you'd better get away from my car if you don't want me to run you down."

"Really? You'd run me over?" He chuckled but stepped away from the vehicle. "And here I thought you were such a nice person."

"I have no idea what your game is, Bert. Whatever it is, don't play it around me. If you've got something I should know about, tell me. If not, get the hell away from me and stay away."

She climbed into the car. But before she could close it, he braced it with his hand. "Maybe I know something you need to know before you finish this puff piece you're doing."

She studied him for a long moment.

"Nice try," she said at last. "But history tells me, if you knew something that hot, you'd already be running with it. Or trying to sabotage my video. Or maybe both. So quit fishing when you have no bait and stay away from me and this project. Do your own story if you want."

He leaned into the car. "How about you get me a meeting with Mr. Wonderful and I will?"

She shook her head. "Are you telling me he won't

see you? Hmm. Seems he has even more brains than people give him credit for. Maybe you should take the hint."

"Maybe I'll ask your ex to open a few doors for me." There was nothing humorous in his grin. "After all, he's still one of the top sports executives in the business."

A muscle cramped in her stomach. "Go ahead. You two deserve each other."

"You know, if we worked on this together, you and I, we could both get what we want."

"In your dreams."

She yanked the door closed, almost catching his hand in it, and cranked the ignition. Once she was off the campus grounds and settled back in her seat, her nerves quit jumping and her body began to relax.

Think about this afternoon. Think about tonight. Forget that jackass. All the jackasses.

Some days she wondered if Daniel would ever really be out of her life. Her job at the station where she now worked was limited. She was lucky they'd taken a chance on her at all. But the general manager had seen her work and was impressed by it, so he'd given her a shot.

During the interview process, she'd sensed that Daniel Forrest wasn't one of his favorite people. That one-upping him would be something he enjoyed. Well, she could get on board with that one, for sure. Doing location spots for the different sports was fun, and she was getting both good reviews and a significant number of followers on social media.

And he'd supported her idea for the documentary. This documentary was her ticket to get back on top, so she wasn't about to let Bert Hoekstra or anyone else screw it up.

But as she headed for home to shower and change, she couldn't help wondering if there really was something in Hatch's life he was keeping out of sight. If so, she'd need to find out before it bit her on the ass.

At home, she stripped off her clothes and treated herself to a long, luxurious shower. Then, bundled into a terry cloth robe, she sat down at her desk, opened her laptop, and began her search on Duncan Jerome Hatcher. After an hour, however, she wasn't much further along than when she started. Almost every article and opinion piece had to do with his football career, from high school right up until his vaunted return to Lakeview University. Anything personal, beyond the basic facts, seemed to have been somehow scrubbed from public record. And she was no rookie when it came to finding what she wanted.

His marriage had happened the second year he was in the pros. He and Alexandra Rombard met at a party hosted by mutual friends, and it was a fast, heady ride to the Hawaiian wedding after that. For the next few years, the media couldn't show enough photos of the two of them—at football events, community events, social activities. As far as Olivia could tell, they looked happy and in love.

Then, it all fell apart, but no one reported the reason. One day, they were seen having lunch in a well-known restaurant. The next, a quiet announcement was issued through Hatch's agent that "It is with regret that Alexandra and Duncan Hatcher announce they are terminating their marriage." That was it. No matter how the media—or the fans—screamed and yelled, the couple remained stoically silent. Hatch moved out of their home, which they sold, and Alex moved back to Texas.

Period.

Finito.

Well, wasn't that just too damn intriguing and off the wall. One minute, he had a great marriage, then suddenly, it was gone. And in a universe where every aspect of celebrity's life was hung out there for the world to see twenty-four seven on any number of social media sites, the reason for the divorce was conspicuous by its absence.

She'd have to find a way to ask him about it, but that would be tricky. It was a dangerous path she'd have to walk with great care. Meanwhile—she glanced at her watch—she had a date to keep. Tomorrow, she could put her brain to work again, look to see what she missed. But tonight, it was all about her body.

She rubbed the lightly scented lotion she favored into every inch of her body and took great pains with both her hair and her makeup. Casual, he'd said. Just grilling steaks in the backyard and enjoying the evening. And discussing what kind of personal information she wanted from him. Okay, then.

She pulled on a pair of jeans that she loved because they didn't make her ass look too big or her legs too muscular. She paired the jeans with a navy tank and a gauzy white shirt knotted at the waist. When she was all put together, she took a moment to study herself in the mirror.

Not bad, for an old broad. Maybe if she stepped up her exercise program…

She immediately gave herself a mental smack. She

was more than not bad, and she wasn't that old. She had to get Daniel's voice out of her head. Not let him screw up her life any longer.

Fine. Good. She'd do it. A dab of perfume behind her ears and at her wrists and she was ready.

She was only a touch nervous as she drove out to Hatch's house and still conflicted about the sudden personal attraction. Would it color her narrative? Affect her objectivity? She had so much riding on this. Was she being stupid to see where the relationship went? She'd gone from nothing to a new career start and a man who made her feel loved and appreciated. She'd better be able to balance both because screwing up wasn't an option.

Saturday night had been one hundred percent spontaneous. Unplanned. Spur of the moment. And it had been the best sex she'd ever had. If she weren't driving, she'd be closing her eyes to remember the feel of his hard, muscular body. She smiled. Hard. Definitely the best word. Hard all over. The feel of his cock inside her, his strong hands cradling her breasts, his hot mouth sucking her nipples, his tongue trailing a line down her belly to her—

The honking of a horn snapped her out of her reverie, and she realized she'd started to drift over the center line. Great. How would she ever explain that?

Sorry, officer, but I was just remembering Coach Hatcher fucking my brains out. You know how it is.

She giggled, but then made a deliberate effort to knock the thought out of her mind for the rest of her drive.

Hatch's house was in a quiet, residential neighborhood, older by the look of the mature trees and landscaping. The houses were a mixture of brick and stone, both one- and two-story. Every house was well kept, the lawns manicured. She wondered why, with the money he was being paid, he didn't go for a more upscale area, but then she realized that it boxed pretty well with her knowledge of the man himself.

The trappings of success apparently weren't important to him. Playing well, coaching well, instilling values in his players seemed to be at the head of his list, from what she could tell during the time she'd spent at practice.

She checked her watch. Seven on the dot. Time to move forward.

Drawing a calming breath, she locked her car and walked up to the front door. Before she could even ring the bell, the door opened and Hatch was standing there, an enticing image in jeans and a Lakeview football polo shirt. His smile made every pulse point in her body thrum with excitement. Lord. She had to get hold of herself.

She grinned. "Were you watching for me?"

"As a matter of fact, yes." He reached for her hand. "Come on in."

Olivia stepped into a small foyer that led into a wide living room. A huge bay window looked out on the front lawn, the drapes drawn to block the view to any passersby. Table lamps poured soft light into the room that opened to the dining room and kitchen, like a huge family room. Comfortable furniture and soft colors gave the whole space a warm, relaxing feeling.

"Nice decorating job," she told him.

He laughed. "You can thank my mother. Yes, even at my age, my mother doesn't trust me to pick out a chair. When I bought the house, she spent a week creating what she called a home befitting my position in life."

"She did a good job." She laughed. "Except for the big whiteboard on the wall. What did she say about that?"

"That I'm obsessed and too old to change." He still had hold of her hand, the contact sending warm tingles up her arm.

"At least she knows you're focused."

"How about a drink? Your choices are beer, wine, bourbon, or iced tea."

"Um, wine, please. White, if you've got it."

"Chilling in the fridge, as a matter of fact. Every possible version of white."

She smiled. A man going out of his way to make sure she had what she wanted was such a pleasant change. "Sauvignon blanc, please."

He got down a wine glass, opened a bottle of sauvignon blanc, and filled the glass for her. He grabbed a beer for himself, popped the top, and touched the bottle to her glass. "To a great evening."

"I'll definitely drink to that."

He took a long swallow but kept his eyes on her, the dark chocolate of his irises warm with heat and the flare of hunger. An answering heat rushed through her. She sipped her wine, pulling herself together.

"Like I told you," he reminded her, "a simple meal tonight. Steaks on the grill, baked potatoes, and a salad." He winked. "I make a mean salad."

Olivia laughed. "A talent I appreciate. I'm a big fan of salads."

They were standing barely two inches away from

each other. Hatch put his bottle down on the counter, took her wine glass, and set it down next to it. Then he wrapped his fingers around her wrists and pulled her those last couple of inches until their bodies were pressed together.

"Come here, you." The words were soft but full of meaning.

She lifted her face to him and welcomed the touch of his mouth against hers, soft at first, gentle, but then the pressure increased.

"Open," he whispered against her lips.

She did, and he ran his tongue over her lower lip before sliding it inside and licking every inner surface. One strong hand cupped her chin while the other slid along her spine to her head, weaving his fingers in her hair. The pulse in her sex kicked it up a notch, and her nipples popped into such hard peaks, they actually ached. And all from one kiss.

Yup. I am in big trouble here.

He lifted his mouth from hers but only enough so he could study her face. "I know we said this would be all about the video tonight, but holy hell, Olivia. I was hard all day just thinking about last night. Tell me you thought about it, too. Just a little?"

Oh, she'd thought about it all right. How could she forget the sensation of his lips and tongue on her sex. She was sure no matter how hard she pressed her thighs together, the pounding wouldn't ease.

"Liv?" he nudged.

"Yes," she whispered. "I thought about it."

"You know, I haven't put the steaks on the grill yet. The potatoes are in the warmer, and the salad is in the fridge."

Reaching between them, he untied the tails of her blouse and slid up her tank top, staring for a long moment. Then he reached behind her to unhook her bra and pushed it up so her breasts were exposed, the heat in his eyes turning almost incendiary and leaving her shivering with need. He took a moment to let his gaze rake over her breasts inch by inch. Then he lowered his head and closed his mouth over one aching nipple.

She arched her back, pressing into his touch at the same time she managed to pull off her blouse and yank her tank and bra over her head. Burying her fingers in the thick silk of his hair, she pulled him harder to her body, silently urging him to suck harder. When he closed his teeth over one nipple and bit down, she couldn't stifle the groan of pleasure.

By the time he'd finished paying attention to both nipples, Olivia was sure she could have come just standing there. She grabbed his upper arms to steady herself, digging her fingers into the hard muscles of his biceps, ready to beg him for more.

When she opened her eyes, she saw such a look of hunger on Hatch's face, it made her weak in the knees.

"I think we need to take this some place where we can be more comfortable. I'm way too old for standup sex."

Olivia giggled. "Maybe we should try it, just to be sure."

"Maybe." He swept her up in his arms. "But not today."

A bedside lamp, turned on low, cast a warm glow in his bedroom. She barely had time to take a look around before he placed her on her feet, knelt down, and with fingers she noted were slightly trembling, proceeded to remove the rest of her clothing. When she stood before him naked, he trailed a line of kisses from her navel across her dark curls as he'd done the night before.

Oh god!

She shook with need, a hunger so fierce it gripped her entire body it running through her. When he rose to his feet, she wanted to protest the loss of his touch.

"Hatch—"

"Gotta get my clothes off."

He swept his tongue across her breasts before methodically and efficiently stripping off everything he wore. He yanked back the covers on the bed, then lifted her and placed her in the center, her head on the pillows. Then he stood and stared at her again, that same ravenous look on his face, before climbing onto the bed and kneeling between her thighs.

He cupped her breasts in his palms, rubbing his thumbs over her swollen nipples. Back and forth, back and forth. Sensations skittered through her, especially when he pinched those hard points to a pinnacle of pleasure/pain. He continued to abrade the tips until she was sure she couldn't stand it any longer.

"Please," she begged, hoping he knew what she wanted,

"No rushing," he murmured, his voice thick. "Nice and slow."

He continued to tease and torment her aching nipples and breasts. When he bent his head and pulled one into his mouth, she tossed her head back, a primitive cry escaping her mouth. Her body trembled as he used his lips and teeth until her nipples ached and her body screamed silently with uncontrolled need.

When she was sure she was reduced to begging, he lifted his head and moved his mouth down her body, using his tongue to draw a line. When he reached her thighs, he nudged them farther apart, reached down, and the tip of one finger homed in on her throbbing clit. He massaged it with a steady, even rhythm, each stroke igniting the fire inside her, tremors racing through the inner muscles of her sex. That was all he touched, just that hot bundle of flesh, but it seemed like only seconds before an orgasm roared up through her body, shaking her. Hatch continued his assault on that hot, sensitive bud, pinching and tugging and rubbing until she was spent. Weak. Panting. And yet, still unfulfilled.

As she lay there, trying to get her breath, riding out the tremors, he licked his way along her nerve endings again, tormenting her with his teeth until he'd coaxed another orgasm from her.

This time it took her longer to come down. Hatch straddled her, cradled her head in his palms, and lowered his head to brush a kiss over her lips. "I sure do love to watch you come, Liv. You hold nothing back."

"Not with you I don't."

He looked as if he was about to ask her a question but just kissed her again, instead.

She drew in a deep breath, put her hands on his hard, flat chest, and pushed him onto his back.

"What? What's going on?"

"My turn." She grinned as she managed to lever herself up and kneel beside him.

She loved the feel of his body beneath her touch as she ran her hands over him, mapping every curve, every dimple, every nerve ending. Her fingers barely around the length of his swollen cock as she stroked from root to tip, gripping the hard length and sliding her hand between his thighs to stroke his balls. She closed her eyes, lost in the rhythm of her movements, feeling him react to her, when he grabbed her wrist.

"Enough," he growled.

She opened her eyes. "What? No. I mean—"

He locked his gaze with hers, the hunger fiercer in his eyes than before. In what seemed like seconds, he had lifted a condom from the nightstand drawer, rolled it on, and positioned her over him. With great care but agonizing slowness, he lowered her onto his shaft, one inch at a time. When he filled every bit of her slick channel, she squeezed him with her internal muscles.

Oh, Jesus! Oh, sweet lord!

He was thick and hard and hot, filling every bit of her. With his eyes still on her, he began to move, his body hard and muscular against hers.

Olivia lost it. Up and down, up and down, his cock driving in and out of her willing, waiting body. He gripped her breasts, as if to anchor himself as she rode him hard and deep. She felt the climax roaring up through her, building until, with a flick of his finger on her clit, she exploded, taking him right along with her. The walls of her sex spasmed all around him as the tremors of the orgasm shook her again and again.

While the pulsing subsided, she collapsed forward onto him, the soft hair on his chest tickling her face. They lay, spent, weak, for a very long time. At last, he lifted her and eased her from his body, placing her gently beside him. He leaned over her and brushed a soft kiss on her lips before heading to the bathroom to dispose of the condom.

Olivia did her best to pull her scrambled brains

together. So much for a quiet dinner and a long discussion. They were like two bunnies who couldn't seem to turn it off the moment they laid eyes on each other.

Hatch padded back in from the bathroom, lay down beside her, and with a gentle tug pulled her into his arms.

"Hatch, I—"

He touched her lips with the tip of one finger. "Please don't say a word. I'm not sure what's going through your brain. Maybe the same thing going through mine. Neither of us was looking for this, but here it is. Let's just see where it goes. Can we do that?"

"We can't—" She began again, but he shook his head.

"I know. This should never have happened, but it did. And we both know it was like a stick of dynamite going off. You've got the documentary, for me football season is two seconds away, and we both know how this town likes to gossip. I don't want to do anything to damage your situation, Liv."

"I feel the same way about you." It was hard to be smart.

"Until after the season and the video," he added and brushed another kiss over her lips.

"Until then." But it would be damn hard.

"Meanwhile, I don't know about you, but I can really use that dinner now. Especially the protein."

She laughed. "Works for me."

As she dressed and pulled herself back together, she thought about Bert Hoekstra and Daniel Forrest, two men who'd like nothing better than to destroy both her and Hatch. They were doing the right thing. But damn, it hurt.

****

Olivia had arranged another viewing of the recent video Drew had shot and was glad she'd have something to take her mind off the turn of her situation with Hatch. Except all she could think was she was twice as determined to make this a top drawer video.

"Do you have time to look at the new footage?"

"Sure. I can move some things around."

"Oh. No, I don't want to—"

He held up a hand. "Not a problem. This is important to me, too. Say about an hour?"

She nodded. "That's fine. And thank you."

This would be her first viewing of shots of Hatch since things had changed between them. Drew was a master at getting the right shots so that wasn't what worried her. Would she be objective in looking at the tapes? Would the shots she requested convey the message she was looking for? Worst of all, had she lost her touch?

Once again, Drew had everything ready in the viewing room for her, tapes in the machines and queued up. He smiled as she took her seat.

"Don't worry. You still got game, Olivia. The shots you asked for this time…well, take a look for yourself."

She took out the spiral notebook she was keeping her notes in, turned to a blank page, and wrote down today's date. Then, wetting her lips, she nodded. "Let's have it,"

As the tape rolled, she wondered again why she was so nervous. Drew was an artist with his video, capturing mood and action like a master painter. At certain spots, she had him stop the tape, back it up, call out the frame numbers to her. Just seeing Hatch on the tape, despite the unsettled situation between them, sent a little thrill racing through her. This was going to be good. Oh, yes. She still had the touch.

"The shots in his office show that coaching is not all just work on the field, and they show his intensity and commitment to what he's doing."

"I have to say," Drew said, "I was surprised. I'd always had the impression he was pretty shallow, like so many athletes, and focused mostly on his ego, but that's not true. He really cares about these kids and the program."

"He does," she agreed. "I'm hoping this will show that to everyone and also let the kids at the university see he's someone to admire, respect, and follow."

"Well, we're getting there, for sure."

"Thanks for everything, Drew. I'm still a little rusty, and you've made this sure smooth for me."

"My pleasure. You're easy to work with. Let me know when the next shoot is."

"I have to check with Hatch, so I'll text you, okay?"

"Sure thing."

I know he'll like it, right? Fingers crossed.

Chapter Nine

It was a comfortable, familiar sensation. Maybe too comfortable, but Hatch had felt the need to test himself. To see if the low-key environment would awaken the sleeping troll or if he could manage the temptation he honestly believed he had under firm control now. If not, he promised himself he'd give it up. It was a challenge he faced every day and no poker game was worth sacrificing the rebuilding of his career and his life.

What he really wanted was the feeling of companionship with these men that a friendly game of nickel poker would invoke. He wouldn't make it a regular habit, but if he could handle it once in a while, it would be a big step forward for him.

Cards in hand, drink—ice water—at his elbow. The fragrant smell of cigars. The low, chuckling laughter of men gathered around a felt-green-topped round table. The clink of the cheap betting chips between his fingers. God, he had missed this. All of it. Up to and including the fact that, nine times out of the average ten, he was a dead ringer at this game.

"Call," he said, flipping a couple of the chips to the pile in the middle of the table. Thankfully, this—his first actual card game in over two and a half years—had been a cake walk. Most of his coaching staff had no idea how to bluff, and he doubted a couple of them had even played more than once in their young lives, which had kept him safe, not needing to take big risks.

Which had also kept the mental rush he'd been dreading at a low ebb. This had been a test to see if he could control himself when it came to gambling. He hadn't so much as picked up a deck of cards or paid attention to a sports book in two years. He wasn't cured—his kind of addiction never went away—but he could control it as along as he controlled his environment.

Numbers played such a major role in his life both on the field and in his head. He could never let himself succumb to that hungry temptation ever again. If the media got hold of his past gambling problems, though, his career would for sure be in the toilet. He had to make sure Olivia never even got a whiff of it or her documentary would turn into a big exposé, which would ruin him but, more importantly, might make her lose face with the sports channel gods.

He actually felt like he was ready to close this down, go home, get some sleep, and contemplate the days ahead without needing more of this sort of input. A true breakthrough, he knew. The weeks and months of court-ordered therapy he'd endured had given him a fair bit of insight into this fact.

He had a dummy hand but already knew every single tell around the table and had figured out that not one among them had anything better. Two of the coaches folded with groans and murmurs of, "I gotta go home while I still have rent money." The two others, George, tonight's host, and Tomas Alvarez, his newest hire at the quarterbacks coach job, stayed. Both men tossed in chips. At the last minute, Tomas pushed his remaining pile of chips to the middle.

Hatch raised an eyebrow at him. The dude had been one of the sorriest players of the night. But he could've been pulling a scam. He shook his head at himself. He was way out of practice if that were the case.

Of course you're out of practice, you numb nuts. Remember why?

He smiled and pushed his entire, much larger, pile of chips in. They were only playing for nickels so at the most he was out fifty bucks. The money wasn't the point.

It never had been.

"All right, gentlemen, let's see 'em." He put his hand down. He was only holding two weak pairs, threes and fives—treys and nickels. But he was an ace bluffer. George groaned.

"Jesus, Coach, you could've warned us you were about to rob us at this game." He tossed his down. He had a pair of tens.

He was reaching for the pile when Tomas placed his hand on top of it. "Sorry, man."

"Shit," Hatch said, leaning back and staring at the guy with admiration. "Nice. I thought I had you nailed."

The other man shrugged and put his elbows on the table, his gaze sharp and knowing in a way that made Hatch uncomfortable all of a sudden. Hatch stared at the winning hand. It was only a lousy straight—five cards in sequence, different suits. A chump hand. He never should've fallen for it, but he'd been on a mild high, enjoying everything about this night too much. He'd dropped his guard.

"So," Tomas said as he divided the kitty up between the men so that they all had their original stack of chips in front of them again. Hatch started to protest, but Tomas held up a hand. "Can we talk about the game now?"

"Sure," Hatch said, downing the rest of his water to cover up his aggravation at the deviation from poker etiquette. A win was a win. No give-backs. At least, that's how he'd been taught to play. "When did you learn how to bluff like that?"

Tomas leaned back, took a puff on his cigar and a sip of his soda before answering. "College," he finally said. "Too many late nights spent working on it, frankly." His brown eyes shone as he stared at Hatch so long, he had to look away.

Tomas Alvarez was the youngest member of the coaching staff. His resume, while somewhat football spotty thanks to four years spent as an active duty Marine, was stellar otherwise. He'd been the QB at Stanford, where he'd graduated with honors, accepted to four law schools as well as promises of a decent pro draft position. Instead, he'd enlisted.

Hatch knew most of the backstory except for the reason behind that move. When he returned, Tomas had been hired as assistant O-line coach for the expansion team in Las Vegas. He'd spent two years there before moving to QB's coach in New England. Hatch had been watching his meteoric rise through the assistants ranks and had never in a million years thought the guy would consider, much less accept, his offer to move to the mild Midwest and take on a once-proud, now flailing D1 program.

Luckily for him, Tomas had wanted off the pro coach hamster wheel. He had a wife, a toddler, and another kid on the way and was eager to set down his family's roots somewhere sane. Hatch had made it his business to know all of these facts about his new coach and had played to the strengths of settling down, until realizing that he didn't even have to try that hard.

But now, with the younger man's dark gaze pinned to him like a pair of magnets, Hatch was uneasy. It was as if the guy was reading him like a book and didn't care much for the plotline.

"Okay, we're gonna go around the table and each of you will tell me what you think went wrong today and how we're gonna fix it." He got up and poured himself more water from the kitchen sink. "Oh, sorry, Abby. Are we being too loud?"

George's wife smiled at Hatch, shook her head, and wandered back upstairs in her robe, her own water glass recharged. He turned to face the poker table. His nerves were zinging. His body felt hot, then cold, then hot again. He drank half the glass, refilled it again, then walked back into his unofficial spring game team meeting, wishing they were playing cards and knowing that he might have reopened his own personal container of demons.

But today's game, their first in a long string of what should be gimmie wins, had been a long slog toward eventual victory. They'd been sloppy, saggy in the O-line, porous in the D-line. They'd been damn lucky to yank a win out of it, ten-seven. He was pissed, so he'd suggested they do a bit of bonding over cards, not talking about it at first. It seemed to have worked. They were loose, and not from booze, since he'd insisted it be an alcohol-free game.

He walked into George and Abby's kitchen and grabbed the expensive bottle of bourbon he'd brought, plus a handful of rocks glasses. When he returned, he plunked them onto the green felt and splashed a bit of the brown liquor into each one, then placed a glass in front of each of his coaches. He lifted his glass, meeting the eyes of all his staff. They lifted theirs.

"To the win," he said.

"Cheers," they replied before drinking.

Hatch let the hot booze roll around in his mouth, coat his tongue, and burn a trail down his throat. He put his glass down on the table.

"And now," he said, before putting the bottle on the breakfront behind him, "I need each of you to tell me how you're going to improve your area so we don't almost lose to some god damned, half-assed D-2 school next week." He sat. "Talk to me, guys. Tell me what went wrong."

They had won the game, but each and every one of them knew that it might as well have been a loss. So they talked well into the night, finishing off the bourbon between them.

He was up early in the morning, ran ten miles, showered, ate a bowl of oatmeal, and drank two cups of extra strong coffee. Then he sat on his back patio to ponder his dilemma. While sipping his third cup, he felt inspired or perhaps over-caffeinated, but whatever it was, it got him up and over to the giant whiteboard in his living room. It took up most of an entire wall. Where normal people would have displayed family pictures, or grandma's paintings, he crafted football strategy. It was a good place to play with the numbers that fascinated him and put his innate ability to good use.

Two hours later, he had a solution to at least one of

his problems—how to bust out a decent offense without a strong center and with an O-line as porous as a damn sponge but with a senior quarterback whose penchant for ducking his head and running for the goal line himself was something just short of legendary. And annoying. At least until right this minute.

He sent a quick text to Tomas and George, asking if they had a few minutes to stop by and talk it through with him. They did, of course. He was their boss after all. Plus, they wanted their inaugural season as coaches to be as successful as he wanted it to be.

By three p.m., the men were laughing and slapping high fives and eager to get back to the gridiron. They had a long week ahead, full of potential potholes to dodge, considering that said senior QB, while classroom smart, was a total idiot in his personal life. God knew what sort of trouble he'd get himself into.

But Tomas had made a point to bond with the kid, as well as his eager, about-to-be-sophomore back up. Hatch felt the man would keep it all under tight control. The kid was local, which helped. And he was bound and determined to work himself into pro playing shape. Hatch planned to use all that energy to create a brand spanking new offense and put it into action after one week, now that he'd concocted it out of thin air.

Relieved, he plopped down on the couch, feet up, and closed his eyes. He'd been the king of catnapping in college and had only perfected his skills at the pro level. For the first time in what felt like weeks, he could relax, having solved his core problem.

No, you have a couple of others, Hatch, remember? And one of them is female-shaped.

He frowned even as his mind drifted into semi-sleep. He covered his eyes with his arm to block the late afternoon sun streaming in through the glass door. Rest. It'll be the best way to tackle the other issues.

But sleep wouldn't cooperate.

After his allotted forty minutes, he sat, put his feet back on the floor, and glared down at his hands. What in the name of all that was holy had made him think continuing to get closer to Olivia was a good idea? He'd avoided her after the game, and she'd been savvy enough to understand that he hadn't wanted to talk, that he needed to be with his coaches so they could work through all the problems. And in the interim few hours, he'd convinced himself that to get to know her any further—the way he truly wanted to—would only result in disaster for them both. He knew himself too well. He'd ruined one perfectly good relationship already.

"Shit," he said, rising slowly.

He took a moment to ponder his options. On the one hand, Olivia was hands-down the most amazing woman he'd ever known. She was smart—and not just about sports—funny, athletic, everything he loved. On the same hand, she was too fucking sexy for her own good. On that exact same hand, if he closed his eyes, he could still taste her, smell her, feel her skin under his fingertips.

He sighed and commanded his body not to react the way it already was doing. After three cold glasses of water, he thought he'd mastered that problem. Now, back to the options.

She should be off limits and not just because of his basic relationship disability. She was making a documentary about his program. One she hoped to use to get a leg up in the sports journalism business. If word got out that they'd been screwing around, she'd never be respected. And he didn't want that for her.

Plus, Tank had provided him with some disturbing intel about her ex-husband. Information that made him so god damned angry he'd almost put his fist through perfectly decent living room drywall. He hadn't. But it had been a close-run thing for a few seconds.

They were supposed to have dinner again tonight. He loved planning these encounters with her, surprising her with out of the way places he'd find within an hour or so drive, BBQ joints with food so amazing it melted off the bone in one's mouth. A killer Indian food restaurant a couple of towns over. An actual drive-in movie they'd giggled and necked their way through after downing fast food cheeseburgers and sugary colas. Tonight, she was making dinner and had made it perfectly clear what was for dessert.

The woman was, in a word, incredible. He was self-aware enough to admit he could, quite possibly, be in love with her. Which was why, tonight, he was going to tell her that it had to stop. While he wanted to say the words that had sprung to his lips when she asked him in the afterglow the week before, their faces close on the pillows, if there was anything about his past he wanted to tell her. Anything she needed to know in order not to get blindsided by lurking scandal that was something best kept to himself. He'd managed to do it this long. There was no compelling reason not to keep up the subterfuge that he was a normal, functioning adult.

He leaned against the kitchen countertop and allowed himself to relive their intense, short-lived relationship so far. The first time they'd made love, it had been a moment he'd initiated. The times after that, she'd met him more than halfway. The shower, her bedroom, his kitchen, on his couch, and once, memorably, in his damn office. He was simply incapable of not touching her, kissing her, caressing every inch of her whenever she was anywhere near him.

But the decision he'd made was best for both of them regardless of how they felt about each other. They had to let it go. For a lot of reasons. She had too much at stake. Far more than he did. Plus, now that he knew what a shithead her ex was, and the power he still wielded over her future success, he had to end it. Tonight. It was the best thing for her, and that's all he wanted. To protect her—from him and his ability to screw things up, as well as from the possibility that, by having a relationship with him, she was putting her reviving career at risk.

****

Olivia pressed the End button on her cell phone and, with great effort, restrained herself from throwing it across the room. She was getting really, really tired of Bert Hoekstra. She was sick of finding him leaning against her car when she attended practice at the university. Annoyed at his phone calls at inopportune times. And damn tired of his sarcastic innuendo.

She had always tried to make it a habit to stay on good terms with others in the industry. When she was married to Daniel, the asshole—that was his permanent name in her mind, Daniel the Asshole—it had been a continuous battle. He didn't want her too friendly with the other broadcast staff. They might try to take advantage of her connection to him. Or people from other stations and networks. They might try to steal her secrets. Or his.

As the thoughts raced through her mind, jarred loose by the sound of Bert's unpleasant voice, she wondered if killing him would be classified as justifiable homicide. He was such a thoroughly dislikable and despicable person, she thought perhaps people would cheer. But then she'd be left with all the messy cleanup, and she'd dealt with enough messes in her life. Her marriage and divorce were at the top of the list.

Sometimes, she wondered how she could have been so stupid. No, not just stupid. Idiotically stupid. But she'd been so focused on her career and so flattered that Daniel Forrest—*the* Daniel Forrest—had been interested in her, she'd bought his bullshit hook, line, and sinker. Six months into the marriage, she'd discovered what a controlling jerk he was, but by then, he had so many strings on her career, she couldn't just walk away. And then the humiliation began when—

Stop! Get him out of your head!

But Hoekstra had brought it all back. For a long time, he'd been one of Daniel's sycophants, practically sucking his dick for a chance at the headline projects her ex was famous for. Or a spot as a guest sportscaster. Or anything that would drag him from a low-level obscurity to the spotlight. But he hadn't had the goods then, and he didn't have them now. All he could do was try to destroy others and use them as stepping-stones.

Well, she wasn't having anything to do with him. He could tease her all he wanted about some deep, dark secret Hatch might have, but she wasn't biting. She was sure his goal was to embarrass her and ruin the documentary. Then he thought he'd insinuate himself in at the station and tell them he had a real exposé to sell them? Didn't he understand that people didn't always want to destroy hometown heroes?

She needed to be on her toes with him, and that wasn't going to be so easy. *After the video. Then we'll have plenty of time to see what this is.*

She was pretty damn sure the university had done its due diligence on Duncan Jerome Hatcher. If they didn't find anything, as far as she was concerned, there was nothing to find. Besides, hadn't she asked him if there was anything? If there was, she'd given him plenty of opportunity to tell her. Hoekstra could try to spread his poisonous innuendo, but she wasn't buying. If he showed up on campus again, she'd be forced to ask Hatch to have the campus police escort him off, and none too politely.

With deliberate effort, she put the man out of her mind. She had things to do for tonight, and she'd best get busy.

Tonight!

Her insides quivered just thinking about it.

Tonight, she was making dinner for the two of them. Cooking had been her emotional release when she was going through the divorce, and she'd gotten pretty good at it, if she did say so herself. She was making baked brie with cranberry sauce as an appetizer, followed by individual beef wellingtons, spiced potato balls, and green beans, and for dessert she'd given in to temptation and picked up a sinful chocolate mousse cake from the bakery she loved so much. She had a bottle of her favorite shiraz open on the kitchen counter to breathe.

Too much? Too fussy? Scrap it all, and do steaks and baked potatoes?

No, that was a Hatch-prepared dinner. She hadn't had anyone to show off her culinary skills for in a long time, and she was excited about the opportunity. Besides, she thought it nothing short of a miracle that this was happening between them with everything that was going on. They both had obstacles to deal with, but she was glad they were figuring out how to make it work. Right?

After making sure everything was ready in the kitchen, she hurried to run water for a bath and stripped off her clothes. Luxuriating in the tub helped work all the kinks and knots out of her muscles. It also gave her time to think about the night ahead. One she was positive would end with more addictive sex.

Damn! She was getting to the point where she could almost reach orgasm by thinking of Hatch and the things they did in bed. Never in her life had she been so uninhibited or felt so completely adored. Addictive barely described her craving for him. She wasn't exactly sure where this was going, but she was most definitely going to enjoy the ride.

And yes, whatever asshole Daniel Forrest might think or intimate, she could keep a wall between her personal and private lives. In fact, she was so energized, she was sure the documentary would turn out even more spectacular than she expected. Life was good. She took particular pains with her makeup, using it sparingly. They were, after all, dining in. Her hair cooperated by falling into perfect, casual curls.

Except for the night he'd taken her to dinner, she always wore slacks or jeans. Now, she pulled a swishy little casual cotton skirt out of her closet that she paired with a gauzy blouse tied at the waist. Golden hoops at her ears, a spritz of perfume, and she was ready.

Oh, man, was she ready.

She had just finished arranging the appetizer tray when her doorbell rang. Pressing a hand to her stomach to quell the unexpected butterflies, she hurried to the door and opened it. And barely stopped herself from drooling. He looked particularly mouthwatering in gray slacks and a black soft collar shirt. The whiff of his aftershave drifting across her nostrils set every nerve to tingling and that drumbeat between her thighs to accelerating.

Damn!

At this rate, she might not get through dinner. She let out a slow breath and smiled. "Come on in."

She'd thought he might give her a hello kiss and frowned when he just smiled and walked in, handing her the bottle in his hand.

"You said beef so I brought a cabernet I thought you'd like."

"Thank you. I have a shiraz breathing so we might get good and looped tonight." She moved a little closer to him. "Not that we ever need alcohol to help us along."

Again, she expected him to kiss her, but again, he simply smiled and followed her into the living room. There was something stiff about his posture, and his smile looked forced. Was something wrong, or was she just being overly sensitive?

Wine and food. That would help. Maybe it was her imagination. She hoped. Her hands fluttered. "I'll get the corkscrew so you can open it and let it breathe while we start on the shiraz."

"Okay. Good. That's good."

She was hit by an attack of nerves as she dug out the corkscrew and took it in to him, then busied herself setting up the appetizer and the wine on the cocktail table. She was glad he did the pouring, because for some reason her hands were unsteady. Sitting on the couch next to him, she lifted her glass and touched it to his. "To a great evening."

Hatch said nothing, just nodded and took a long sip of his wine.

Okay, enough.

Olivia set her glass down and turned to him, hands twisted together to calm herself. "What's wrong? Please don't tell me there's nothing, because it's written all over your face. You looked tense and uncomfortable the minute I opened the door. You didn't bother to kiss me hello, which you've been doing every time we get together since... Well, since. And to tell the truth, you look like you'd rather be anywhere but here. I don't have time for bullshit, Hatch. So tell me what gives."

He took another sip of his wine, then set the glass on the table and looked down at his hands. "Liv, I..."

"What?"

"I'm not sure I know exactly how to say this."

That knot forming in the pit of her stomach got suddenly bigger and tighter. "Just spit it out, for god's sake."

"Okay. Here it is." He blew out a breath. "I don't think we should see each other anymore, outside of work on the documentary. That is, until the documentary and this season are both finished."

Olivia stared at him. She'd had the very same thought herself, so why did hearing it from him hurt? Hearing him say it first colored the situation.

"Not see each other?" She repeated the words, just to be sure.

How had he reached this point? She had a sense of losing control.

He nodded, once, a stiff jerk of his head. "That's right. I think it's best."

Wow. Okay, then. Now she wondered how the situation with him would color the project as far as the station was concerned. And of course, ultimately, the national sports channels.

She wet her lips. She could handle this. "I wasn't exactly expecting this. I have some thoughts on the matter, but I'd like to know what got you to this point. Straight answers, Hatch. No lame excuses."

He took a deep breath. "I think it would be bad for you professionally if people began to gossip about us. You're working hard to get your career back on track, and nothing should affect the impact of this video. It can be your ticket back to the big time."

Olivia took a deep breath and let it out slowly. For a déjà vu moment, she had a sense of being back with Dan again, This was the kind of thing he would do. Then she pulled herself together. "All right. I hear you. Yes, this video is important and could open doors for me. My boss believes in it and me. What is the problem, exactly?"

"Okay. People love to gossip. What happens if people start saying you got the documentary access because you slept with me? That it was the only way you could agree to get me to do it? How does that look for both of us?"

Olivia thought for a moment she might throw up. Then a hot rage boiled through her, and she knew what people meant by "seeing red." This was why he wanted to break this off? She stood up so fast she almost knocked over her glass of wine.

"I can't believe you are even thinking, much less saying this crap. Are you implying they'll think I'm some kind of whore?" She shook with anger but tried to remain calm.

"No." He shook his head. "No, no, no. That's not it at all."

"Well, that's damn sure what it sounds like." She curled her fingers into fists, trying to grasp her rapidly disappearing self-control.

"Please, Liv. I'm just trying to think of you." He reached for one of her hands, but she jerked her arm way.

"Are you? Are you really? Or are you just thinking of yourself and what might blow back on you, the great Duncan Jerome Hatcher. Idolized player. Revered coach." She wanted to smack him.

"Of course I'm not." His voice was low and even. "Listen. I just want the best for you."

"The best? The best?" She could hear herself screeching now. "Are you afraid if we keep on seeing each other—make that sleeping together—that somehow I'll turn out a video that's a piece of shit and it will look bad for you?"

"Please. Just listen to me. I—"

"Or maybe...maybe people will say you only got the video because you were sleeping with me?" She knew how insane she sounded, but she couldn't seem to stop herself. It was as if someone else had taken over her brain and vocal cords.

"Stop." He grabbed her hands. "Just stop. Please.

142

It's not that at all. You know there are people out there just waiting for you to fail. Waiting to pounce."

"Oh." She took a deep steadying breath. "Wait a minute. This isn't about me. It's about you." She slapped her forehead. "You're afraid people will say you slept with me so you'd be the star. God." She shook her head. "I am so stupid."

"Olivia. Liv." He reached for her again.

She slapped his hands away. "Don't touch me." She took a step back. "Do. Not. Touch. Me."

"I'm just trying to tell you what would be best for you. You have to be sure you've put yourself in the best position."

"And you don't think I'm doing that? Who are you to tell me how to live my life?"

He lifted his hands, then let them fall. "I should go. We can talk about this when you're a lot calmer and willing to listen."

Olivia picked up her glass of wine and drained it, then set the glass down on the table.

"There. I'm calm. But I'm done with this. Quit trying to manipulate me the way Daniel did. You want this to be over? Fine. It's over. Finished. We will only see each other by appointment until the video is done. Now get the hell out of here."

"Liv, please. I want this video to happen for you. I just don't want other things or people to do or say anything to detract from it."

"Out." She pointed toward her door. "Now." When he didn't move, she repeated, "Get the hell out. Right this minute."

He looked at her for a long moment, then shook his head and walked to the door. After he opened it, he turned and looked at her, opened his mouth but didn't say anything, then walked out and closed the door behind him.

Olivia watched Hatch go, her emotions roiling around inside her like a tornado. Then, as if someone had pulled the plug, all the energy drained from her.

What was she supposed to do now? How was she supposed to finish this documentary that was going to be her opportunity to give Daniel the finger and put herself back on top? Would Hatch even plan to let her continue? What was she supposed to say when she called to set up their next meeting?

God! How was this happening? And who had been putting a bug in his ear?

She collapsed onto the couch, dropped her head into her hands, wondering if it was possible she could wake up tomorrow morning and it would all be a bad dream.

****

For two days, Olivia stayed away from the university and football practice, knowing that seeing Hatch would be painful. There was always the uncertainty of his reaction to her if she showed up. He hadn't cancelled the documentary, thank the lord, but how could they possibly work together? How did she do a documentary about a man when the man had decided to hold himself at arm's length?

She had asked Drew to spend another afternoon shooting B roll footage of the university itself. She also thought about contacting others on the athletic staff to get their opinion of having Hatch as the coach, and she made a note to clear it with the athletic director. She hoped Hatch hadn't said anything to him or indicated he might want the project cancelled.

Her stomach cramped at the thought. Although Hatch had not been nasty or demeaned her in any way, she was suddenly faced with the diminishing sense of self-worth she'd had with Daniel. This project was so important in reestablishing herself and her reputation. She had to find a way to make it work. Maybe after a few days, she'd text or email him and try to set up another meeting.

Meanwhile, she spent another afternoon in the editing room with Drew. This was the part of the job she really loved, had always loved, even more than being on camera. Looking at what the photographer captured and putting the pieces of it together so the finished product projected the message she wanted the audience to see.

She wanted to get just the right flavor of the background, of the place that had made Hatch who he was and now welcomed him back. This video wasn't just a retrospective and return of an honored player and coach. She had come to terms with the fact she was damn good at what she did, and she hated the fact she'd let a man make her question herself and nearly run her out of a profession she loved. She had to fix the situation with Hatch, but she didn't know how.

The video Drew had shot was wonderful just as she'd expected, and they went back and forth choosing exactly the right scenes to interweave with the shots of Hatch. She could feel in her bones that the project was coming together just the way she wanted. Drew had even taken a half hour before she got there to roughly string some of the clips together so she could see what they were creating and make sure they'd picked the best scenes.

The station manager popped in, naturally curious about how the project was coming, and stayed to view about fifteen minutes of video. He, too, approved of the B roll Drew had shot and the direction the video was taking. He stood there for a few moments, watching the part of the tape running across the screen.

"I can smell national on this," he told the two of them. "Can't wait to see the finished product."

She managed a smile. "Neither can I."

"Olivia, I think you've outdone yourself on this." He smiled. "I have to admit I had misgivings when you pitched this. Probably because…" The smile disappeared and he looked uncomfortable.

"Because of all the crap Daniel was passing around about me," she finished for him.

"Well…" He rubbed his jaw. "I mean…"

"It's okay." She really wanted to get Daniel out of this. "I'm aware of what he's done and said, and I am truly grateful that you took this chance on me. I doubted myself for a long time, but I think this video is going to make a difference."

He nodded, the stiffness gone from his shoulders. "I took a chance on you, and now I'm glad I did."

"Thanks. That means a lot."

By the end of the session, they'd selected some killer video, but no matter how much she concentrated on her project, Hatch still sat front and center on her brain. But now the pleasure she'd shared with him was coated with pain of missing him.

****

All day she'd replayed her conversation with Hatch over and over in her mind. She totally ignored the fact she'd been about to put on the brakes herself and focused only on finding the reason for his decision.

At home, she showered, tried to eat something, but finally slipped into her comfiest sweatpants and T-shirt. Grabbing her cell, she nestled in her pillows with a glass of wine. She punched the speed dial for Lee Ann. Then she spent five minutes examining her situation from every angle.

"Call him," Lee Ann urged. "You have to speak to him sooner or later."

"I know." Olivia chewed a thumbnail. "I just have to figure out exactly what to say."

"How about, 'Hello, Hatch'?" Lee Ann's giggle vibrated over the connection. "Sorry. I couldn't resist."

"First, I have to see if he's even willing to let me near him. We haven't been face to face in more than a week." She sighed. "I wasn't sure what to say if we were. I've avoided going out to the university, but I can't do that much longer. Not if I want to finish this video."

"Listen. I have an idea. Let's have a girls' weekend away like we used to. I'll call Dana and Cissy, and we'll all head to the Petoskey Inn and Resort. Spa treatments. Massages. Mani-pedis. Swimming in their gorgeous indoor pool. Just for a weekend."

"Oh, I don't know if—"

"Oh, come on. You need to put this aside for a couple of days and get yourself together. You'll be all fluffed and buffed and ready to face Hatch when we get back."

Olivia sighed. "Okay. You're probably right. Make the arrangements, and we'll go."

Chapter Ten

"What?"

"I said, where'd you go, man? I thought we were in here to work."

Tomas' lips twitched just enough so Hatch knew he was only half kidding. But he'd been more than half out of it for at least the last five minutes and he knew it. "Sorry. Sorry, guys. I'm not…anyway, sorry." He could feel his face flush as his coaching staff stared at him, most of them mildly curious, a few of them smirking, which immediately made him nervous.

Was it that obvious he was having a sex flashback day-dream? Because that is exactly what he'd been doing. Ever since that night at Olivia's place when he'd ended things with her, he'd been miserable, not to mention horny as hell. That's what happened when he tried to do the right thing. Never mind he still didn't quite understand why he'd done it, at least at this stage of the post-breakup.

"All right, where were we?" He leaned forward on the large tabletop and attempted to look engaged.

"Um…" George glanced around at his fellow assistants, then back at Hatch. "You were about to tell us what your goals were for the weekend."

"Right. Yes. That. Thanks." He smiled at the table in general, mortified at his lapse but determined to get the kick off to this off-site, coach-bonding, working

148

weekend done right. "I wanted to take the opportunity to get away from the usual office, locker rooms, and fields so we can talk seriously about our goals for the rest of this season. And have some fun in the process."

He'd concocted this early-season, bye week off-site with a full realization of what each of his coaches' family lives were like. He knew most of them had school-age kids and which of them had spouses who worked outside the home. He also knew that he planned to work everyone's tails off for the remainder of the season, so he'd planned a getaway at his own personal expense for all of them, families included. He'd also invited his personal secretary and the team's equipment managers and their families.

The Petoskey Inn and Resort had been the obvious choice. He'd been there several times, usually to play golf with old friends when he was sick of the rat race that was his life as a pro coach on the rise. It had everything. An award-winning eighteen-hole golf course, a huge indoor/outdoor water park complex for kids, access to a pristine Lake Michigan beach, a five-star spa, which he personally planned to use for a deep tissue massage, and four different restaurants. Plus meeting rooms where he'd been guaranteed complete privacy for daily meetings with his staff and a team building and visioning guru he'd hired for a couple of days' worth of thinking outside their usual boxes.

It also had a small casino. Something he'd somehow forgotten when he'd booked it. But he'd be plenty busy enough to withstand the siren call of the poker table. Or at least he'd make sure he stayed that busy.

Gail, the secretary he'd inherited from the previous

coach, had set it all up for him and been pleased as punch when he leaned out his office door and reminded her to be sure and include herself and her husband, Mike.

It was an expensive way to try and defuse upcoming drama, but he figured it would be well worth it. They'd had a decent start to the season, winning their first three games, each more decisively than the last. But the rest of their schedule was going to be hard as hell. And he wanted everyone to feel bought in, engaged, and empowered. Frankly, the team had over achieved, well beyond everyone's expectations so far. And he wanted—no, he needed—for everyone to keep up the positive momentum. Hence, this little off-site gathering.

Once he'd been jolted out of his Olivia-induced reverie, he rallied like a champ. With the help of the visioning guy he'd hired at astronomical expense, they'd all written their own separate visions for the second half of the season. That coalesced into an official team mission statement. A little corporate-sounding, perhaps, but he could tell all the guys and the one woman around the table under his immediate supervision enjoyed it. They broke for lunch, which he had brought in so everyone could be done by four and enjoy the evening with their families.

After inhaling his turkey sandwich and fruit, he spent the rest of the break time talking with Susan Rockford. She'd been the team's head trainer for years, and he considered her a wealth of institutional knowledge about the existing players, as well as some of the coaches that he'd kept on. She and her wife Paula Harrison owned their own physical therapy company and had been expanding for the last four years throughout the west side of the state. He respected her, her talents and opinions enormously.

He rapped his knuckles on the table for attention.

"All right, let's finish up. I want to talk about shifting the starting lineup, based on the new offense we worked out after the first game. Hit me with names. We'll talk about the why's and why not's later." He was at the giant whiteboard, marker in hand, grinning from ear to ear. This was his world and he loved it. While it might not be a perfect season, it wasn't going to be for lack of trying on his part.

Three-and-a-half hours later, the table was strewn with printouts full of stats and previous game data, the kinds of numbers he should stick to. The whiteboard had been wiped off at least four times, and they had their new plays outlined and their mission statement. Tomorrow, they'd watch film of previous games played against this year's opponents on the second half of the schedule.

Now, it was time to relax.

"Okay, everyone, remember. There's a bonfire for us at eight down on the beach. Dinner's right before under the pavilion on the lawn—barbeque pork, chicken and yes…" He pointed to Tomas, his resident vegan. "I ordered up something special for you. Soy-based, just the way you like it."

"Thanks, coach," Tomas called out. "I'm captain of one of the volleyball teams," he added, looking around the table. "George is the other so you guys better start sucking up to me 'cause my team is gonna dominate later."

Everyone in the room chuckled and rose from their

seats.

"I claim Hatch!" George said.

"Ah, you can have him," Tomas said, smacking his fellow coach on the shoulder. "Hatch sucks at volleyball."

"We'll see, we'll see."

Hatch shook hands with every member of his team, feeling so good about what they'd accomplished and what they'd continue to work on this weekend he could barely stand it. The staff hustled in to clean up the snack trays of fruit and brownies and the empty water bottles and coffee cups. He had declared that all the family events, like tonight's BBQ, volleyball game, and bonfire would be alcohol-free. If anyone wanted booze, it was on their own dime.

"We still have an eight a.m. tee-time, buddy?"

"What?" He jumped when a hand landed on his arm. It was mid-September, and they'd been lucky with the weather this weekend. It was warm, in the high seventies, with only the slightest hint of cool in the evenings and early mornings.

"You know, golf?" Scott mimed a swing.

"Oh, uh…yeah. Sorry."

He'd not directly invited the A.D. but had told Scott he was welcome to stop by any of their meetings and offered to pay his way too. Scott had refused his offer but said he'd love to play eighteen holes on the Friday morning following their first working session on Thursday. "Then I'll shove off and let you guys plan the rest of our winning season."

Glancing at his watch, Hatch remembered he had a ninety-minute massage scheduled, and he wanted to shower first.

"You all right?" Scott peered at him.

"Yeah. Fine. Sorry. Exhausted. It was a long day but a good one. A really good one."

"I mean, with there being a casino here."

Hatch flinched. This time, he managed to knock a half-empty water bottle to the floor. A staff member hurried over and scooped it up.

"Yeah," he said, his voice rough. "I'm fine with it."

He sometimes forgot that Scott was one of the few people who knew his full story. He had to know about it of course. The man might be a glad-handing, money-raising, former basketball stud and semi-genius when it came to hiring decisions, but he was no fool. He'd demanded to know about the whole, ugly affair start to finish.

"Great. Okay, then. See you at the bonfire?"

"See you there."

Hatch headed up to his room, which he'd had Gail book in a different wing of the resort from everyone else. He leaned back against the elevator railing, his heart racing, his mouth bone dry, never readier for a massage in his life.

The Petoskey, as it was called, was an enormous complex, with over two thousand rooms and suites. It encompassed several acres that included the water park, golf course, and private beach. The spa that was Hatch's destination was on the fourth floor, along with a huge exercise facility, state-of-the-art spinning and yoga rooms, an indoor pool, multiple hot tubs, steam rooms, the works.

He waved at a few of his coaches who were grunting their way through weight lifting or sprinting to nowhere on the treadmills. He knew two of them were here alone. One was single, the other newly divorced and on a serious prowl for women. Another was his strength coach, the father of four, who claimed when Hatch passed by him that his wife and kids were nowhere to be found so he wanted to get in a few reps before dinner.

Hatch had taken a shower. A hot one at first until he'd made the crucial error of recalling his night with Olivia at her place. That had demanded a hard and immediate burst of ice cold water that left him shivering but somewhat less fraught. Redressed in a pair of navy shorts and a polo, he'd pocketed his phone and room key and headed for ninety minutes of mindless bliss under the capable hands of the masseur. He was tense as hell and he knew why.

Olivia Grant was consuming him, body and soul, and he had no earthly idea what to do about it now. Why he'd given the stupid speech about staying apart for the sake of her career and the success of the documentary he had no clue. But he'd done it. And probably ruined everything.

Now all he could think about was all the times they'd been intimate.

Perfect.

Ideal.

Sexy as all fuck.

It was all he could think about waking or asleep, and he'd blown it big time.

He had to get a grip.

If forced to admit it, he'd even hoped getting away from his house, his office, all the places where he could now picture her would help. So far, not so much.

"Hey, coach," the receptionist greeted him.

"You're here for a ninety-minute—"

"Beating? Yes." He grinned when she flashed him a glimpse of the Lakeland U tattoo on her biceps. "With Hans or Franz or—"

"Arnie, actually." A huge, intimidating looking guy emerged from a door behind the desk.

"Arnie. Perfect. Let's get to it, shall we?"

"Right this way, Coach."

The next ninety plus minutes were pure, pain-induced bliss. He'd had his fair share of massages, both pleasant and therapeutic, and it remained one of his second favorite ways to truly relax.

"All right, Coach. You're all set." Arnie ran his capable hands down Hatch's legs one last time, gripped his ankles and gave a quick jerk, which made Hatch's left hip—one that always gave him trouble—settle nicely back into a somewhat normal position. His body would never be right, thanks to the abuse he'd endured. But he wouldn't trade a minute of it.

"Thanks."

"Feel free to lay here a few minutes. I don't have another client for about thirty."

"Will do."

He was groggy, sleepy, and figured he'd be sore in the morning. Arnie knew his shit.

After about fifteen minutes spent dozing, he got up slowly, redressed, and drank the sweating bottle of water Arnie had left for him. He wandered down the long, lavender-scented, soft-music-infused hallway, calm and blissed out beyond belief. As he emerged out in to the lobby, he pulled his phone from his pocket, equipped to handle anything its sometimes-nagging screen could throw at him.

He scrolled through the messages and other crap, his mind at rest for the first time since…well, since laying eyeballs on Olivia Grant.

"Oh, excuse me, I'm sorry," he muttered when his phone and nose mashed up against a soft spa-robe-clad back. "I don't usually run into…people."

His victim turned to face him. His mouth dropped open at the sight of her, of Olivia, standing there and staring at him in her fluffy blue spa-labeled robe.

"Oh. Hello." His voice broke. Everything he'd managed to sublimate, to bury under piles of guilt and remorse, came roaring up and out, claiming his brain and rattling his cage like a randy lion.

Her hair was tugged back into a utilitarian ponytail, which reminded him of their first time together, after that damn over-the-top dinner. Her face was pale, clear of make-up, the way he actually preferred to look at a woman. As he stared, a pink flush crept up her chest and neck to her face. She had her hands jammed in the robe pockets, her feet in spa slippers.

"What are you—" he asked.

At the exact moment, she asked, "Why are you—"

He smiled, but it was no use. He wanted to rush forward, grab her, crush her to him, and kiss her until she begged him for more.

Oh, boy, Duncan Jerome. You're thinking way too hard about this. Get a grown man grip, already. You ended it, remember? And she made it perfectly clear how she felt about that.

"Staff retreat," he said. His voice sounded strangled. He cleared his throat and forced his gaze to remain on her gorgeous, still-blushing face and not to move downward to areas of her body he knew well by now.

"Girls weekend," she said, her voice low.

"Ah, okay, then. Great. Well, good to see you, um… Next week for more work on the video, right?"

He groaned in his mind at his oafishness.

When she smiled, he had to curl the fingers of both his hands into tight fists to keep from reaching for her. She was probably only humoring him after all. They hadn't exactly parted on *smiling* terms, in his humble opinion.

"Yes. See you then, Coach." Her voice was pleasant but reserved. "Have a nice…retreat."

He nodded at her, trying to keep his reaction neutral, even though it took every ounce of willpower he possessed before turning on his heel and run-walking out of the place. She was here. At the spa. He was assaulted by images of her naked under that robe. He was being punished. That was all he could think about. Punished for all the stupid things he'd done in life. Punished for screwing everything up with Olivia. Punished for not doing what he wanted, for what he honestly believed they both wanted, the rest of the world be damned.

****

Lee Ann was already back in the room they shared, having gone for a swim after her massage.

"I feel as limp as a noodle," she told Olivia as she lay on the bed in a robe, a towel wrapped around her head. "And it feels damn good. How was the massage? Did it get rid of the million knots you're tied up in?"

Olivia flopped down in the comfortable chair and sighed. "For a while. Yes. And then…"

"And then what? Did something happen?"

"I ran into Hatch."

Lee Ann sat up. "What the hell? What's he doing here?"

"It seems he and his staff are here on a retreat." She made a face. "Just my luck, right?"

"We need a meeting." Lee Ann grabbed her cell and texted Cissy and Dana. "I told them to get their asses down here ASAP."

"Oh, they'll love that." Olivia snorted.

But when Lee Ann explained the situation to them, after soundly cursing him, they decided this was a sign. A symbol.

"Of what?" Olivia asked.

"That you guys are supposed to be together, of course."

Cissy and Dana chimed in their approval.

"Look." Lee Ann reached out to take Olivia's hand and tugged her down on the bed beside her. "Someone has to make a move here, or the two of you will be at a stalemate forever. Do you have the guts to make the first move if he doesn't? This place is perfect for it."

"God, I don't know." She raked her fingers through her hair. "I just don't know."

"You could call him and ask him to meet you for a drink," Cissy suggested.

"Okay, but what if he turns me down?"

"I bet we can find out his schedule," Dana offered. "Then you could arrange to bump into him again."

"But what if he just nods and walks away from me? And there's no one I can call and ask to set something up." She shook her head, all those old feelings of insecurity welling up. "Not that I would anyway."

"So what's left?" Cissy asked.

"It has to be something that he won't run away from," Lee Ann said. "That will give you the chance to reconnect with him." She took Olivia's hands in hers. "Liv, look at me. You know I only want what's best for you, and I think that's Hatch."

The other women murmured their agreement.

"Okay, here's my idea."

As she listened to Lee Ann's plan, Olivia had to finally agree there was no success without risk and she'd certainly be no worse off.

****

The BBQ was interminable, but Hatch had fun playing an hour or so of beach volleyball. By the time the bonfire was lit, he had made it a point to speak with every significant other who had made the trip up and most of the kids. At least the ones who'd allow themselves to be corralled away from all the fun and games being thrown at them.

And the entire time—a solid three hours of food, iced tea, games, and chatter—all he could think about was her.

Olivia.

Her long, lean muscled legs, her strong, slim arms, the way her hair slid through his fingers like silk. Oh, and her lips. Yes, those. Not to mention her ass…and the way she'd—

"Hey, Coach!"

He jolted away from the post he'd been leaning against, lost once again down sexy memory lane. "Shit." He looked down at his shirtfront, now dripping from the half bottle of water he'd dumped on himself.

"Throw a few with me?"

He grinned and ran down the expanse of lawn away from George's oldest, a lanky high school freshman with serious throwing potential.

"Hit me, Paul!"

An hour later, he sat at the bonfire, staring into its dancing orange, yellow, and red depths, willing Olivia out of his head. It worked about as well as every other time he tried to do that. He rose, stretching and wincing at the various sore places he'd developed thanks to Arnie.

"Gonna call it. You guys enjoy. I'll see the staff at noon for a few hours of film study. I'm golfing early so I'll be hard to reach, just FYI."

Various choruses of "Good night!", "Sleep well, Coach!" and other farewells filled his ears as he made his slow way toward the resort.

****

Hatch walked into his suite in a daze, stomach full, mind spinning with the fact that she, Olivia her own self, was wandering around under the same roof as he was, right now. Albeit with her friends, who all, no doubt, hated his stupid guts after hearing about how he'd behaved.

He sighed and dropped onto the couch after retrieving and opening an overpriced craft beer from the minibar fridge. It went down fast and eased his fevered brain a bit. He grabbed another one and pointed the remote at the television.

The next thing he knew, he woke to a loud banging on the door, and a full beer spilled onto the couch beside him.

"Crap." He jumped up, confused for a moment as to exactly where he was. "Ow!" He limped to the door, his abused calf muscles twanging and cramping. "Hold your damn water. This had better be an emergency. You're about to break the damn thing—" He yanked it open. "—down."

"Hey, Hatch." Olivia stood there, a tentative smile on her face. She waved a couple of the minibar fridge beers in hands that trembled just the slightest bit. "Wondered if I could interest you in a nightcap."

"Thank Christ," he muttered to himself, not even the least bit willing to think this might be a mistake. He'd missed her, even for the short time they'd been apart. Damn the consequences. He took the unopened beers in one hand and her arm in the other. "Get in here already."

She gasped when he dropped the beers onto the carpeted floor and yanked her to him right in the doorway, unable to stop himself.

"I thought maybe it was a sign of something that we're both here." She bit her bottom lip. "I wasn't sure if I should kill you after what happened or…or I don't know what, but I convinced myself you really didn't mean what you said. About us not seeing each other."

"Worst mistake I ever made," he agreed. "Forget I ever said anything. Please? I need you."

They fumbled around with each other's clothes, teeth and lips crashing together like rookies. At one point, when they made it as far as the thick rug in front of the couch, he shoved the coffee table aside and eased her down onto her back, covering every damn inch of her with kisses and small bites, something he knew she liked.

"Oh…yes, Hatch." She sighed as he settled himself between her legs, eager to provide her with the sort of pleasure he was feeling, simply by existing in the same room with her again. Her heels dug into his back and pounded there when he drew a lovely, shuddering orgasm from her.

"Wait," she said as he moved up her torso, needing to be inside her, connected with her, so badly it hurt him all over. "I—I brought some supplies."

He blinked, confused all over again, and watched her wiggle out from under him and pull a strip of condoms from her jeans pocket.

"I'm impressed." He grinned. "And she's a girl scout, too. Lord help my poor heart." He crawled over to her, every inch of him wanting more, wanting to make love to her all night, to sleep with her in his arms, wake up and start all over again.

"That's me. Always prepared," she said, walking backward toward the room where the bed awaited them.

He jumped up and ran for her, tossed her over his shoulder, and carried her to the bed. He had every intention of losing himself in her for hours or maybe days. But he wanted to take it slow, to savor, to enjoy every last minute of this night and, in so doing, prove something to them both.

When he dumped her onto the bed, she gave a little bounce and squealed in a way that almost forced all his "go slow" intention to the back of his brain. She was so damn gorgeous, and so his.

"You kind of look like the big bad wolf right now. Not gonna lie." She put her hands behind her head and bent one knee, giving him the sort of view he couldn't have planned better himself.

****

He woke up to the sound of his blaring phone

alarm, aware that he was sticky, sorer than ever, and more sexually sated than he'd been in his whole damn life. And that he was alone in the bed.

He rolled over and dragged the pillow to his face, sucking in huge breaths of her, then got up to shower and play golf with Scott Durbin. He grinned when he picked up all five of the empty condom packages and tossed them into the trash. Olivia. She was here. It hadn't been his imagination. And she'd come to him this time.

Maybe this could work after all. Even Alex hadn't affected him this deeply or emotionally. With careful deliberation, he stuffed the warnings in his brain into a hiding place. Was it possible this could work? He hoped so, with everything he had.

He spent the next two days focusing his goals for this getaway with his staff. He and Liv managed to spend two incredible nights together. Nights that Hatch knew was setting him on a path to something he wanted to admit to her but figured it could wait.

By the time they checked out, he was exhausted from the long days and lack of sleep at night, but it was the sort of exhaustion that felt well-earned. He didn't even want to think anymore about the fact this—whatever he and Olivia had going on—might be a mistake.

They checked out separately as agreed upon. The plan was to meet about a mile down the Interstate at a diner for a leisurely breakfast. Hatch was on edge the whole way there and almost passed the exit. He braked at the last minute, waved an apology to the cacophony of honking behind him, and parked his truck next to her hybrid car.

"Hey," she said from a booth with cracked red leather seats. "Thought you were going to stand me up."

"Nah," he said, sliding in next to her draping his arm around her shoulders and nuzzling her neck. "We need to talk about something. Something important."

"Okay. But after we eat. I can't take anything important as hungry as I am."

"Deal." He noticed that she was wearing a Jaguars T-shirt and grinned. "Really getting into the whole thing, aren't you?"

"You bet. After all, I plan to be your number one fan."

He loved that she ate like a normal person. Being a former athlete would do that. Their conversation was deliberately casual as they ate fluffy omelets and thick slabs of toast smeared with real butter and cherry preserves. Both tried to ignore the elephant in the room.

"This is the best damn coffee I've ever had," she declared, resting her elbows on the table.

"It's just all those orgasms," he said, their thighs and arms touching as he finished his admittedly perfect brew. "They make everything taste good."

She grinned, but he could sense her lust rising to meet his. Damn, but they were gonna be hurting the next few weeks. There was no way to sneak around in Avon. He was already concocting another getaway long weekend when the quaint little bell over the door of the diner jingled.

"Oh shit," Olivia blurted out and ducked her head. "Oh crap. Oh hell. You were right. This is a bad idea."

"What? What's wrong?" He stared at her, his hand still resting on her leg. She had her eyes tightly closed, like a little kid thinking she could hide from the grownups if she couldn't see them. "Olivia? Honey?"

"Yes, Olivia," a strange male voice said from somewhere nearby. "Whatever could possibly be wrong, honey?" The stranger turned to him right when Hatch forced himself to look away from Olivia. "Well, hello there, Coach." The guy stuck out his hand. "My name's Bert. Bert Hoekstra."

Chapter Eleven

For an insane moment, Olivia thought she was going to throw up her entire breakfast on the table. Bert Hoekstra? Here? What in the ever-loving hell?

Hatch's face set in its usual, pleasant public mask, but his eyes were stone cold. He stared at Bert, as if by just looking at him he could pulverize the man. He made the handshake as brief as possible.

"Nice to finally get to see you, Coach. I've been trying to get an interview." He gestured at the booth. "Mind if I sit down with you guys for a while? Share a cup of coffee?"

"Actually, yes." Gone was any vestige of pleasantness in Hatch's expression. "I do mind. We're having a private meal."

Hoekstra threw a nasty glance at Olivia. "You shouldn't be wasting your time with has-beens, Coach. Not if you want to get the kind of recognition you deserve."

"I'm getting plenty of the right kind of recognition. Thanks, anyway. And I suggest you think twice about throwing stones at people. I, for one, don't react well to back-biting."

"Yeah?" Bert lifted an eyebrow. "Interesting. Did she crawl into your bed to get your agreement to do her video? Which, by the way, I can promise you will go nowhere if Daniel Forrest has anything to say about it."

Olivia clutched her hands in her lap, twisted them together to keep them from shaking, as much from anger as fear. How dare this scum of the earth lowlife say this? She was about to snap back at him, but Hatch looked at her and gave his head an almost imperceptible shake.

"Here are a few things for you to know, Hoekstra." His voice was stone cold. "One, I don't react well to people who throw dirt on others. Two, I don't talk to reporters except at press conferences or by appointment. Three, if you ever have a hope of even getting on the university campus again, you'd better apologize to Olivia right now."

The smile on Bert's face turned into a sneer, and something dangerous flashed in his eyes. "Fine. I can promise you it won't be a problem to dig up dirt on both of you. I have plenty of news outlets that will jump on it with me." He looked down at Olivia. "And Liv? I can promise you the last thing Daniel Forrest wants is for that video to see the light of day. So work your cute little ass off on it, but no one will ever see it." He stepped away from the booth. "Hope you enjoy my columns when they come out."

By now, Olivia was shaking so badly, she wasn't sure she'd be able to walk to the car. She kept hearing Hatch's words from that disastrous night at her house and realized how right he was. Would Hoekstra go to her boss? Or worse yet, go to Daniel?

In a fog, she watched Hatch pay their bill. Then, with his hand on her arm, he guided her out the door to where their cars were parked. When they reached her car, he turned her to face him and cupped her chin with one hand.

"Can you drive?" Concern etched his words.

Could she? She swallowed, then drew a deep breath and let it out slowly. Her insides were still shaking, and she was afraid any moment she might throw up, but outside, she was steady and together.

She nodded. "Yes. I can drive." She reached for control. She wasn't going to let that little asshole screw things up. "Listen, Hatch, don't worry about Hoekstra. I—"

"Ssh" He touched the tip of a finger to her lips. "I'm not worried about him. Not for me, anyway. I've weathered anything he can throw at me and worse. I'm just concerned for you."

"This is what you were trying to tell me the other night, isn't it?"

"Forget about the other night. I was…" He shook his head. "Are you clear for the rest of the day?"

"I am. Why?"

"Can you follow me to my house?"

She frowned. His house?

"Liv?" His voice nudged her back to reality. "My house? Okay? I want— There's something we need to talk about."

An unhappy look on his face made her stomach knot. She nodded and swallowed the last of her coffee. "Yes. Your house. I'm good. Let's go."

"Okay. But stay right behind me."

Olivia settled herself in her car and pulled out of the parking lot right behind Hatch. She turned left as they headed down the highway. He was driving like a little old lady, as if afraid she wouldn't be able to stick with him otherwise. But her shakes were gone now, replaced by a growing surge of anger.

Bert Hoekstra had always been a thorn in everyone's side and had a reputation as a muckraker. She'd once heard Daniel chew his ass out and tell him not to show up again. That neither the station nor the network had any interest in his kind of reporting. She'd bet even money Hoekstra had been looking for a chance to get her out of the way and take over her slot. But at the time, she'd still been Daniel's puppet and he wasn't in a mood to give her up.

Then memories of the last two nights with Hatch flashed through her brain. She could tell he was sorry he'd gotten into it with her the night he came for the dinner they never ate. He said as much. What she didn't know was if he was sorry he'd thought those things or sorry he gave voice to them. That was one of the first things she wanted on the table when they were alone at his house.

She was so busy focusing on the tail end of his car and having a one-sided discussion with herself that they were at his house before she realized it. Hatch pulled into his garage and motioned her into the driveway behind him. Then he led her inside through the garage. The moment they were in the kitchen, he grabbed her purse, put it on the counter with his keys, and pulled her into his arms. No kissing yet, just a hug that made her feel warmer than any kiss he could have given her.

"Let me say this first." He rested his chin on her head. "I made a big mistake the other night. I should have thought it through before opening my stupid mouth, but I was only thinking of you." He huffed a laugh. "Well, mostly."

"You had good intentions," she murmured against his chest. "And I hate to admit you were probably right.

169

That is, if I'm being sensible. I'm glad we had the last two nights, but if you think we—"

"You know what they say about good intentions," he interrupted her. "The road to hell is paved with them, and that's what I was in, until we were together this weekend. Hell."

She sighed. "I wasn't exactly nice about it—"

"Hush." He stroked her back. "I could have said it a lot better. It was just my crude self coming out. This video is important to both of us for a number of reasons. I just didn't want anything to screw up the opportunity. Gossip can spread and be very destructive."

"Tell me about it. So tell me why we're here."

"Okay." He gave her another quick squeeze, then stepped away from her. "After Hoekstra showed up this morning, something became very clear. He and your ex aren't going to let you climb the ladder of success again without doing their best to destroy you."

Her heart gave a painful thump. "I've been worried about the same thing. I'd love to know what Bert was doing in Petoskey and how he just happened to show up where we were having breakfast." She swallowed. "But right now, I just want you to hold me. Okay?"

"The hell with that. I want to do a lot more than hold you." He pulled her body close to his again. "Maybe, after I tell you what I have to say, you won't want this anymore."

She took a step back and looked up at him. "I can't imagine what could be that bad."

"After you hear it, you can let me know. Until then…" He swung her up in his arms, carried her into his bedroom, and set her on her feet beside his bed. He stared into her eyes for a long moment, then took her mouth in a hungry kiss. He broke it after a few lovely moments. "I want this, Liv. No, I need it, because it might all be over after you hear what I have to say."

God. What on earth could be so terrible?

"I'm sure it can't be that bad." She reached to pull her T-shirt over her head.

Hatch brushed her hands aside. "Let me. Please."

She let him tug the shirt over her head. This was much different than the last two nights. That had been about wiping out anger and bitter emotion and frustration. She had been tentative and nervous, and he had been excessively welcoming, the sex hot and hard and heavy. Today, however, there was a tenderness in his touch and it awoke all kinds of emotions inside her.

He tossed the shirt aside and kissed the upper swell of each breast before he unclasped her bra and sent it to join her shirt. His palms were warm as he cradled her breasts, kneaded them with gentle squeezes as he took one pebbled tip into his mouth. The suction as he pulled on it arrowed heat straight to her core, and the pulse in her sex throbbed with need. She gripped his upper arms to steady herself.

When she was sure she couldn't stand one more minute of his sucking and biting her nipple, he switched to the other one and gave it the same treatment. By the time he lifted his head, she was already quivering with need and her panties were soaked. She looked up at him and saw an answering hunger blazing in his eyes.

The rest of her clothes were gone before she could take another deep breath. Then he sat her on the edge of the bed, knelt between her legs, and pushed her thighs apart. His mouth on her sex was warm, and she shivered when he took a long, slow lick with his tongue.

Oh god!

She fell back on the bed, splaying her legs even farther apart, and closed her eyes, giving herself over to the very intense pleasure. He knew exactly where and how to touch her with his mouth and his hands, lapping and nibbling and stroking until she was nearly out of mind with desire. She heard little sounds of need in the air and realized they were coming from her.

When he slid two fingers easily into her greedy sex, she pushed against them as hard as she could. He added a third finger, stretching her, then began to push them in and out, in and out, driving her up to that elusive edge. Her whole body quivered with want.

Then he pinched her clit, hard, and she exploded, riding his hand as her climax surged through her. He curled his fingers, scraping that sweet spot, and that set her off again. Her body shook with spasm after spasm until she had no breath left and lay exhausted, spent.

Hatch rose from his kneeling position and lay against her, cradling her head in his hands. "You taste just as good now as the first time I did that." He brushed his mouth over hers, sharing her flavor with her, then licking her lips with a lazy swipe of his tongue.

"I think you destroyed me," she told him in a breathless voice.

"Better not. We're just getting started."

He shed his clothes, smiling as she devoured him with her eyes. She was sure she'd never tire of seeing him naked—the broad shoulders, flat chest, ripped six-pack, and a cock that defied description. Her mouth watered just looking at him, and on impulse, she pushed herself to a sitting position and reached out to wrap the fingers of one hand around that thick swollen shaft.

It was hot and pulsing in her hand, and a tiny bead of fluid sat on the slit. She leaned over and licked it, making a humming noise of satisfaction. She would have done it again except he lifted her and rearranged her on the bed.

"Next time," he growled. "This time I can't wait."

She gave a thready little laugh. "Even after last night?"

"Even after." He pulled a condom from the nightstand drawer, tore open the foil, and rolled it onto his shaft. Then he lifted her legs and rested them on his shoulders so she was totally open to him, took his hard length in hand, and slowly eased himself into her hot, tight clasp.

Positioned as she was, he had complete access to her body, and the feel of his cock inside her was unbelievable. He filled every inch of her as he always did, and her inner muscles clasped around him. He hovered over her, hunger and heat flaring in his eyes. When he flexed his hips and drove into her even deeper, she caught her breath.

"Hold on tight," he told her. "This ride's gonna be hot and fast."

He wasn't lying. Olivia could do nothing except lock her ankles behind his neck and take the ride with him. He thrust into her again and again, his cock dragging on her inner walls with each retreat, then scraping every sensitive nerve as he thrust in again. Over and over, never breaking rhythm, and she reached for the climax hovering just out of reach.

And then, with a final plunge, he took them both over the edge.

His cock throbbed inside her and heavy spasms shook her body. On and on it went. When she was sure she couldn't stand another moment, it eased, slowly subsiding. As the tremors slowed and faded, his shaft inside her softened. He held her so close she wasn't sure whose heart was beating so hard or whose breath sounded so fractured.

Finally, they were both limp. Spent.

Hatch looked at her, as if trying to read something in her eyes. Then he kissed her, a hard, almost desperate connection, thrusting his tongue inside to lick every inch of her. With a sigh, he lifted himself and eased from her body, then headed to the bathroom to dispose of the condom. When he walked back in the room, she had plucked his shirt from the floor and slipped it on over her nakedness.

"That looks better on you than it does on me." He grinned, then his smile faded. "Liv, we need to talk."

Every muscle in her body tensed. "Not that same shit you threw at me the other night, I hope."

"Yes, but in a different manner. As long as I'm breaking my resolution to stay away from you until the video is done, I might as well share something with you if we're going to take this any further."

There was no mistaking the serious tone of his voice or the lines of strain on his face.

"Um, okay. Do you want to put your boxers back on, or would you rather be naked?"

"I'd rather we both be naked, but that would be too distracting." He pulled on his shorts and jeans. "Let's go into the kitchen and get some coffee."

When they were sitting at the kitchen table with full mugs, he took one of her hands and brushed his thumb over the knuckles.

"Are you going to tell me you killed someone?" She tried to make her tone light and joking, but at the look on Hatch's face, she wondered just how devastating the thing he wanted to tell her was.

"No, but you may want to kill me when I tell you."

She took a swallow of her coffee and waited.

He raked his fingers through his hair. "I'm not sure where to begin, exactly. I guess at the beginning."

She nodded. "That usually works the best."

"Okay." He blew out a long breath. "You know, my whole life is numbers. Scores. Yards gained. Yards thrown. Number of games ahead. Rankings. Stats. It's never ending."

"I know that." She took his hand and gave it a gentle squeeze. "But that's not all of it, right?"

"Right. I guess it started in college when a bunch of us got together to play poker. Nothing much, mostly penny ante. It was just for fun."

"Okay." She nodded. "A lot of guys do that."

"Right. But when I was drafted, people asked me if I played. Big money people." He raked his fingers through his hair. "I knew I should have said no, but I was at the top of the world and relishing my newfound financial windfall and fame. I got invited to some games that were much higher stakes." He looked down at his hands. "I couldn't believe what a rush that was. The thrill of winning, of besting other people at the table. Of raking in all that money."

Olivia frowned. "But you were making a huge salary. Why did those games excite you so much?"

He shrugged. "The thrill of winning, I guess. I don't know. If I had an answer, I probably wouldn't have gotten in the mess that I did."

"Mess?" She rubbed her forehead, where a slight headache was beginning to generate. "What kind of mess?"

"High stakes gambling. High dollar games. Private games in hotel suites where the buy-in was ten thousand."

Olivia nearly knocked over her mug. "Ten thousand dollars? Holy shit, Hatch."

"Yeah," he agreed. "It's even worse when you consider that's the minimum. Sometimes there was more than a hundred thousand on the table."

She was speechless. What could she say? She swallowed back the rising nausea. This was not at all what she'd expected.

"Anyway, I hit a game every chance I had. And then I started losing. Big time. Lots and lots of money. But I just couldn't stop. It got worse when I was allowed to play on credit. But what they say about credit at a casino is exactly right. It's not something you ever want."

"Oh, Jesus," she whispered. "What did your wife say?"

"Oh." He snorted. "She didn't know a thing about it. She only found out when she was checking our bank accounts and our investments and discovered how much I'd been pulling out."

She stared at him. "You kept it from her?"

"I did." A muscle in his jaw twitched. "I was afraid to tell her. I kept thinking I'd win it all back and never have to spill the beans."

"So what happened?"

"She listened to every word, then told me if I'd stop we'd be okay. We could get past this. She made me promise, and I did for a while." He raked his fingers through his hair. "But then the team was playing an away game and some people invited me to dinner and to one of their private games. I was so sure I could control it."

Olivia blew out a breath. "But you couldn't. Right?"

"Right." Again he ran his fingers through his now thoroughly mussed hair again. "In fact, I lost big time. And Alex, who had by then developed the habit of checking all our accounts regularly, found out." He looked out the window, his jaw clenching and unclenching in a way that hurt her heart.

"I'll bet she was none too happy."

"Ha." He snorted. "That's putting it mildly. She wanted a divorce, and I couldn't talk her out of it. We just both agreed it would be best to claim irreconcilable differences, which we did. A quiet divorce made the whole thing go away. Well, almost, considering how much money I owed to some, ah, fairly angry individuals."

She reached out and put her hand in his. "Oh, Hatch, I am so sorry."

"Yeah, well, me, too. Of course, the team owners found out about it. Nothing happens in a vacuum, you know."

"What did they do?"

"We were smack in the middle of a season, so they agreed to let the contract run to the end, but that was it. By that time I was too scared to try sneaking in a game or two. I think that was the worst year of my life."

Olivia's heart hurt for him. "I'm sure it was."

"You can bet I've stayed away from high stakes poker since then. The only numbers I've focused on are those in the playbook and on the schedules." His mouth curved in a wry grin. "I actually played some penny ante with my coaches, just to see if I could control it."

"Tempting fate?"

"Yeah. It was okay, but I know the itch is still there, so I probably won't be doing that again. I came clean with Scott Durbin when I was hired, and he appreciated that."

"What did he say?"

"That everyone takes a wrong step once in their lives, and if I could promise him I'd stay away from it, he was okay. He said this was a new start for the team and for me." He looked directly at her. "But there's probably a better than even chance that Bert Hoekstra will dig it up. If he does, you know he'll hotfoot it to your ex."

Olivia was silent for a long moment, mulling it over in her head.

"And," Hatch continued, "if he does, that's going to affect you and the video. From what I've learned about your ex, he wouldn't be above using that to pressure your bosses into tossing the whole project. Or if they didn't, making sure it got a lot of bad press. He's obviously a manipulative asshole of the first order."

"That he is." She frowned. "Wait. What you learned about him?"

"Don't get mad," he pleaded. "But you said he'd made your life miserable and I just wanted to get a handle on it, so if he tried to cause trouble, I'd be in your corner. But I could see this whole thing blowing up in our faces, especially yours. You being pushed to dump the documentary or they'd be sure everything got out in the media."

Olivia didn't know whether to laugh, cry, scream, or hug the man.

"Okay, we'll get to that another time. But let me get this straight. You wanted us to end our personal relationship because you thought my ex or Bert would use that to muddy my name and by extension the video, so it would go nowhere."

"That's right." He took another swallow of coffee. "I just wanted to protect you."

She shook her head, speechless for the moment. She wanted to tell him she'd wrestled with the same conflicts. Had the same worries about the video but for different reasons. Her concern was that a relationship would taint the project in the eyes of her boss and maybe kill it. It would certainly give her ex plenty of food for gossip.

"That's very noble of you, Duncan Jerome Hatcher, but I'm done letting Daniel Asshole Forrest try to manipulate my life. I'm not the weak pushover I used to be, so if he tries anything, I say, bring it on."

"But—"

She held up her hand. "No buts. And let's not worry about Hoekstra. I have an idea about how to handle him."

"Yeah?" He cocked an eyebrow. "Like what?"

She shook her head. "Not right now. I have to think about it a bit. But I'm not letting either of those two scumbags dictate my life. The important thing here is to make sure they don't ruin yours."

179

"I can handle it," he began.

She held up a hand. "I'm sure you're right, but let's not take any chances. This is a whole new beginning for you, Hatch. Let's make sure it works."

His mouth curved in a lopsided grin. "I have to say your ex certainly had you pegged wrong."

"And I'll be happy to let him find out. Meanwhile, you have to promise me something."

"What's that?"

"No more nonsense about us not seeing each other personally. I don't know about you, but I get the feeling we have something good here. We're not kids anymore, and this is a second chance for both of us. I refuse to let jerks like them ruin it."

He laughed, a full-throated sound. "I still think it's dicey, but if you're all in, so am I."

"I might need protection, but not from them. At the appropriate time, I'll let my boss know what's going on, but I refuse to be scared away from something that feels so good."

Hatch rose, put his hands under her elbows, and lifted her from her chair.

"I won't deny I'm nervous," he told her, "but at the same time, the last thing I want is to stay away from you."

"Good, because you're stuck with me. We'll get through this together, right?"

She grinned. "You got it, Coach."

Chapter Twelve

"You know what I don't want? Anyone got a guess? Anyone at all?"

Hatch slammed his office door and looked at the coaches he'd pulled in with him from the locker room. He met every pair of eyes in front of him, all of them filled with varying degrees of dismay and frustration. He figured it was all reflected in his, too, but right now, what he felt most was anger.

Raw, roiling, gut-clenching fury was more like it.

He took a long deep breath, closed his eyes, then reopened them. "Can anyone in this room tell me what I don't want right now?"

The coaches all looked at each other, the floor, the middle distance, none of them meeting his gaze. Until Tomas did.

"Excuses, Coach," the young man said. "You don't want excuses."

"Damn right," he said, smacking the flat of his hand against his desk before curling his fingers into fists and leaning them on the glass. "That is the correct answer, Coach, thank you. So. We've got that out of the way. Talk to me about solutions."

They'd made it all the way to the final third of their season undefeated, deep into the conference, riding high on a wave of successes. Then, somehow, everything had skidded off the rails. One loss hadn't fazed him too much. It was against a team he'd worried about from the get-go and sure enough they'd read every play, shut down every defensive gambit thrown at them, and left the Lakeland Jaguars with a humiliating twenty-eight to nothing loss.

Not a huge deal, as far as losses go. And frankly, Hatch had been shocked they'd made it this far into the season without one, considering the gaping holes in both their secondary and special teams. He already had his eye on four players he'd be working on for next year to fill those very gaps. He'd conducted the requisite triage and re-hash of that game, spoken to the necessary players who'd made errors, and basically felt convinced that he'd dealt with it all.

Apparently, he had not.

The season was sliding off the edge, and with it his determination—no, his need—to hit the jackpot not only for the team but for himself. The team's success would be his. There was a real problem here. He had to correct it, to right the ship, before the season went down the drain, and with it his career.

"George," he barked, after dropping into his large leather chair. "I want to know straight up what in the name of all that is holy is wrong with my quarterback? He's gone from the top to the bottom. I swear, I've talked to that kid until I'm blue in the face, and I'm done coddling him. Unless there's something I don't know about."

"I'm afraid that anything I say is going to sound like the very thing you don't want to hear right now, Coach." George met his gaze.

Hatch frowned. "I don't like the sound of that."

"I mean, it's not much to do with anything other

than, you know, the usual issues he has."

"Usual issues. That girl? Jesus. Please don't tell me he's still—"

"Fighting with his center over her? Yeah." George made a sound of disgust.

Hatch blew out a breath. Tony and Josh had not let up for one second. Hatch didn't like the ugly, blatantly misogynistic thoughts that rose in his mind about the girl in question, so he shoved them down deep and leaned forward on the desk. Two of the game's most crucial moments had come in the red zone. Both times Josh had bobbled the snap, leaving Tony either empty handed or scrambling for the ball. And both times, the other team had converted and scored.

"I honestly don't know what to do about this. Can anyone in here give me some insight?" He blew out a breath of exasperation. "Because if those two don't get their heads out of their pants, we are never going to make a bowl game."

The group made random noises and glanced around at each other.

"Fine. I'll solve it right now," he said, getting up and coming around to lean against the front of his desk. "Meeting's over."

Everyone filed out in silence, happy to give him space.

Hatch knew he was letting his emotion—anger, primarily—get the best of him, and he knew damn good and well that he shouldn't be making any crucial decisions right now. He needed to decompress. To go home, take a hot shower, have a beer, and talk to Olivia. Not exactly in that order. And he probably wouldn't be doing much talking at first. He knew himself well enough to admit that. He needed to touch her, to hold her. To fuck her until he could barely walk. She grounded him, soothed him, made him center himself. Then he could think a clear-headed thought, maybe.

After a few minutes, he grabbed his phone and tapped out a quick message to his right-hand man, George.

"Ignore everything I said. I need a night to think about it. I'll get back with you in the morning. But I won't be meeting with the team tonight. They can take that however they like."

"Got it, Coach," George responded within seconds. "Leave them to us tonight."

Hatch tossed the phone onto the desktop and leaned forward, willing himself not to lose it. He knew his team was green, mostly untested. He and his staff had worked their tails off getting ready for the season, and until the last few weeks, it had all seemed worth it. Some of the young men were too stubborn to coach, but they'd worked through that. He knew he'd be dealing with a team the likes of which he would never have put together. It was part and parcel of taking over a D1 program.

But this whole fighting over a girl thing was simply not something he was prepared to handle, nor did he want to. His entire focus had to be on transforming the team. He wanted to crack their fool heads together. To tell them a lot of truly awful things about how this girl was playing them against each other on purpose, to cause this sort of strife that threatened to tear the team apart at this crucial juncture. To channel the absolute worst of the worst of himself to convince them that she was simply not worth it, at all, for any reason.

"Damn it," he muttered as he rose to his feet. It felt weird to be leaving so early. But there was no way in hell he could face the team without losing his temper in a way that would do no one any good. It was for the best.

His phone buzzed with a text. Distracted, he grabbed it as he was heading for the door. Walking down the darkened hallway, his mood matching the low lighting and freezing cold temperatures, he looked at the name of the sender.

Olivia.

Exactly the medicine he needed.

Her text read, *Hey, Coach. Sorry about the game. Let's curl up in front of a fire and deconstruct it together.*

He climbed behind the wheel of his truck, touched the ignition button and waited while the heater got to work. He'd managed to leave his coat in his office; he'd left in such a snit.

Shaking his head at himself, he picked the phone up and texted his reply.

Yes. Please. All of the above. I'll be home... He paused, his thumbs over the tiny screen's keyboard, pondering that four-letter word.

Home.

He smiled to himself. She hadn't moved in with him or anything but had made an enormous deal about installing a toothbrush in his bathroom and several sets of lingerie and a robe in his bedroom. It was one of the happiest days of his life when she'd done that. Sappy, he knew. But the god's honest truth.

She'd taken over his kitchen, too, which had meant

he had delicious meals pretty much every night and normal, healthy breakfasts every morning she was around. Even if it meant she'd tossed out his three boxes of sugary, kiddie cereals with a look of disgust, he was thankful for her efforts to take care of him via his stomach. Not to mention all the other ways she took care of him.

He'd kidded her about how they'd eased into stereotypes, but she'd insisted that was silly. She loved to cook. She didn't love laundry. He could handle that for them. And he did. He'd do anything for her.

They still were low-key about the whole thing. The less Hoekstra and Forrest knew about it, the better. They were smart enough to handle that.

He smiled as he turned down the road that led to his neighborhood. He'd caught himself pondering engagement rings on the internet the other day, which made him nervous until he admitted to himself that he had every intention of presenting her with one for Christmas, once they got past this hell of a first season.

He hung his keys on the rack in the mudroom, shucked out of his shoes, and wandered into the kitchen. It was full of delicious smells. A fire was indeed crackling in the grate. A bottle of cabernet was open and breathing on the high eating bar. And the lovely Olivia was stirring something on the stove, her back to him.

He allowed himself a few seconds to admire that view, stopping just short of licking his lips at the sight of her full hips flaring from her waist. She was still dressed in dark jeans and a Lakeland sweatshirt from the game but had obviously left in time to get home and make things nice for him here. Something warm and somewhat shocking filled his chest and throat as he contemplated this and mentally increased the carat size of the rock he wanted to slap on her finger in a few months.

She turned to face him. A few tendrils of her dark blonde hair had escaped the tieback and framed her face. Her face was flushed from the steaming stovetop. She smiled and held out her arms.

"Whatever that is smells great, babe, but would you mind turning it off? I'd hate for it to burn." He scooped her up and carried her into the bedroom, needing this raw physical connection with her now. Not after a meal and a few glasses of wine. It was fast, a little rough, and fully satisfying. He always made sure that was the case for her.

As he lay with her draped over his bare chest, their breathing calming in unison, sweat drying on their skin, his head finally began to clear.

"Okay, that was fun," she said, kissing his shoulder and draping her leg over his under the soft sheet. "Now, talk to me. What is going on with Josh and Tony?"

He sighed and pulled her closer. "A girl."

She smacked his chest.

He groaned. "I mean, a woman."

"Still?"

"Yeah. And I'm at a total loss what to do about it. I mean, it's not like I can tell them what I really think, you know?"

Olivia rose on her elbow, her eyes bright. He mentally bit his own lip and braced himself.

"Oh? And what, pray tell, do you really think about it, Coach?"

He ran his finger across her cheek. She moved ever

so slightly out of his reach. He decided that she might as well know what he thought. If he planned to spend the rest of his life with her he had no intention of hiding anything.

"I think that girl is messing with my kids, and it's pissing me the hell off. Not to mention how pissed you are right now, because I said such a throw-back sexist thing."

She flopped back down. "You're right. But I'll let it slide for now." She played with the hair on his chest for a moment. "Did you ever consider that they could be messing with her? I mean, do you have the whole story? As in her side of it?"

"No, and I don't want it. I'm only concerned with what's going on with my players."

"Okay, but just listen for a second, so you don't risk being a total asshole." She ran her fingertip across his bare chest, distracting him just enough. "How about you get one of your assistants to talk to her? I mean, what can it hurt?"

"It can get the program in all kinds of trouble, that's what," he said. "What if she claims we intimidated or harassed her?"

"Then let me talk to her. I'm not affiliated with the program in any official way."

Hatch took her hand and pressed it to his lips. "I don't know, Liv. That could put you in a tough position. What if she feeds you some story about them, and then you tell me and I have to do something about it."

She scrambled out of his arms and stood up, drawing her discarded sweatshirt down her bare torso before he could say or do anything.

He sat, watching her stomp around the room. "Olivia, calm down," he said before he could stop himself.

She jammed her feet into her jeans, hopping around with her back to him. But she whirled to face him, her expression one that did not bode well for that whole cuddling by the fire thing later.

"You do know how unwise it is to tell an angry woman to 'calm down.'" She hooked her fingers around the last two words. "Right, Coach?"

"Yeah, actually, I do know. And I'm sorry. Come back here. Let me try to explain."

"No, I get it. It's all about winning games. Screw anyone who might be hurt by anyone on your precious team."

"Liv, how in the world did we get from my QB and center acting like a couple of idiotic Tom cats to someone being hurt?" He rubbed his cheek. "Honestly. I'm confused."

Her shoulders slumped, and she flopped into one of the leather chairs by the window. "I don't know. I guess I'm projecting. I'm sorry. But I think I should talk to her, don't you? Instead of someone from the team?"

Hatch turned and put his feet on the floor. "Can we talk about this later?"

"Fine," she said.

When he got up to face her, she'd left the room. Cursing under his breath at his idiocy and the way he'd fumble-fingered the whole conversation, he took a quick, hot shower, and got redressed. This wasn't how he'd pictured this evening progressing. And he had no one to blame but himself.

Funny thing was, he thought as he ran his fingers

though his hair and stared at himself in the mirror, he didn't mind it. Relationships were, by definition, a challenge. Two human beings would never get along a hundred percent of the time. But if one truly cared about the other human in the equation, sometimes disagreeing was as much fun as agreeing. Determined and refreshed, he headed back to his kitchen.

Olivia was still there, so that was a victory. She was sipping wine and picking at a plate of something that looked Italian and smelled incredible. When his stomach rumbled, she glanced over at him. "I didn't mean to insert myself into your team's issues, Hatch. It was unnecessary, and I'm sorry."

He grinned and walked over to her, pulling her to her bare feet and wrapping his arms around her.

"I really love how passionate you are. About everything, including my team's love life."

He held her close, relishing the press of her breasts against his chest, her breath on his neck. "But I need to ask you something important." He felt her stiffen. He grinned and pointed to her plate. "Can I have some of that? Because as much as I would really like to make love to you again, I might pass out if I do that before I eat."

She smacked his ass. "Sit down. Relax. Talk to me about something other than the game."

"Gladly," he said, sliding into his seat and pouring himself a generous helping of wine.

They ate—a glorious, rich and cheesy eggplant parmesan with homemade bread and a dark green salad—and talked about nothing in particular for an hour. Hatch would swear he'd never felt more comfortable with a woman in his life. Olivia had a way about her that put everyone at ease, something that came naturally to her that she'd honed as a journalist. And she never failed to coat his twanging nerves with a sort of emotional salve.

He reached across the table, took her hand, and twined his fingers in hers. His need to have her, to keep her in his life, his bed, his home forever was a bit of an old school throwback. And something she'd likely reject on principal if he knew her, and he believed that he did. Not making assumptions about her was key.

"I think you're right," he said, unable to take his eyes off her.

"Of course I'm right," she said, licking a bit of butter off her other hand, which made his cock leap to attention under his well-worn jeans. "But about what?"

"About talking to the girl."

"The woman, you mean," she said, keeping their fingers linked together.

"Of course that's what I mean. I want you to talk to her. See if she can give you any insights into what in the hell's going on, so I can deal with it on the guy side of things. I need them focused. Not wandering around the field worrying about when they're going to get laid next."

Olivia glared at him, but her gaze softened when he put her knuckles to his lips. "Can we go back to bed now?"

"Oh, I see." She let go of his hand and stood up, slowly, like a cat unfolding itself from a nap in the sun. His mouth watered, and not for Italian food. "I make your dinner, pour your wine, fuck you, feed you, and now I get to fuck you again?"

"Something like that," he said, leaning back as she

wandered over to him. The shoulder of her sweatshirt slipped down. He reached for her, trying to draw her into his lap.

"Nope, sorry mister. But we have to clean the kitchen first. I cooked. That means…"

"Yeah, yeah, I know." He picked up their plates and headed for the sink. "Go on and relax, Liv. I've got this."

She picked up her wineglass and sat at one of the tall bar height chairs. "What do you want me to say to her?"

Hatch mulled it over in his mind as he loaded the dishwasher, put the leftovers in plastic dishes, washed the pasta pan and the cheese encrusted casserole dish.

"I just want to know her side of the story, like you said I should. And…" He dried his hands and hung the towel on the stove handle before coming around to kiss her temping, exposed shoulder. She made a lovely, low, sexy sound as he did it. "And I also want you to know…" He slid his hand up under her shirt and cupped her bare breast. She shifted in her seat, that amazing sound she made when she was turned on burrowing deep into his libido. "That if she says anything that she doesn't want me or the other coaches to know, you don't have to tell me."

"Wait." She turned and rose to her feet so the tall chair was between them. "You mean, you're okay if I tell her what she says can remain between the two of us?"

"I am." He was working hard to keep from launching himself at her and dragging her to the nearest available horizontal surface. "If it's something you think is critical, I know you're smart enough to figure a way to tell me without involving her."

"Then, I guess, as long as you mean that…"

"Well, don't lead with that if you don't have to. I'm hoping she'll be willing to open up and give us some insight into how I can help Tony and Josh focus on football for a few more weeks. But if it's something she'd rather me not know, well…" He shrugged. "I get that, too. But if she needs some other kind of help, can you get it for her and keep me out of it?"

She frowned.

He held up both hands. "You have to understand that if those boys have hurt her in any way, she has to take that directly to the University. Then I'll deal with it. And trust me, I will deal with it. But I don't want it to just come to me first. I want the proper authorities to know first."

"Do you think…"

He sighed and his shoulders slumped. "God. I hope not," he said. "But if that's the case, I want it known at the highest possible level first so there's no reason for anyone to cover it up. They'll be gone before sundown if that is the case, I swear it to you."

"Okay," she said, her voice soft.

"George knows her name, and he can get her phone number or email for you."

"Fine," she said, staring down at the floor. He thumbed her chin and lifted it so she met his gaze. "I feel like I'm being too nosy or something."

"I love it when you're nosy," he said, watching the way her expression changed, relaxed, and her full, delicious lips lifted in a smile. "In fact, I love a lot of things about you, Olivia." He shoved the chair to the side and stepped into the space between them. "Like these." He kissed both her cheeks. "And these." He lifted her shirt up and off, exposing her breasts and lowering his lips to one of her rock-hard nipples. "And this," he muttered as his hands slipped around her waist to cup her ass.

He lifted his head to kiss her mouth again, drowning in her, losing himself gladly in their sweet contact. He broke the kiss and cupped her cheek. "I…I love you, Liv," he said, his voice hoarse. "I can't believe I'm even saying this, but it's what I feel. And I didn't want to keep it to myself any longer."

He hadn't meant to say that out loud for a while, but really, what the hell. For one brief moment, it scared the shit out of him, but then he made himself relax. This was a new start, a new life, and a new woman.

She smiled and put her hand against his. "I know you do, Hatch. I…I don't know…"

"Shh," he said, meaning it. "You don't have to say anything yet. Not until you want to. But I want you to know how I feel. It's important—" His voice broke. He swallowed, embarrassed but somehow not at the same time. "I need you, Liv. All of you. Everything about you. Even the nosy, hyper-feminist, bossy parts."

She pretended to frown, but he saw the tears in her eyes. He swiped them with his thumbs as they fell. "I don't make women cry, Olivia."

"Yes, you do," she whispered. "Now, take me back to bed, already, will you? I'm tired of waiting."

He did just that. He was, after all, at her service by now. Or maybe it was love. He decided to ponder that…later.

Later, he woke in the wee hours of the morning,

startled from a strange dream. It involved him beating the ever-loving shit out of Olivia's ex-husband while his buddy Tank watched and cheered. The fact that she was still here next to him, wrapped in a sheet and nothing else, her hair draped over her face as she slept, made him what had to be the happiest man alive.

Chapter Thirteen

Olivia sat in a back booth in the little coffee shop just off campus. She knew it wasn't a place where students hung out so there was little danger that anyone would spot Angela Pierson meeting with her. She figured the girl was already edgy about this meeting, and she wanted to create a comfort zone for her. She couldn't help wondering what Angela was like, who had two jocks fighting over her. Was she enjoying the competition? Encouraging it? Was it the highlight of her semester?

According to Hatch the two guys were bright, excellent football players, and up until now, highlights of the team. But things had escalated so much he was ready to bench them both, which would be a serious problem for a team on the verge of the level of success he'd personally not expected during this, his inaugural year as its coach.

Glancing at her watch, she noted that Angela was fifteen minutes late and wondered if she'd had a change of heart. She'd just taken another sip of her coffee when the door to the place opened and a young blonde woman hurried in, bundled into a jacket and a Jaguars scarf and carrying a backpack. Olivia had sent a picture of herself so she'd be recognized. The girl scanned the customers, and when their gazes connected, Olivia waved her over.

"Hi." Angela slid into the booth, dropping her backpack on the seat and unwinding the scarf.

"Hi, yourself. Angela, right? Or do you prefer Angie?"

"Angela, please." She grinned, a too cute dimple flashing in one cheek. "I plan to be a lawyer so I'm practicing using my professional name."

All right, then. Maybe not such a fluff ball after all.

Olivia smiled. "I wish you good luck."

"Thank you."

"What can I get for you?"

"Oh, a skim milk mocha latte, but I've got it." The words came out in a rush, an indication of underlying nervousness.

"Nope. My treat." She waved at the waitress heading in their direction. When she'd placed the order, she turned back to Angela. "Thank you so much for meeting with me today, Angela. I really appreciate it."

The girl busied herself, rearranging her jacket and her backpack, giving Olivia a chance to get a good look at her. Long blonde hair framed a face that bore little sign of makeup except for mascara on already thick lashes framing electric blue eyes and tinted gloss that accented bow-shaped lips. Even though the girl was sitting down, Olivia could tell she had a toned body that went with the fresh good looks.

Lordy. Was I ever that young?

Yes, and foolish, even when I was older than that.

She stifled a sigh.

By the time Angela settled herself, the server had brought her coffee. Angela took a sip of it and sighed. "My very favorite," she confided. "You can take away everything else from me, but if you dare to touch my latte, I might have to kill you." She grinned to show Olivia she was joking.

"I appreciate you giving me a few minutes of your time. I wouldn't bother you if it wasn't important."

"Sure." She looked around. "But is there some reason we're meeting here rather than on campus?"

"Most of those places are jammed all the time, and it's easy to get distracted." She shrugged. "But we can go someplace else if you'd feel more comfortable."

"No, no. This is fine. I come here once in a while when I want to get away from the crowds, too." The girl took another long sip of her drink. "I have to say, I was real surprised when you called me. I mean, we don't even know each other. But everyone knows you're doing some kind of video on Coach Hatcher." She grinned. "And we're all excited about this. He's the big hero here, you know."

Olivia smiled and blushed despite her efforts not to do so. "I do know that. It's one of the reasons I'm doing the documentary."

"I don't know what I'd have to do with that. If you don't mind my asking, how did you even get my number?"

Olivia grinned. "Being friends with the football coach has a lot of perks. He has friends in high places."

"The coach himself?" Angela chewed on her lower lip. "Am I in some kind of trouble with him?"

"Not at all." Olivia studied the girl. "What made you think that?"

Angela took her time answering. "I just don't get what this is all about."

Olivia chose her words carefully. "Angela, I say this only as a point of fact, not to make you

198

uncomfortable. I understand you're dating two of the members of the football team."

"That's what this is about?" The girl's jaw dropped. "I didn't think it was against the rules to date any of the athletes." Her eyes widened. "Wait. What's going on here?"

Slow and easy. She's not doing anything wrong, at least, that you know of.

"Coach is a little concerned because the two guys don't seem to be as focused on their playbooks as they should be. I'm sure you understand what an important time this is for everyone. He thought maybe you could give me some insight, and that you'd feel more comfortable talking to me rather than him."

"Coach Hatcher wanted to talk to me himself?" Angela's eyes opened wide. "Are you kidding me? Does Coach Hatcher think it's my fault we lost the last couple of games? Ohmigod. I can't believe that." She smacked her forehead. "Those two damn idiots. I told them and told them, and they just won't…"

"Just won't what?" Olivia prompted.

Angela leaned against the back of the booth and blew out a breath. "Look. You seem really nice, and everyone says what a big deal you and this video are. If I tell you anything, it's not going to end up on television, is it?"

"Lord, no." Olivia laughed. "That's the last place we'd want it. What's going on, Angela? Is there something serious for you with one of these guys? And I'm not asking just to be nosy, because for the most part, your private life is just that. Private. But I think we have a problem here that I hope you can help me with."

"It's just so stupid," she said at last. "I'm

embarrassed to even tell you about it. I should have been able to stop it right away."

"Have they hurt you?" *Please say no.*

"No, no, nothing like that." Angela shook her head.

"Because if it is, you know it should be reported. If you don't want me to tell Coach, then at least let me take you to the right people."

"It's nothing like that. It's just so stupid." Angela drained the last of her mocha and set the mug down. "Okay, so it was great to have two of the team stars asking me out. I won't lie about that. But it was just for fun. I mean, I have one more year of undergrad and then I'm hoping to be accepted to law school. I'm not looking for anything to complicate my life." She fiddled with her empty mug. "It was kind of flattering having two hot football stars both into me, but I think they need to do some growing up."

"I probably agree with you, but I need some details, Angela. Hatch is very concerned about these two guys."

Angela sighed. "Okay, here's the deal. Tony, the quarterback, is in my economics class. It's a required course, and he was having some problems, so he asked if we could study together for the first exam. I agreed. Somehow, after a couple of weeks, it became a habit to meet at the library at night to study together."

Olivia cocked an eyebrow. Study dates sounded harmless enough. "So, what happened?"

"In the second week, Josh showed up with him and asked if he could join in. I said sure. I mean, it was no big deal." She sighed. "Then Josh caught me after a class and asked me out for a coffee that night. It seemed harmless enough. I texted Tony to say I wouldn't be at the library and that Josh and I were going out to grab coffee. That's when everything went to hell."

"In what way?"

"Tony got all proprietary and chewed Josh out, and they practically got into a fist fight at the coffee bar. I threw down money for my drink, told them to grow up, and walked out. Now it seems they're in some kind of contest. I stopped going to the library, because they started causing a scene. Both of them were texting me so much I had to block their numbers." She leaned forward. "Miss Grant—Olivia—I haven't even gone out on a real date with either of them, and now, for sure, I never will. Yet they're fighting over me like two dogs over a bone. To tell the truth, I'm glad Coach is getting involved, because I was getting ready to call him myself."

Interesting. "Sounds like Tony has a little possessive streak about him."

"No kidding." Angela flipped her long hair over her shoulder. "I'm sorry I ever agreed to study with him. Look what it started."

Olivia nodded. "I'm thinking there's a little more to this than squabbling over a girl. Not," she added quickly, "that you aren't worth the battle."

Angela heaved a long sigh. "Believe me when I say this whole thing doesn't stroke my ego. This is not what I'm looking for from guys."

"I wouldn't think so."

Angela looked at her watch. "I hope I'm not being rude, but I do have to be someplace in fifteen minutes. Is there anything else you need from me?"

"No." Olivia shook her head. "Thank you so much for meeting with me and sharing the information."

"If you can get those idiots off my back, I will be very grateful."

"I'm sure, when Coach Hatcher gets through with them, they won't be bothering you anymore. Again, thank you."

"Oh, sure. Nice to meet you." She flashed a grin. "We all can't wait for the video to come out."

"It won't be until after the season," Olivia told her. "But I promise, there will be plenty of publicity about it to let you know it's out. Again, thanks for your help."

"Sure." Angela slid from the booth, grabbed her backpack, and hurried out of the coffee shop.

Olivia sat for a moment before reaching into her purse and pulling out her cell phone to text Hatch. "*Met with Angela. Nice girl. Have stuff to tell you.*"

After a long moment his answering text popped up. "*How bad is it?*"

"*I think nothing a good stern lecture won't cure. Want to come over for dinner tonight?*"

Another long minute.

"*Sure. Seven okay?*"

"*See you then.*"

She hoped that the pause before his answer had more to do with the fact he was busy than that he was backing away from their relationship yet again.

After collecting her stuff, she headed home, stopping to grocery shop along the way. Drew had emailed her a couple of files with some raw footage of the games they'd shot so far, and she wanted to start viewing it. She was starting to put the actual pieces of the video together and was excited at the way it was falling into place.

Tonight would be a good time to tell Hatch what

she wanted to add to the documentary. She just hoped he didn't go off the rails when she brought it up. In her mind, she saw it as a segment that would add richness and depth both to the video and the image of who Hatch was. A man who had found his inner strength and was rebuilding his life as he rebuilt this team. The big question was, how would he feel about it?

Between watching the video clips and mulling over how to sell her idea to Hatch, the afternoon nearly got away from her. With the lasagna in the oven and the salad in the fridge, she treated herself to a hot shower, then dressed in silky slacks and a matching top. By the time the doorbell rang at seven, right on the dot, she had the table set and the cabernet open and breathing. She flung open the door and gave the man standing there a huge grin.

And why not. He looked totally delicious in his trademark khakis and a black soft collar shirt. His hair, as always, was neatly in place, and when she looked at his eyes, she blushed at the heat simmering in the dark chocolate irises.

He was holding a bouquet of wildflowers, which he held out to her. "I figured you had the wine thing covered, but I wanted to bring you something."

She took the flowers from him and stood on tiptoe to kiss him. "I love flowers. Thank you so much."

Maybe tonight wouldn't be the best time to bring up her ideas, she thought, as she found a vase for the bouquet and poured a glass of wine for each of them. Just enjoy the dinner and being together. He'd already be pissed off enough when she told him what Angela had said.

"We've got about fifteen minutes until dinner is

ready," she told him. "Let's take our drinks into the living room, look out the window, and enjoy the view of the sky."

"I don't think anything can beat this view right here." His voice was low and warm and sent a tingle along her spine. "And I want to do this first."

He tilted up her chin with the tips of his fingers and pressed his warm lips to hers, a gentle pressure at first, but then he slid his tongue along the seam, urging her to open for him. When she did, he slid his tongue inside and licked every inch of her inner surface. Her nipples hardened at once, aching in their need to be touched, and the heavy pulse in her sex throbbed like a drumbeat. Lordy! How easily this man turned her on, from zero to a hundred with just a touch.

He cradled her face in his palms as he tasted and tasted until she was weak in the knees, gripping his upper arms for support. She blinked, and when she looked into his eyes, she saw that same intense heat and hunger that made her entire body flush with need.

"I think we'd better eat dinner," she murmured, "or it might burn."

"I'd rather eat what's right in front of me." The deep, hoarse timbre of his voice vibrated through her. Was it possible to get any more turned on?

"Um…" She licked her lips. "Hold that thought."

She managed to disengage herself from him and moved into the kitchen to serve their meal. They were about five minutes into dinner when Olivia decided this might be a good time to share with Hatch what she'd learned from Angela.

"Well." He took a swallow of his wine. "I'm sure glad it wasn't anything worse than that. Dealing with sexual harassment or sexual aggression in collegiate athletics is a giant snake pit of trouble."

"Don't I know it." She swallowed a bite of lasagna. "So where do you take it from here? She really doesn't want anything to do with either of them, and is sorry she ever started anything. I'm sure she didn't expect to be dealing with two immature nitwits. It's important to impress on them, however, that if they do try to hassle her about this, there will be consequences."

"Don't worry about that." Hatch snorted. "They don't want to be kicked off the team and lose their scholarships. That's exactly what I'll tell them will happen if they don't cut it out."

"Oh, yeah." She grinned. "That's the last thing they want."

"God save me from nitwits and immature kids." He blew out a breath. "I will definitely make them understand that their immaturity affects the entire team. That if they don't start playing the way they're supposed to and work together on the field, they are definitely out."

Olivia nodded her agreement. "Kids that age don't often think about how their actions affect others."

"I'll call them to come to practice early tomorrow, and we'll have a little Come to Jesus meeting, along with some head knocking. And also please assure Angela they won't be bothering her again. We'll figure out a way to handle the class they're in together."

"I know she'll appreciate it."

"You know how important the success of this team is to me," he reminded her. "I'm putting everything into it—heart, brain, body, and soul. This is a relaunch for both the team and me, and I don't intend to fail."

She smiled. "I'm pretty damn sure you won't."

And she would do everything on her end to give him whatever help he needed. Which meant waiting to bring up to Hatch the bit about confessing his gambling problem on the video. The team was coming off a bad loss and had two crucial games to play before the end of the season. They were already bowl eligible, but their final record could determine what quality of bowl they were invited to.

And she had some lead-time on her project. She planned to attend the bowl game and have Drew get good footage to use. Hopefully, the Jaguars would win and give the video the kind of ending audiences liked.

"Mighty quiet over there." Hatch's deep voice broke into her concentration, startling her.

"What?" She blinked. "Oh, sorry. Just thinking about the video."

"I hate to say this, but the next two weeks my time really isn't my own. And then getting ready for the bowl will be even tighter, depending on which invite we get."

Well, I guess that answers my question.

"Just thinking about everything you've got ahead of you." She smiled. "And wondering what I can do to help."

There was that hungry look again.

"As a matter of fact, if we can finish this dinner, I can show you."

She smiled. "Funny you should say that. I was just thinking I've had enough to eat…of food."

His answering grin was positively smoldering. "Me, too. Let me help you clear the table so we can get that out of the way."

"Yes. The faster the better."

A shiver raced over her skin as she thought about the evening yet to come. Yes, after the bowl would be a much better time to present her plan to Hatch. Show him the value and get him to buy into it. By then her boss would have seen the raw footage and gotten a feel for how good this was going to be.

And she hoped, in the meantime, Daniel didn't decide to try and throw a monkey wrench into her life.

Chapter Fourteen

God save him from stubborn young men.

Hatch watched Tony and Josh settle themselves into seats across from his desk, keeping as much distance between them as they could. He'd understood them to be good friends, not unlike he and Tank had been, with Josh being the non-partying, more studious type and Tony taking Tank's nagging-him-to-go-out-more role. But after getting the low-down from Olivia on what was really going on, he knew theirs was a different dynamic.

He'd talked with the entire coaching staff, and they'd decided as a group that this discussion had to be between the players and their head coach. They were at a moment in the season where bowl games would be decided, and now that he was so damn close to one, he wanted it. Bad. Hence his decision to break with his usual MO and meet with these men in private.

Once his star players—the ones responsible for racking up the most crucial numbers—had their backpacks set aside and themselves sorted out and ready, he leaned forward on the desk's pristine surface, meeting first Tony's eyes, which were slightly hooded and wary, and then Josh's. That kid's body language screamed "wigged out," complete with a sheen of sweat on his forehead and a jittering knee.

Hatch took a breath and dove in.

The thing about D-1 scholarship-worthy football players, he thought when he had to launch himself around the desk and separate the two of them within ten minutes of the start of their meeting, was that the same stubbornness many find frustrating was what drove them to succeed. They refused to give up. They threw, ran, sat up, pushed up, lifted weights, and then ran some more in an effort to get themselves to the place where they were now. Both of them easily qualified to play at the next level, after a year or so spent on NFL practice teams. And yet neither of them was willing to give a damn inch on this Angela Pierson issue.

As he held Tony back from throttling Josh for saying something not-very-polite about the girl in question, he made a snap decision about how to handle this mess.

"Sit," he said, pushing both of them back into their seats with a firm hand on their shoulders. "I'm going to send you both to the sports psychologist. I need you to get past this. And nothing I say is going to do that, obviously." He stood between them, keeping his hands on their shoulders. "I want you to go separately first, then together. And I want it done in the next two weeks." He tightened his grip on them briefly, then let go and returned to his seat.

"But, Coach, I have to study," Josh said.

Tony rolled his eyes.

Hatch tried not to overreact. This was, after all, his first year. And these were not players he'd recruited. They were succeeding beyond everyone's wildest expectations, and while he realized that part of that was pure adrenaline on the part of the players, he didn't want to be the one to pop that particular bubble. Which was why he'd made the call not to threaten the revocation of scholarships or playing time—yet. Neither of them had laid a finger on the girl, literally or figuratively. If they had, they'd be having a different discussion. But this was something else. Not something he felt equipped to manage.

He picked up the handset of his desk phone and asked his assistant to contact Dr. Lock and ask if he could fit Tony and Josh into his schedule today. Once she'd worked her scheduling miracle, which reminded Hatch to ask the AD to give her a raise, he pinned his players with his gaze once more. Tony still looked defiant. Josh seemed deflated.

"Men, I need you to figure this out. I'm going to work out something with the economics professor to allow you to take the rest of the class online. There are only a few weeks left to the semester anyway. I want you both to steer clear of Angela Pierson. She's not interested in either of you, and if you don't believe me when I say 'no means no,' then you'd better pack up and leave my team right now." He paused for effect. "But beyond that, I want you to spend some quality time with Dr. Lock and show up to practice with your heads on straight."

"I don't need a head shrinker," Tony muttered.

"Actually, I say you do. And right now, the school says I'm partially responsible for your well-being." He'd been shocked at the violence with which the young man had reacted to Josh's comment. Something else was going on with him. And he needed a professional to help sort through it. "I'm here for you, son. You, too," he said, looking at Josh, who looked even more stressed out, if that were possible. "I know how hard this moment in your life is, remember? I've been here, done this. Let me get you both some help."

"Whatever," Tony said. "Are we done?"

Hatch frowned at his quarterback. The young man's brow smoothed out, but his eyes remained stony. Evidence of the previous coaching staff's methods with the team had reared their heads before. The general lack of discipline across the board had been evident early on when he'd established the New World Order of Jaguars Football back in the spring. But it kept rearing its ugly head in clutch moments like this one when he needed the young man in front of him to accept that he needed help and that he, Hatch, was in charge.

Not to mention that he wouldn't tolerate the sort of BS attitude that the kid was throwing at him right now.

He rose, slowly, mostly for affect. He didn't like to play Head Asshole. He was Head Coach. And up until the last two games, he thought he'd established the sort of respect level he expected. Tony blinked up at him, and his shoulders slumped.

"I mean, um…I need to get to class. So that I can make the appointment you just set for me…uh…us." Tony looked down at the floor between his feet.

"Don't drop your gaze, DeLong," Hatch said, using Tony's last name to put things more on familiar ground. He always used last names at practice and during games. He glanced at Josh. "You're good men. Good players. And at least one of you is an excellent student."

They both chuckled, which relieved him.

"We need to get to the bottom of this issue. And you will, starting today. At four p.m. with Dr. Lock. And remember, whatever you say is between you and her. She can't and won't tell me anything so feel free to unload about me, your position coaches, whatever it takes. But talk, okay?"

"Okay," Tony said, meeting Hatch's gaze with eyes that were noticeably less hostile. "Coach," he added, with a quick glance over at his friend. "Josh, I'll meet you there. I'm really gonna be late."

"Go on," Hatch said, waving them out and taking a seat with a loud exhale. He looked up to find Josh lingering in the doorway. "What is it, Josh?" He used the first name on purpose this time, hoping to maybe get something out of the kid.

"Thanks for doing this, Coach. He's… His family's all fu—I mean… His mom just took off with some guy, and his dad's been on a bender, and he's worried about his little brother and sister. I shouldn't tell you, but, uh…"

"You just did," Hatch finished for him.

"Yeah. I guess I did."

"Thanks," Hatch said. "I didn't know any of that."

"He won't tell anyone. I think this thing over that girl…I mean, over Angela, was a distraction for him, maybe."

"So, do you like her?"

Josh's blue eyes brightened. His smile widened. Hatch tried not to react, but the poor kid was so obvious it was painful to watch. "Yeah."

"Okay, here's my completely unprofessional advice. Bearing in mind that I'm one failed marriage into my life and ergo uniquely unqualified to say a single thing about what you should do." He paused. "Leave her alone for a while. Take the class online. Make sure your teammate doesn't fail that damn thing, something that is well within his reach right now. Let her think about how she feels about you a little, with some distance to give her perspective. Then, after the semester's over and we're headed to a bowl game, give her a call or a text or a direct message or however you guys communicate these days. Take her out on a real date. See how things progress from there."

"Thanks, Coach," Josh said, his boy-next-door handsome face positively beaming. "I'll do that. Thanks…Coach," he repeated. "Gotta go."

"Go, go, but don't let Tony fail that class, got me? Do some talking with him. He's your friend. And that matters right now."

"You got it. See you later, Coach"

Hatch glanced down at his phone, which was blowing up, as usual, with messages from his staff. When he looked back up, his doorway was empty. He sighed and sank into his leather chair. As hard as this was, he thought as he opened his laptop to start responding to emails and working on the plan of action for the week, he'd take coaching these kids over the prima donnas in the pros any day of the damn week.

He smiled when he saw the text from Olivia pop onto his screen.

"Well? How did it go? Knock heads or wipe tears?"

Something about her easy, casual manner gave him pause. As a card-carrying, born-again, commitment-phobic bachelor, he knew he should be alarmed by how great he felt at the mere sight of her words on his phone screen. As much as he had loved Alex at one point in his life, he'd never truly felt this way about his ex-wife. Olivia was definitely more his style. Dare he even think, mate of his soul?

He shook his head. They were playing with fire, and he knew it. Between the precarious nature of her situation with the documentary and his need to keep certain things from the public eye, they had exactly zero business getting this deep into something that, for him, went way beyond a mere sexual arrangement. Although… He grinned and had to shift in his chair as his newly revived libido gripped his consciousness.

He realized he'd been holding his phone in one hand while running all this around in his mind for a solid five minutes. Damn. He jumped up from his chair and wandered to the window that overlooked the state-of-the-art practice facility. This was his life and he loved it. Football, football players, football coaches, football games—this was what got him up every morning, period.

After another long stretch, during which he tried to come up with a legit reason to break it off with her, for her own good, he glanced down at his side, confused by pain in his fingers. He'd been clutching the damn device so hard, his knuckles were aching.

"Lighten up, Hatcher," he muttered. He realized that he was projecting. It was one of his long-established bad habits. Things going wrong on the field? Take it out on anyone and anything handy. No good, he knew. But the fact that he didn't feel good about himself right now was spilling over into his worry over Olivia and what she might be sacrificing to be with him.

He'd sworn off this sort of thing, or so he'd believed, when his fairytale marriage had crumpled under the weight of his personal failings. He'd promised never to inflict himself on another unsuspecting female. And since he was the polar opposite of his friend Tank, he'd not buried his unhappiness with random hookups. He'd buried it in his quest to be a better man.

But had he succeeded?

He glanced at his phone screen again. He owed her an answer, but he felt frozen. Hamstrung by his own disbelief that she existed in his universe, much less had slept in his arms the night before. And he'd confessed everything to her, too. Told her more about his life as an addict than he'd told anyone, including his lawyer, which was saying something since that guy knew an awful lot about him. He'd never known that level of trust with anyone.

He was tapping out an answer to her, jaw clenched in aggravation at himself for overthinking everything as usual, when George burst into his office with a fresh crisis to manage. By the time he circled back to the fact that he hadn't answered her text, he'd supervised the day's light practice—carefully observing Tony and Josh as they tiptoed around each other in a way that he didn't consider much of an improvement—and was tossing his laptop into his leather backpack, preparing to go home.

"Shit," he muttered when he noticed she'd sent two more unanswered messages.

"Hey. You all right?" and *"I'm making pesto for dinner. See you soon?"*

They populated his screen along with a bunch of other random messages from office staff, plus another one that caught his eye as he scrolled down. Frowning at the unfamiliar number, he swiped the message to open it. It took him a solid two minutes to figure out who it was and what, exactly, he was saying.

"You need to be careful when dealing with Olivia. She's way too devoted to reviving her career on the back of your story for you to trust her. I know how ruthless she is when it comes to her own future. No need to respond. Just consider this a friendly heads-up about a woman who doesn't deserve your full attention. A woman I trusted. And a woman who can sometimes distract you with her…various talents."

His face flushed hot as he read the message for the fourth time. It was that shithead ex-husband of hers. It had to be. How the hell had he gotten this cell number?

Hatch pulled his laptop back out onto the desk and did some digging around, trying to trace the number, but the guy was obviously savvy enough to know how to block his number. His pulse raced as he read the text again, then once more. His natural tendency to protect Olivia, to defend her, warred in his brain with his extreme compulsion to get in his truck and drive straight to where this guy sat and punch him.

At that moment, as he sat with his jaw clenched and his fingers balled into tight fists, the phone rang.

Olivia.

He touched the button to send it to voice mail, paused a few seconds, then sent her a text.

He repeated the apology, paused, then hit Send, packed up his stuff, and headed for his truck. He sat behind the wheel, fuming in the cool, late-fall evening. Finally, he called up a name, closed his eyes, and waited for his friend to answer.

"Hey, loser. What up?" Tank said, over a cacophony of chatter and computer keyboard noises.

"I need you to talk me out of something really, really stupid," he said, his voice choked with emotion.

"Hang on." Tank had obviously heard the urgency in his tone and was acting accordingly. Hatch smiled in relief as he waited. "Okay. I'm alone now. Talk to me. Are we gonna go bust some heads? Get shit-faced? Pick up random chicks using our old football player charm? I'm down for whatever, my man. Talk to me."

Hatch sighed and told Tank about the text.

"Dude, he's obviously intimidated by you, by your celebrity, and pissed as hell that his ex isn't cowering in a corner after the divorce. I think that's why he's taking a chance by initiating contact. Pretty risky, considering."

"Yeah." Hatch ran a shaking hand down his face. He touched the button to lower the window and sucked in breaths of cold Michigan night air. "And so I need you to tell me not to point myself toward Detroit and have a face-to-face with the guy. I won't let him bad mouth her that way. And he needs to know that."

"I feel you, Hatch. But I'd advise you instead to go find said lovely lady who obviously has captured your soft and squishy heart and take her to bed instead. Don't start something that would be a mess to finish."

"Yeah," Hatch repeated, sensing the adrenaline whoosh out of his body at the sound of his friend's solid advice.

"I mean, she's obviously settling for your weak-ass skills. I say enjoy that instead of working yourself into a stroke over some tiny-dick ex-husband who's trying to get you to do something stupid. Feel me?"

"Yes, I do. Thanks, Tank."

"I'm here for you. I'll send you a bill for my therapeutic services tomorrow. Be ready to cough up some serious dough."

Hatch pressed his aching forehead on the leather steering wheel. He was a mess over this woman, that much was certain. And at that moment, all he wanted was to see her, hold her, kiss her, and take Tank's advice about heading straight for the bedroom.

"You're not gonna go confront the guy, right?"

"No, I'm not. You can stop worrying, Mom."

"Yeah, your mom says hi. She's back at my place, smoking a cig in the afterglow."

Hatch grinned. Good old Tank. He could always trust him to come up with a distraction, complete with crude, "your mom" jokes.

"Go on. Find your woman. Bury your face between…"

"Gonna go now," Hatch said. "Thanks. Good talk." He ended the call and headed toward Olivia's place. He was sick of hiding, tired of worrying about who might see them together or catch his truck still parked in front of her place in the morning. He wanted more. He needed it. And he was going to ask her tonight.

He made two stops before heading to her house. One was to a florist shop. Just like the other night, he was sure flowers would be good for this situation. The other was to a local jeweler he'd spent a bit of quality time with a few nights prior. He'd made his purchase but left it there to keep himself from thinking about it or pondering his motivation for a few days.

Now, waiting at a stop light, he tugged the soft, velvet bag containing a small box out of his pocket. He held it tight in one hand all the way to Olivia's apartment, his heart pounding, pulse racing, and a smile stuck to his face.

Chapter Fifteen

Olivia was annoyed to notice that her hands were shaking as she finished crushing the pine nuts into a paste. The mound of minced basil leaves and bottle of premium olive oil were at her elbow. Pasta was burbling away in the pot. Even a deep breath didn't seem to settle her nerves, so she pulled out the bottle of white wine in the fridge and poured the last of it into a glass. Two swallows and a deep breath, and she had herself back under control.

Almost.

What was wrong with her? This was just a dinner, for the love of God. Period.

No, Olivia, it's more than that, and you know it.

Things had been going so well for the two of them, better than she ever could have expected. Never in her wildest dreams would she ever have thought the personal side of their relationship to grow and develop the way it had. And that was indeed an unexpected pleasure. After Daniel, she hadn't been interested in anything with anyone for a long time. Maybe not ever.

And then, this thing with Hatch exploded.

He was so different than Daniel, both in attitude and behavior.

After she popped her confession-on-film idea he might walk out. That would be the end of the video, of Hatch, and of her rejuvenated career. She'd be just another newly-single, middle-aged female scrabbling for her place in life and relegated to the fringes of her industry. This was going to come out, this thing about his past sitting at the front edge of her brain. No question about it. Bert Hoekstra was going to dig it up, if he hadn't already, and use it as the lead to the piece he hoped would jump start his career. No matter if it destroyed both her and Hatch. Or maybe that was his dual intention.

They had to get out in front of it. Tell people. Everyone had skeletons in their closet, and by comparison, this wasn't nearly as bad as many others. So he had a gambling problem. Okay, a big one. One that likely derailed both his pro coaching career and his marriage.

But still, when it broke his marriage and nearly destroyed his life, he'd gotten control of it, and this was his new, fresh start. All the other pieces were falling into place. If she could just convince him that talking about it now would shortstop many problems, and he could emerge from this a hero on so many fronts.

She only hoped that, in fighting down his objections and convincing him to do this, he didn't get the idea the video was all she wanted from him. Now that she'd admitted to her feelings for him, she knew she wanted him in her life. Permanently. Wanted a man who treated her with respect, who admired her, who also had introduced her to the best sex of her life. They were getting there, one step at a time. She didn't want to kill it.

God. Why does everything have to be such a problem?

She checked the time. Hatch would be here any

minute. She had a baguette and some of his favorite Irish cheddar cheese waiting. A bottle of wine was breathing nearby. The salad was made. She planned to mix the pasta with each of the ingredients once he got here, so it would be at its freshest. Making one last check of the pan, she popped it in the oven and set the timer. She had just washed and dried her hands when the doorbell rang.

Showtime!

Folding the dish towel she'd had tucked at her waist, she hurried to the front door and pulled it open. And had to take a minute to admire the man standing there, all six foot two of lean, toned muscle, his dark hair freshly combed, humor gleaming in his dark eyes, his dimples winking as he smiled.

"Hi!" He thrust a wrapped bouquet of flowers at her. "For you. Something special for a special evening."

Olivia quirked an eyebrow. "A special evening? It's only pasta, mister."

Heat flared in his eyes. "Maybe I plan to make it special. How about that?"

Her heart took an extra beat. What did he have in mind? And how would it go with what she had planned?

"They aren't nearly as beautiful as you are," he continued. "And don't smell even half as good, but I thought they'd make you smile. I love to see you smile."

Olivia took them, feeling the heat of a blush creeping up her cheeks. Holy crap. Blushing over flowers at her age?

"Thanks so much." She took a step back from the door. "Come on in. I have the wine open and some nibbles."

"Sounds good." He followed her inside, but as soon as he closed the door, he pulled her into his arms. "But first, there's something else I'd rather nibble on."

Being careful not to crush the flowers, he tugged her close to him and pressed his mouth to hers, taking little bites of her lips, then soothing them with his tongue. Fire streaked through her from that simple touch, and she opened her mouth, eagerly accepting the way he slid his tongue inside. For a moment, she forgot where she was and what they were doing, so befuddled did she get at just his touch and a simple kiss.

After. Let me tackle the elephant in the room, and then we can get back to this. I hope.

"Wow." Her breath hitched. "That's some potent kiss." She grinned. "And the flowers are a nice touch, too. Let me put them in water and get the wine."

He nibbled the lobe of her ear. "There's more where that came from. And a little something special, too, after dinner."

"Oh? Care to give me a hint?"

And I hope I don't screw it up when you hear what I have to say.

"Nope. You'll have to wait, just like kids do at Christmas."

"Tease." She grinned. "Okay, have a seat. I'll be right back."

She found a vase in the cabinet, arranged the flowers, and set them in the middle of the dining table. Then she picked up the tray with the cheese and bread, wine and glasses and carried it into the living room.

When they each held a filled glass, Hatch touched his to hers. "Here's to a special evening with a special lady."

"And a special guy," she added, hoping he'd still think she was special after she dropped her request on him. She was so damn nervous. She was afraid he'd be able to read it in her eyes.

The wine slid easily down her throat, its warmth easing her nerves and the tension somewhat. Hatch seemed as wound up as she was. What was that all about?

Olivia sat on the couch, curling her legs beneath her, hoping she looked more relaxed than she felt. "How are things going with your two horny players since you banged their heads together?"

"Josh and Tony?" He grinned. "I made it clear that their behavior was distracting them from team business and they weren't showing much respect for the young woman in question. I told them they better get to their butts to the therapist to work it out and leave her alone for the time being or they were off the team."

She laughed. "That had to be enough to quiet their hormones."

Hatch nodded. "Without a doubt. Let's hope we've heard the last of this. We're already bowl eligible, but I'm hoping to end up ranked high enough for one of the better games."

"You're good enough to play almost anyone, that's for sure. I've watched every game and then reviewed the videos to see what we could extract for the documentary. You've done an incredible job with these guys, Hatch. The university is more than getting its money's worth."

"Let's hope they think so." He took another sip of his wine, then leaned forward and set the glass on the coffee table. "Listen, Liv. There's, uh, something I want to talk to you about."

"You do?" She studied his face for clues, wondering what this was all about.

"Uh huh." He sat down next to her and took her hands in his. "Liv, this thing between us just exploded right out of the blue, agreed?"

Her heart did a tiny somersault. Was he going to tell her he couldn't see her anymore? Didn't want to? That they should keep this thing between them strictly professional? What had flipped the switch?

The sex between them was off the charts, and they'd become comfortable in each other's company. She certainly hadn't been looking for anything more. She'd pulled herself together after her disastrous marriage and divorce, and both her professional and personal lives were unexpectedly looking up.

Did he think they'd moved to fast? Did he want to put a pin in it until after the season was over?

Oh, God! The video. How would that be affected?

"Um, yes, it did." Her mouth curved in a tiny grin. "And I think exploded is probably the right word." She wet her lower lip. "Do you think maybe too fast?"

"Fast, yes, but not too fast. I just—" He rubbed the back of his neck, a gesture she'd come to understand meant he had something to say and wasn't sure how to phrase it.

Ignoring the sinking feeling in her stomach, she forced a smile. "Maybe I can help you out here, since you seem to be struggling. Should we back off a little, maybe until the season is over? Did you bring me flowers to soften the situation?"

Besides, after she dropped her bombshell on him,

he might want to call it off forever.

"What?" His eyebrows rose. "Hell, no, Liv. Just the opposite." He squeezed her hands. "I never thought I'd be lucky enough to have any relationship again after my marriage fell apart. But then here you are, apparently willing to put up with me in spite of my history, and I thought, well, moving forward—"

Moving forward?

"Hatch, wait." She held up a hand. "Stop. Are you talking about taking things to the next level? I mean, whatever that means. Oh hell, you know what I mean." Her face got even hotter.

His eyes lit up. "Yeah! Now you get it. I guess I'm not very good at this, but—"

"Stop," she repeated and shook her head. "I can't—I don't—" She let out a breath. "Before you say anything else, please listen to what I have to say."

"I hope you're not going to tell me you don't want to see me anymore, because that's the furthest thing from my mind." He rose from the couch and began to pace. "This isn't going at all the way I planned. I was going to wait until after dinner, but I just got ahead of myself. Liv, I—"

She jumped up and placed a hand over his mouth. "Please let me say something, okay? Please?"

"Okay." But his body was suddenly stiff and unyielding, and his face had set into that expressionless mask he used when he was trying to control his emotions. "Let's have it."

Now it was her turn to pace. She had to phrase this just right. "You know Bert Hoekstra is sniffing around this whole thing, hoping for some kind of dirt for his podcast."

Hatch nodded but didn't say anything.

"He'd feast on the story of your gambling problem and how it affected your job and your marriage. You talk about how football is a numbers game and how it directs your life. Well, you've got issues with other numbers, specifically, the gambling. Knowing Bert, I'm damn sure he'd wait until the video is released and he can use his story to throw mud on you. We don't want him to do that right?"

"Of course not," Hatch agreed. "But what do you suggest we do about it, short of strangling the guy. I've asked about him and talked to our director of public relations about the situation. But otherwise, I don't know what to do about him."

"We need to find a way to make sure he can't dig that up. And since that's next to impossible, I have a, um, different suggestion."

He studied her face with those all-seeing eyes of his. "Which is?"

She drew in a deep breath and let it out slowly. "I think you should talk about it on camera. Just put it out there and tell people the truth. They'll—"

"No." The word exploded from him. "Jesus, Liv, that's a terrible idea. Tell the whole world I was a gambling addict? Still am, if I don't control it? Lay it all out there? I could lose my job. You realize that? At the very least get scorched by the university and the alumni and the donors. Shit! I can't believe you even suggested it."

"But don't you see? It's the best way to get out in front of this. We'll make sure the people who need to know about this in advance, like Scott and others at the university... Wait. Are you telling me the university knows nothing about this? That you hid it from them when you interviewed for the job? Never said a word?"

Hatch shook his head. "No, that's not what I'm saying. Of course I told them. The key people, anyway. You think I'm such a piece of shit I'd hide something like that? I couldn't afford for them to be broadsided. Besides, that's not who I am."

"I didn't think so. I believe you're an honorable person who wrestled with a problem in his life." She managed a smile. "And you'd be an inspiration to people who're fighting other addictions, knowing you took steps to keep yours under control. Think about it, Hatch. You'd be a hero to a lot of people."

"A hero? Are you kidding me?" He took a step back from her, then began to pace the length of her living room.

"No, I'm not."

"I...I can't do it. It would ruin me right when I finally got my life back together." He sucked in a breath. "Listen, I came over here tonight to propose to you. I even brought a ring." He stopped his pacing and stared at her, a strange look on his face. "If you must know, your ex warned me not to trust you. He said you put your career ahead of everything. Told me that's why your marriage fell apart. I guess I should have paid better attention to what he said."

"My ex?" Olivia's vision narrowed down to a tiny tunnel. "You spoke with Daniel? Are you joking? How did that happen?"

"He sent a text message. He wasn't shy about telling me be careful because you'd do anything to make a success of this documentary. That it was your ticket back to the big time."

Olivia couldn't believe what she was hearing. "Damn it, Hatch. He treated me like shit from day one and always held my job over my head. If I didn't let him control every single moment in my life, he could blackball me in the industry. I'd never work again. I thought you…"

What had she thought? How much had she held back about her toxic first marriage?

"Olivia," he began, a helpless look on his face.

She swallowed hard, reaching for some measure of composure and failing. "Did I make any secret of this from the beginning that I wanted this to be picked up by a national sports network? I was completely honest with you, right?" When he said nothing, she repeated, "Right?"

"Put yourself in my position." His voice remained hard and uninflected. "I've already been screwed over by enough people that I know to be careful. I just didn't want to believe it about you, but then you pull this out of thin air…"

"You honestly think I made the suggestion about confessing your gambling addiction for me? For publicity for the documentary? Damn it, Hatch. After everything, you still don't know me." She stomped to the door and yanked it open. "You can leave. Right now."

He stood there, and she sensed all the conflicting emotions chasing each other in his eyes.

"Okay, maybe I was a little hasty—"

"A little?" She did her best to conceal her disappointment. "Not exactly the word I would use. But if that's what you want, by all means go. Go on." She made a shooing motion with her hands.

He opened his mouth to say something, then apparently thought better of it and headed toward the door.

"We're not done here," he snapped

"I'll be the judge of that." She slammed the door and turned the lock with a vicious twist.

Then the anger drained from her, as if someone had pulled a plug. She moved to the couch and sank into the cushions, head in hands. Her throat was tight with unshed tears, but they were more tears of anger than anything else. How stupid she was, to be taken in by yet another high-profile man.

Dumb, dumb, dumb.

She sat there for a long time, trying to sort everything out in her swirling mind and in her pounding heart. At last, she rose and went to pour the ruined pasta into the garbage. Not that it mattered. Her appetite had certainly disappeared. Then she refilled her wine glass and sat down at the kitchen counter. She had to pull this back together. This video was all she had left now, and she wasn't about to let Hatch sabotage it.

She'd fix it. Somehow. And her rotten ex at the same time.

Chapter Sixteen

The whistle pressed against his tongue as he gripped it tight between his teeth and stared out at his team. They were going through their final practice of this, his debut season as their coach. He felt good about them. No, he felt great. This was it. They'd win this last game, end the season six and two. And he'd by god be taking them to a bowl game, the first for his alma mater in over a decade.

"Do it again!" he hollered around the whistle before blowing into it.

A couple of his coaches shot him a look. He glared back at them. This was what he had. This was his life. He'd been a total fool to think there was anything out there for him, after the stupid shit he'd done to ruin everything he'd had before this.

The young men's shoulders slumped as they trotted back to the line of scrimmage. He watched. They ran the play again. And again.

"Hey, uh, Coach?"

Hatch flinched and turned to find Tomas behind him, his dark eyes full of concern. "What? Do it again, damn it."

"No. They can't. They're gassed."

Hatch locked eyes with the man, one of an amazing team of assistants, with whom he could credit a hell of a lot of the success this season. They were all his, either handpicked from the previous staff or hired by him. He trusted them and had told them that, more than once. He felt himself deflate as he glanced out over the field at the team of utterly exhausted players, hands on their hips, heads low, every single one of them ready to "do it again" if he demanded it.

"You're right. I'm sorry." He put his hand on Tomas' shoulder and sensed the man lean into him, as if trying to take some of his weight, to take pressure off an injury. That gesture, one he'd both given and received as a teammate from a young age made him realize that he had to get a grip. Ever since walking away from Olivia's house three nights prior, he'd been running on an average of two hours of sleep, strong coffee, and antacids. His pulse was racing. His head pounded from lack of food. His guts felt like they were coated in gasoline.

His coaches could tell he was off. And if they could, then so could his team.

"I'm gonna…" he began.

Tomas spoke at the same time. "Let us wrap it up, Coach." He gave Hatch's shoulder a quick pat. "I don't know what's going on with you, but I have a guess. And I suggest that you go…walk or run or shower or nap or whatever it is you need to clear your head."

Hatch closed his eyes. "Yeah. You're right. Thanks, Coach." He smiled at his assistant, his actual problem remaining unspoken.

"My pleasure. If you ever want to, you know, talk about it…"

"I'll be sure and call you, Tomas."

It took every ounce of energy he had to walk away from the group without a word, his mind on nothing but a hamburger and fourteen straight hours of sleep. He barely recalled the drive home, which was probably not safe, but he made it. He stumbled into his front door, drank half a gallon of milk from the jug and passed out, face down on his bed.

His dreams were a jumble of images—football fields, stands full of fans, whistles, yelling, and of course, Olivia. The sight of her face, unhappy and pissed off at him, and the sound of her voice, jolted him awake. When he realized it wasn't the sound of her voice that woke him but the shrill ring tone of his phone, he rolled onto his side and grabbed it with a groan. "What?"

"And good morning to you, Prince Charming."

"What the hell do you want, Tank?"

"Damn, Hatch. Why so grumpy?"

He sat up, confused by the fact that it seemed so light in the bedroom. "What in the hell day is it anyway?"

"You tie one on, my man?"

"Yeah, right. That's so like me." He got up, wincing at the soreness in his neck and back from staying in one position for so many hours. "God."

"Yeah, that's who I am. But besides that, I'm wondering if you could use my help."

"Uh…" He felt fuzzy, addled, like he was still half asleep. After stumbling into the bathroom and emptying his bladder, he splashed cold water onto his face to try and clear the cobwebs.

"Yo!" Tank's tinny voice filled the bathroom from the phone he'd set on the vanity. "Are you taking a piss while you're on the phone with me? That's rude, man."

Feeling marginally more human, Hatch picked up

the phone and wandered toward the kitchen. "Dude, we used to shower in the same room."

"Don't remind me. So do you want my help or what?"

"Help with what?" He stared at the contents of his fridge, willing something to jump out to him. There were several tidy plastic bins full of Olivia's leftovers, but the sight of them only made him mad, or sad, or something in between. "Shit."

"Help with that sorry excuse for a team. You know, at your last, most important, most challenging game?"

Hatch grabbed the half empty milk jug and took a long drink. "You think I need your help with that?"

"Nope. I know you do. I know you, Hatch. I'm willing to bet you're running on zero food, too much caffeine, and too little sleep. Am I right or am I right?"

He leaned against the counter, the empty jug dandling from his fingers, feeling just as depleted as he had on the field, however long ago that had been. "What the hell day is it anyway?"

"It's Thursday. You have two more days to prove you're worth that no-doubt obnoxious salary our alma mater is overpaying you. So I'll ask again. Do you want my—"

"Jesus, Tank I screwed up. Big time."

"I have no doubts about that. I've been watching the games, and I think you need to utilize your strong safety more. And what is up with your center? He's pretty unreliable."

"No, no, just shut up a minute, will you?"

He dragged a hand down his face. He had to make this right. He had to get Olivia back. But there was no way in hell he'd do what she'd asked him to do. He couldn't. He'd spent too much of his life's energy putting the past behind him.

Dropping into a chair at the dining room table, he rested his forehead on his arm. "I fucked it up with Olivia. Big time."

"You?" Tank barked a laugh. "Messed it up with a woman? I can't imagine that."

"Yeah, well, imagine it."

Tank sighed. The noises behind him silenced, letting Hatch know he'd gone into his private office and shut the door. "Okay, spill it, Romeo. Let's see if we can fix it."

"It's unfixable."

"Nothing's unfixable. That's one thing I can guarantee. Break it down for me. We'll come up with a game plan."

"She wants me to confess to my gambling, on TV. I mean, on the documentary she's doing."

Tank let out a long whistle. "Wow. That's...something."

"Uh huh. So about that game plan?"

"Tell you what. Why don't I jump on a plane and help save your sorry ass on the sidelines instead?"

"I figured as much." He got up and limped into the kitchen. "But yeah. Come on up. I'd like to see you, and I might even give you access to the team. If you promise not to warp them, that is. They are somewhat malleable at this age."

"Ha! I remember being malleable."

"I don't think you ever were, Tank. You were born fully formed, like some kind of a demi-god, all your thoughts, ideas, and pre-conceived notions in place."

"It's about time you recognized me as a god. I'll be

there tomorrow afternoon. You'd better have something nice ready for me for dinner."

"Yeah, yeah." But the sound of his best friend's voice and knowing he was coming, that he wanted to be a part of the end of this winning season, made Hatch feel better than anything had in a long time.

"Remember, I like my steak rare and my beer cold."

"Do I need to pick you up from the airport?"

"Nah. I'll rent something fun to drive. See you soon, Hatch."

"See you soon, Tank."

****

Olivia had been ten kinds of miserable since she'd thrown Hatch out of her house. One minute she wanted to pat herself on the back for standing firm. The next, she wanted to kick her own ass for the knee jerk reaction. Maybe she should have tried to talk calmly to him, but everything in the past with Daniel seemed to color her reaction to Hatch. And that was a damn shame.

She finally called Lee Ann and begged her to come over, even though begging was definitely not her style. But she badly needed her friend, if only to bounce everything off her and get some sane advice.

"It would be easier for me to commiserate with you, honey, if I had some kind of idea what you were so miserable about," Lee Ann told her. "What is it you asked him to do?"

Olivia sighed. "I wish I could tell you, but it's really not my story to tell. I can't break his confidence."

She stared at Olivia for a moment, then nodded. "Okay. Then let's pour some medicine and see if that helps."

Lee Ann sat with her all through her pity party, the two of them killing a bottle of the wine they both loved, alternately cursing Daniel Forrest and Olivia's apparent inability to handle episodes like this with Hatch.

"I seem to keep getting myself in the worst possible situations," she moaned. "How do I do that? Am I such a bad judge of men?"

"No, honey," LeeAnn soothed. "No more than the rest of us. We all make mistakes. Sometimes, we learn from them. Sometimes, er, we don't."

"I guess I'm still learning" she moaned.

"Daniel was such an asshole," LeeAnn reminded her. "It's tough to get past that. We'd all have a problem."

"And you think I'm looking at Hatch the same way?" She drank more wine, hoping enough of it would erase all this tension.

"I think you may not be objective about this. Give it a little room. See what happens."

"We've about talked this to death," Olivia sighed. "I've been debating with myself all day about going to videotape the Jaguars final game. On one hand, I have a gut feeling we're going to win and it would be an exciting finish to the season. It would all lead into bowl game selection. On the other, what could I possibly say to Hatch? Even more, what could he say to me?"

The question rattled in her brain even as she tried to fall asleep that night. The wine hadn't done much good after all. She didn't think she slept more than thirty minutes at a time as scenes kept replaying in her mind. They were still there in the morning so the first thing she did was call Lee Ann.

"I'm a wreck and I feel like an idiot. Maybe I should have led up to what I said a little better." She traced a circle on her knee with the tip of a finger. "You know, not just jumped into it the way I did."

"And, as I said ten times last night, maybe you should have been slower to jump all over him and his reaction," Lee Ann reminded her. "You're so good with people. Always have been, except when you were with Daniel. I think a lot of how it hit you is based on the situation with him. But Hatch is not Daniel. His response had nothing to do with his feelings for you or a dose of unmitigated arrogance, like your ex. Whatever his problem is, he's probably worried about it affecting his new job and his relationship with you. Think about that."

"Yeah, yeah, yeah. I hear you." Her off the charts reaction probably had more to do with Daniel contacting Hatch and doing his usual asshole thing. She needed to stop caring about what he could do and take the power to upset her away from him. And if he decided to stick his nose in her business again and attack Hatch at the same time, well, two people could use the power of the press. She had to remember that.

"You have to go to that game today," Lee Ann pointed out. "It's a key piece of the video. The climax of an incredible season for the Jags."

Olivia sighed. "You're right, and I know it. What if he bars me from the field?"

"He won't. He's got too much class for that. Besides…it would generate questions neither of you want to answer."

"Right again." Olivia continued drawing the meaningless circles on the bedspread, trying to pull her brain together.

"Do it, Liv. Get past this and move forward, with your career and Hatch. You'll regret it if you don't."

"And what if he doesn't want to move ahead with me? Just saying the words made her nauseous. Her emotions had been riding a roller coaster ever since she first connected with Hatch, and damn it, memories of her relationship with Daniel were tainting her opinions and her view of the situation.

"Only one way to find out."

"Yes. Double yes." She swallowed a sigh. "Okay. But you'd better have a cellar full of wine ready if this blows up in my face."

"That's a deal. Now set it up."

****

The day couldn't move fast enough for Hatch. Tank's presence on the sidelines at their last, helmets-only run through before the game helped a lot. The team was suitably impressed by him and the urban legends that swirled around him. From star football player, to Navy SEAL, to owner of one of the biggest and most successful private investigative and security firms in the world, the guy cut an imposing figure without a doubt. Hatch even let him give a pep talk, but only a short one, in case it turned into something that could get him fired.

Later, they sat in front of a dancing bonfire in Hatch's backyard, full of steaks, beer, and memories. Tank tossed another log onto the flames and leaned back in his chair, a bottle of water in one hand. The silence between them was both comfortable and not. Hatch knew his friend was waiting for him to spill it, but he felt hollowed out, exhausted in body and spirit.

Unable to think about her—Olivia—and how badly he'd handled himself when she made her suggestion.

"It probably doesn't help that I haven't even tried to contact her since…since our disagreement," he said, more or less to the grass between his feet.

"You are correct about that. Women require communication. Even I know that."

More silence.

"I was going to propose. I had a ring and everything." Hatch heard the whine in his voice and knew he was going to pay for it. He braced himself for the Tank-style mocking as punishment.

The other man leaned forward, elbows on his knees, his gaze trained on the fire. "That's pretty serious, man. This woman must be—"

"Amazing? Perfect? Everything I've ever wanted? Yeah. That about sums it up."

Tank took a breath.

Hatch waited for the teasing to commence.

"So, what happened exactly?"

Hatch shot his friend a pointed look. "Seriously?"

Tank grinned. "Yeah. I'm here to help, like I said. I straightened out those kids for you, didn't I?" He ran a hand down his Lakeland University-sweatshirted front. It was one of Hatch's, and hence, way too tight for his huge torso.

Hatch rolled his eyes and leaned back in his seat with a loud sigh. "Damn."

Tank shook his head. "Enough with the whining and sighing. What are you? A teenager? No. You're a grown-ass man, or at least, that's what everybody else thinks. So it's time to own your screw up. Tell Uncle Tank all about it."

"It's complicated."

Tank's chuckle rumbled deep in Hatch's chest, setting him oddly at ease. He gave a half sigh, caught Tank's murderous look, and stopped himself.

"Nothing about you is uncomplicated, Duncan Jerome. Remember, I was there from the beginning. Spill it, Romeo. I'll bet if we brainstorm, we can come up with a way to get her back for you."

"Right. Okay. So...she's doing this documentary on the team and, well, I guess me, mostly."

"That should be a short film," Tank snorted.

"Shut up if you want the story."

Tank mimed zipping his lips together and throwing away the key.

"It wasn't... We weren't supposed to, you know, be... Ah shit. I never should've...I don't know."

"Damn. I hope you're a tad more literate on camera. I think you may have switched bodies with one of your college students."

"I know. It's got me turned inside out. Anyway, we did get, you know, intimate."

Tank had taken a long drink of his water but seemed to choke on it and spewed it toward the fire, causing the flames to splutter. "You are too cute when you use dirty words. So you guys...you know..." He mimed sex with his fingers.

Hatch rolled his eyes. "Yeah. But it's more than that, you know? And I...I wanted her to know how I felt. I was going to propose, but her damn ex-husband—"

"Ah. The ever-popular Daniel Forrest. The guy I looked up for you."

"That guy, yeah. He actually sent me a text running

her down, you know. That was before I headed to her place for dinner, with a ring, ready to…" He groaned.

"You're a hopeless romantic, Duncan. We all know that. But do go on."

Hatch took a long breath, and the whole story tumbled out in a rush. How she seemed uptight, stressed, which set him on edge immediately, thinking she was going to end it or something, based on the fact of their professional relationship. Even though they'd worked their way past that. Then the whacked-out, untenable suggestion she made, which quickly pre-empted his marriage proposal. Followed by his stupid confession about Daniel's text, along with the stupider shit he said about her motivation for making the suggestion that he confess on camera.

He rose and began to pace, anticipating his oldest friend's explosion of support for him, of his disdain for Olivia's nerve, asking him to do such a ridiculous, career-killing thing. Even as he knew damn good and well his reaction to it was, in a word, horrible. When he turned around to see what was taking Tank so long to react, he was shocked to find the man sitting, staring at him, his expression one of "Yeah? And what else?"

Hatch's shoulders slumped. He leaned back against the tall, wooden fence and closed his eyes. "I really screwed this up, didn't I?"

"At the risk of erring on the side of understatement, my friend, yeah. You did. With a vengeance." He whistled low in a "wow, I can't believe it" sort of way. "I mean. Seriously, dude. You're lucky she didn't brain you with a cast iron pan on your way out."

"Right. So, what can I do about it, smart ass?"

Tank boomed out a laugh, got up, walked over to

him, and slapped him so hard on the back he stumbled forward. "Duncan, if I knew the answer to that one, I'd not be two ex-wives into my life as committed bachelor, now would I?"

Hatch glared at him. "Then why in the hell did you demand that I tell you about it? I thought you were going to actually have something helpful to say."

"Proves what a dumbass you are, as if your behavior with what sounds like a pretty damn great woman didn't." But his grin belied his words.

Hatch felt the anger drain out of him, leaving him limp, like a week-old forgotten party balloon.

Tank walked back to his chair and flopped into it. "Damn, I forgot how cold it was here. Ugh."

He shivered and tossed another log onto the fire. Flames shot up into the dark sky, framed by thousands of sparks as the fresh fuel ignited. Hatch wanted to move, to walk, to sit, to drink another beer. But he was frozen, his feet stuck in some kind of emotional bog he figured he'd never escape now.

Because how in the world could he ever convince Olivia that he didn't mean to be such a shit, such an unmitigated jerk. His fingers curled into fists as his brain settled one thing he could and would do. He could pound her smarmy, trouble-making ex into a pulp. Oh hell yes, he could.

He didn't realize he'd made his way to the back door of his house from across the lawn until he felt Tank's hand on his chest. "Hold up there, tough guy. Let's think this thing through first."

"Get your hand off me, or I'll break it." He kept his voice low and as calm as he could manage.

"I have no doubt that you would." Tank patted him

again, then grabbed his biceps and dragged him back to their fire-gazing chairs. "Sit. Good boy." He patted Hatch's hair, turned his chair so it was facing the other one and sat. "While beating Daniel Forrest into a bloody pulp would do the entire world a favor, best I can tell, that's not the answer. You won't prove anything to her by whaling on her ex-husband, no matter how much he deserves it."

Hatch stared at his clenched fists a few more seconds, then released them, slowly, wincing at the effort. "What in the hell are you talking about?"

"I think you should do it. You should let her film you talking about your gambling problem. About how it ruined your life. And how she, Olivia, has brought your life back to you. You know, romance shit. Chicks love that."

"I...can't do that, Tank. It's too... I mean, what if... Oh shit." Hatch dragged fingers through his hair over and over again.

"You can, Hatcher. And you will. Hear me out."

Hatch accepted the fresh beer Tank held out to him, took a long drink, and attempted to accept his new reality. Because he knew, as well as he knew the sight of his own face in the mirror or the feel of Olivia's face under his palm, that his friend was right. He had to do it. It was time.

"I won't...until after the bowl game. I can't let my stupid mistakes screw with my players' opportunity to play on a huge stage, you know?" He dropped the half empty beer to the grass at his feet and put his head in hands. "Oh God, Tank. What have I done?"

Tank put a hand on Hatch's shoulder. "It's not what you've done. It's what you're about to do to make it right. It's time, Hatch. You can't pretend it never happened anymore. Olivia's right. People will find out, and it could ruin all the work you've done with the team this year and what she's done with this docudrama thing about you."

"Documentary," Hatch mumbled.

"Nah. With you, it's always gonna be drama. Do you have anything stronger? I think this calls for a real drink."

"Bourbon's in the cabinet in the dining room."

Tank whooped and headed for the house. "That's what I'm talkin' about."

He looked up when the bottle of Jefferson's Reserve appeared in front of his face. "This bottle cost me two hundred bucks."

Tank waggled at him. "All the more reason to suck from the neck of the damn thing, my man. Go on. You first."

Hatch took it, downed enough to heat him from the inside out, and handed it back. "I'll do it. But on my terms."

Tank took a drink, smacked his lips, and grinned. "Nah. It'll be on her terms and you know it. Now, we have a bigger problem. The one where you figure out a way to get her to acknowledge your existence much less talk to you again."

"We have to finish the documentary. She has to talk to me."

"Dude, there's talk and then there's...*talk*. You know what I mean."

Hatch held out his hand for the bottle. Might as well get drunk. Because once again, Tank was right.

Chapter Seventeen

Olivia put in a call to Drew to touch base and was relieved he was already on his way to the stadium. She took extra care as she dressed, choosing gray slacks and a white sweater with a small red and gray Jaguar's logo on it. Since she was an alum as well as a reporter, she wanted to show her school colors today. She checked herself so many times in the mirror, she had to force herself to walk away from it. Then she dithered about her hair. Ponytail? Leave it down? Held back with a headband?

Jesus, Olivia. Just get ready, already, and get your ass out of here.

At the stadium, she parked in the special lot she'd been given a pass for. Drew's van was parked beside her, but since he wasn't standing there waiting for her, she assumed he was already on the field. She could hear the noise coming from the stadium, the shouts of multiple voices, the hubbub of a game day crowd.

She developed a mild case of nerves when she entered the gate for media and special guests, wondering if her credentials were still good, but the security passed her through without hesitation. As she headed for the sidelines, she did her best to quell the nerves jumping in her stomach and swallow back the urge to throw up. Good lord. When was the last time she was this unsettled?

Oh, right. When she'd had her last big confrontation at work with Daniel.

Asshole.

She could hear Lee Ann's voice in her mind. *Don't let him take over your life again.*

She found a place on the sidelines, away from the bench and team personnel, unwilling to make herself a distraction. She spotted Drew on the field filming pre-game warmups. Hatch was watching them, analyzing them as he always did. Next to him was a man she hadn't seen since he was a Jaguars player. No matter the age, though, Theodore "Tank" Pasternak was an unforgettable figure. His nickname was totally appropriate. At six-foot-four, with muscles on his muscles, the man was built like his nickname-sake machine, and easily rolled over players from the opposing team in his heyday. It looked like he'd kept in shape.

Olivia knew from her research that he and Hatch had maintained their close friendship all these years. In fact, from what she culled from stories, he was still Hatch's closest friend. She figured he was here to give him support for this, the final game of the season. Had Hatch told him about the debacle of their relationship...or lack thereof?

It's not all about you—especially not today.

She had to keep telling herself that. Tank had surely shown up for moral support in this crucial capper to the season. He was here to provide moral support for the next chapter of Hatch's coaching story. Maybe...

Maybe I should quit talking to myself and get down to business.

The stadium was filled to capacity, the seats a sea

of red and gray. Jaguar caps and sweatshirts were the order of the day, especially in the student section. The cheerleaders were revving up the crowd, and the excitement was a palpable thing. Olivia just watched, taking it all in, making sure Drew got video of the crowd in all its frenzy.

The team had gotten past the dip in their winning streak. This was the biggest game Lakeview University would play this season, the crowning touch to an incredible comeback. The Avondale game was always the biggest of the year, and Lakeview had lost to them for the past seven matchups. Olivia prayed her temper tantrum hadn't affected Hatch's ability to focus and concentrate so he could coach his team to victory.

Okay, so it wasn't quite a temper tantrum, exactly, but she'd been hurt and lashed out accordingly. Now she could only hope that Hatch was able to partition it off in his mind, put it aside until this game was over. Today, they were playing the Avondale University Lions, their strongest opponent. Rivalry between the two teams was decades old, and the desire for revenge by whoever had lost the most recent competition was like a fiery, living thing. She couldn't be a distraction.

She couldn't stop herself from watching Hatch, either, so she noticed when Tank touched Hatch's shoulder and pointed in her direction. For a moment, she wanted to run back to the parking lot and hide in her car until the game was over, especially as Hatch stared at her for an endless moment. Then he nodded his head and actually smiled. She smiled back, and the tension gripping her eased a bit.

But in another moment, she had no more time to worry about Hatch. Whistles sounded, the teams

247

finished their warmups and jogged through the tunnel into the locker rooms, the coaches with them. Olivia waited breathlessly for the formal start to the afternoon, silently praying that it would be a success for Hatch and the team.

A crackling sound snapped through the public address system and everyone quieted. Cheerleaders stood on the sidelines with hands on hips, holding their pompoms. The pep squad lined up in one end zone and the color guard in the other. Anticipation sizzled in the air.

Then the announcer's voice, deep and resonant, came over the loudspeaker system. "Good afternoon, everyone. Welcome to the final game of the Jaguars regular season and the battle with the Avondale University Lions. Band, take the field."

The whistle from the drum major sounded, three sharp bursts, then he led the marching band from the tunnel, all of them high stepping to the triple beat of the drums. No matter how old she got, Olivia would never stop being affected by this sight. Once on the field, in formation, the band marched from one end to the other, playing the Lakeview fight song.

Next came the teams, Lakeview first, running from the tunnel between the double line of cheerleaders and pep squad, the coaches behind them, fans screaming and clapping. Avondale ran out next, and the teams lined up on the sidelines. This was followed by the presentation of the colors, the playing of the national anthem, and the traditional coin toss. Today well-known alumni represented both teams for the ceremony, and then it was time to play ball.

Lakeview kicked off and the game was on.

Olivia was riveted to the spot. She could tell just by looking at them that the Jaguars were revved up for this. Avondale went three and out on the first possession, then Lakeview got the ball. In six plays, they moved the ball down the field, capped by a twenty-yard pass that the receiver caught and ran into the end zone. The crowd screamed, Olivia along with them.

The rest of the first half was like that. The Lions apparently woke up after the first score, realizing this was a revitalized Jaguars team they were facing, and they needed to get their shit together. Before Olivia could blink, the score was tied, and then it was all-out war on both sides of the ball. The air was filled with the constant sound of screaming fans.

She was torn between seeing the game and keeping her eyes on Hatch in his familiar game stance, bent over, hands on knees as he watched the team. She was relieved to see him completely focused on the action and interested to note Tank staying close to him. Every now and then, Hatch turned to the man. For advice? A pep talk? Whatever it was seemed to be working. Hatch was all in and the Jaguars played harder than she'd seen all season.

The quarterback was right on the money today, completing eighty percent of his passes, and the running backs moved as if they had wings on their feet. The Jaguars defense played tougher than they had all year. At halftime, when the teams jogged off the field, the score was tied at twenty-one all. Olivia thought it interesting that Tank accompanied the Jags to the locker room.

Drew captured the teams running off the field

before walking over to where she stood. "I got some great footage, Liv. Man, this team is really hyped today."

She grinned. "They are looking good."

"Coach Hatcher seems to be at the top of his game, too." He paused. "I don't mean that he hasn't been all season, but today seems…"

"It's okay. I know what you mean." And she gave silent thanks that her meltdown hadn't affected his ability to coach this game.

"Isn't that Tank Pasternak with him?"

Olivia nodded. "I believe so. They've been good friends since their college days. I guess he's here to give Hatch some moral support."

I wonder if Hatch has told him what happened.

"Well, we've got some priceless video here. This team isn't just bowl eligible. After today, I'd say they'd get an invite from one of the top events."

"Fingers crossed," she agreed.

The second half was as tough as the first, both teams playing as if their lives depended on it. The crowd screamed incessantly, urged on by the cheerleaders, and every time the Jaguars scored the band played the school fight song with more and more intensity. Olivia was hoarse from shouting.

With less than a minute to play, the score was tied again. Lakeview, having made the most recent score, kicked off to Avondale. The Lions made two first downs, and the tension was so thick in the air she could practically touch it.

Thirty seconds to go.

Lakeview called a time out, and Hatch huddled with his team. When they took the field again, Olivia found herself mouthing silent prayers. Overtime was always chancy and well-avoided.

The Lions quarterback dropped back and threw a pass similar to the ones he'd been succeeding with all day. Olivia held her breath as the receiver reached up to grab the ball. But at the last second the Jaguars defender leaped in front of him, grabbed the ball out of the air, and headed downfield to the end zone. It looked like a free for all on the field as the Jaguars offense went into defense mode to protect the runner. A Jaguars player ran backward toward the end zone, motioning with his hand to the runner who poured it on in the last ten yards.

When the ball-carrier crossed the line at the final second, scoring a touchdown that won the close game, the crowd went nuts. They screamed and yelled and hugged each other. The band played the fight song three times while the teams lined up for Lakeview to kick the extra point.

The moment the ball sailed over the crossbar of the goal posts, insanity erupted. The players on the sidelines dumped the traditional bucket of Gatorade on Hatch while those on the field were jumping up and down and racing around like kids. The fans were yelling the words to the fight song and pounding each other on their backs.

Hatch looked like Santa Claus had just arrived. His coaches all hugged him, people clapped him on the back and cameras began flashing. After the traditional handshake with the opposing coach, he was surrounded by media, everyone clamoring for a statement from him. Olivia knew they'd all be jamming the room where the after-game media conference was held, and she debated whether she should go or not.

"You can't bug out now," Drew said, as if he read her mind. "I need audio from the presser to go with the absolutely outstanding video I got. Holy shit, Liv. You couldn't script an ending better than this."

She managed a smile. "Of course we'll go. I'll bet we get some good quotes."

The room they were directed to was usually big enough to hold whatever media hung around, but today people were jammed in body to body. Olivia had her small recorder on so she could pluck what she needed from it later while Drew videotaped the entire proceeding.

"We'll be spending a lot of time in the editing room," he reminded her as it was wrapping up.

"Works for me."

After taking a few questions, Hatch said he needed to get to his team but promised to come back for a longer press conference in a few minutes. As people were leaving the room. Olivia had stood at the back, trying to be unobtrusive and ease out the door unnoticed. She'd almost made it when a hand grasped her arm and gave it a gentle tug.

"Running out on me?" a deep, familiar voice asked.

She turned and smiled at Hatch, glad to see the excited grin on his face.

"Just giving you space after all this. You'll be a long time coming down off this high."

He nodded. "We're all enjoying it." He paused. "I'm glad you came today. I was afraid you might not."

She wet her lips. "Listen, Hatch. I—"

He touched two fingertips to her mouth. "I've been

doing a lot of thinking." He chuckled. "Rather, Tank's been doing it for me. When this settles down, we need to have a talk. And not a bad one," he added hastily. "I'm sorry I freaked out on you the other night."

"You had every right to," she told him. "I should have presented it better, sounded you out about it first."

"Next Sunday is the bowl invitation show. We'll be watching it in the room in the football center where we usually watch game films." He paused. "I'd love it if you'd join us...and bring Drew to get some video footage."

She was stunned. "Really? You want me there?"

He nodded. "Of course I do."

"Well, then, yes. Thank you."

"I'll add your names to the guest list." He ran a tentative fingertip down her cheek. "But first, how about a more...private meeting?"

Anticipation wiggled through her like an electric thread. She glanced behind him. "Better get back there, Coach. The media awaits you and your players." She kissed her fingertips and pressed them to his lips quickly, then gave him a little shove. "Go. Be the star. You earned it. I'll find you afterward, don't worry."

Chapter Eighteen

Hatch had celebrated his fair share of victories in his career, but this was one he knew he'd never forget. After coming into this job with a team full of morale-depleted players expecting less than nothing from some half-baked coach eager to get a mid-major D1 job, he'd never expected to eke out a winning record, much less the level of success they'd achieved. On one hand, he understood it for a sort of over-achievement typical of once-proud programs like this one. On the other, well, he was by god happy to take some credit.

As he looked around the room, watched his coaches grinning from ear-to-ear and slapping each other on the back, he was filled with the sort of happiness he hadn't felt in in his entire, over-achieving life. The reporters clamored for his attention, shoving phones, mics, cameras straight into his face. But for a change, he didn't begrudge a minute of it. Not one minute.

His team had overachieved, to be sure, and they'd done a great job answering questions afterward. But he was ready to call this whole thing. His brief, encouraging encounter with Olivia had lifted his mood even higher if that were possible. He saw his way clear now for the big gesture that had sprung fully formed into his brain that he'd put in play tomorrow once they got their bowl game notification.

And he was already anticipating a reunion with her tonight, which made him eager to cut the rest of the after presser short, even though he knew he couldn't do that.

He grinned and pointed to a familiar face in the middle of the crowd, calling on the reporter. "Jeff?"

The guy grinned back at him. After a solid fifty minutes of questions, most of them about where he thought they might land in the bowl picture, he held up both hands and met the one set of eyes in the room he wanted to see. Their emerald green energy sent a jolt of lust from the base of his spine to his brain. They also did something else that gave him almost as much joy. Seeing her standing there, smiling at him gave him resolve. He would make this work—the bowl game, the relationship, all of it.

After acknowledging a few remaining shouts of "Hey, Coach!" and "Wait, one more question, Coach!" he stepped away from the podium. He hugged each of the players he'd chosen to participate in the presser, then all his assistants one more time before he caught Olivia's gaze again. He smiled, already anticipating their reunion later.

She smiled, mouthing "Good job, Coach."

He shoved his hand in his pocket, fingers curling around the small ring box he'd kept on him all during the game. He was determined to do this the right way now. And he was ready to seriously consider her suggestion about coming clean on tape. Anything she damn well wanted. Because he loved her and he was prepared to shout that fact to anyone within a ten mile radius.

He turned the corner and ran straight into some guy

in a dark suit, plowing into the stranger so hard they both jumped back with loud yelps of pain.

"What the hell?" Hatch put a hand to nose, which had collided with the other guy's chin or maybe cheekbone. Something hard that hurt.

The other man glared at him, hand to his face. He was taller than Hatch. A full six-foot-six if he were an inch, with jet black hair, small, close-set dark eyes, and a sharp nose. Without even thinking about it, Hatch said, "What the hell are you doing here, Forrest?"

The guy squared his shoulders, shot his cuffs, and furrowed his brow. Hatch tried not to mirror him, knowing these for bullshit alpha male posturing. He was superior to this asshole in every possible way and he knew it. He had nothing to prove to Forrest whatsoever. But that didn't answer the basic question.

"How did you get back here?"

"I guess you haven't heard." Daniel Forrest leaned on his title, as if dissing it. "I do run the biggest regional sports network. Getting passes is pretty easy for me."

Hatch refused to rise to the bait, just waited until the man finished his thought, proud of himself for his extreme self-control. The sound of Forrest's voice—bossy, a tad nasally, and completely annoying—lit a match to the rage that began smoldering ever since he'd seen that terrible text message. But he sucked in a breath, not willing to give away just how pissed off he was.

Yet.

"I see." Hatch crossed his arms and tamped down the increasingly urgent need to plant his fist in the guy's stupid, smirking face. "So. Here you are. What can I do for you? I'm kind of busy right now."

"I can imagine. Congratulations on the win. Impressive for a first season and a team full of second-string players."

Guy sure knew how to get his digs in. Hatch made himself smile. "Thanks. But as I said, I'm pretty busy. If you need information, you can contact the team's press—"

"I don't need information. I'm here to warn you about something." Daniel Forrest took a step toward him, looking almost comically villainous.

Hatch didn't move. He half expected the man to twirl a non-existent mustache and give an evil chuckle. "Oh?"

The crowd began to roil around them as the press room emptied out. Hatch didn't break eye contact with Olivia's ex-husband as he accepted slaps on the back, punches to the shoulder, hollered congrats. It was a surreal moment. He'd reached the pinnacle of his career today. This win, with these gutsy young men would always be more fulfilling than any pro win for him. He curled his fingers around the ring box in his pocket. He was about to invite Olivia into his life for good. He was on top of his personal mountaintop. Nothing this hopped up little Napoleon—okay, really tall guy with a Napoleon complex—might say to him would change anything.

"You should know that Bert Hoekstra is about to break something wide open about you." Forrest had the balls to poke him in the chest with this long, thin finger.

Hatch clenched his jaw and pushed the guy's hand out of his personal space bubble, keeping his calm at least on the surface. "I have nothing to hide," he declared, realizing this for a falsehood, at least right now. His anger had flared from a hot bed of coals to a solid flame and was licking at his brain, urging him forward, to act, to shove this guy into a wall, and get on with his day.

"I've seen his report. And I'd beg to differ with you." The other man's nostrils flared. Hatch had to close his eyes for a few seconds to collect himself. "You're going to regret taking my—"

A flash of denim and cream colored sweater passed between them. "Taking? Taking? Really, Daniel, you think Hatch took something from you? You truly are delusional."

Hatch's eyes flew open, panic hitting his brain like a sledgehammer. Olivia stood in front of Forrest in her dark, skintight jeans and Lakeview sweater with a look in her eyes that Hatch honestly believed Daniel should recoil from. He moved closer to her, to create what might pass for a united front. The sensation of her shoulder touching his provided him with a bit of calm in an otherwise grade five hurricane swirling through his brain and guts.

Forrest sneered. There wasn't a better word for the expression on his face. Hatch tensed, prepared to launch himself at the guy, unwilling to hold back another minute. Olivia put a hand on his arm. He sensed the "stand down" message in her touch, as if she'd come right out and said it to him. He blew out a long breath.

"Daniel, I don't know why you're here or what your motive is for spreading lies and innuendo on a day like this, but you can take it all right out that door. No one here has any use for it or for you." She pointed over his shoulder at the nearest exit.

The look Daniel Forrest shot her was so full of raw hatred, Hatch tensed again.

"Go, Forrest. Before I decide to show you the door myself," he said.

Before he could take half a breath, Daniel reached out, grabbed Olivia's arm, and was dragging her to him. To her credit, she didn't make a peep. The crowd around them was so loud no one would've heard her anyway. The next few seconds were the sort of bizarre slow motion one sees at the pivotal moment of a bad thriller movie.

Hatch moved, but not fast enough.

Daniel shoved Olivia against the wall, his hand to her throat, his thin lips so close to hers Hatch thought the man might kiss her. Spit flew from Daniel's lips as he spoke right into her stoic face. She flinched when he pressed his tall, lean body against hers.

The surreal nature of the whole scene increased by a thousand-fold when the dude had the unmitigated gall to put his disgusting lips on hers. But before Hatch could grab him, Daniel yelled in pain, cutting through the cacophony of existing press people. He stumbled back, hand to his mouth, almost making Hatch fall backward with him.

As Hatch righted himself, Daniel lowered his hand from his face. His lips were covered in blood. Hatch glanced at Olivia, confused, still half-addled with rage and a need to protect her from the shithead cursing his head off from the other side of the hallway. She wiped her lips, and her fingers came away with blood on them.

"Liv?" He reached for her. She moved away from him, tears standing in her eyes. "What did he say to you?"

She shook her head and backed away further, holding one hand in front of her, as if to ward him off. A surge of pride, followed quickly by a tidal wave of protectiveness, washed over him, almost smothering the flames of rage.

"You fucking bitch!" Daniel's shrill voice caused everyone around them to drop almost completely into silence. "You and this washed-up, has-been are going to regret this. I promise you that. Remember what I said, Olivia," he added, as he kept his distance from them both. "I have the power to ruin you, both of you. And you just guaranteed that I will. I don't care how many stupid low-level football games this team wins." He swiped the back of his hand across his mouth, leaving a smear of blood on his cheek

Hatch stared, as if hypnotized by it, as the man kept backing away from them.

"Go, Daniel." Olivia bit off each word. "Leave me alone. I don't love you. I never loved you. But that didn't matter. You loved yourself enough for both of us."

Daniel's sneer returned. "You're a fat, useless, wanna-be, Olivia. The only reason you ever had any play was because of me. Because of what I was. Never forget that."

Hatch clenched his fists and took the five or so feet between them in two long strides.

"You know what time it is, Forrest? It's time for you to shut the fuck up." His fist landed true, hitting Daniel Forrest's nose at the perfect angle, providing him with a satisfying crunch. He smiled even as he pulled back and landed another almost as satisfying upper cut to the asshole's jaw.

He wasn't a hundred percent sure how many times he hit the guy before Tank and George had him pinned against the wall.

"Hatch," his old friend said as he strained against them and almost escaped, eager to pound that useless waste of space into a bloody pulp. "Chill, my brother."

"Let me go, god damn you," he spat at Tank's face. "I'm gonna fucking kill that—"

"Hatch," George whisper-yelled. "Cameras." He jerked his chin to the left where there were, indeed, at least four TV cameras and half a dozen smart phones pointed at their little milieu.

A couple of his trainers stood over Daniel who was lying flat on his back, making moaning noises.

"Jerome, you need to stand down. If for no other reason than your team is watching," Tank said with a calm firmness Hatch hadn't heard from him in, well, ever. He pointed a thumb over his shoulder.

Hatch leaned to the left so he could see past the massive wall of human that his friend had created between him and the rest of the hallway. The team captains were there, in their Hatch-required post-game coats, dress shirts, and ties, gathered at the far end of the hall. He sucked in a breath at the sight of them, their mouths all hanging open in almost the exact same expression of shock.

Then he saw Scott Durbin step in and take charge, talking to the reporters, handling the scene. Hatch swallowed hard and moved back so Tank was blocking him again. Remorse rushed in behind the adrenaline, making him shaky and weak in the knees. He looked down at his right hand. The knuckles were almost unrecognizable. His hearing had gone all wonky. His vision was tunneling. He shook his head and tried to get a full breath.

"Hatch? You all right?"

He held up a hand as he leaned over and attempted not to throw up his guts in front his players. Tank led George and the other coaches away from him, making reassuring noises. "I've got this."

Never more grateful for his friend's take-charge attitude, Hatch rose slowly, forcing the dizziness to subside. Olivia. He had to see Olivia. Right fucking now.

He looked around, seeking her familiar form and face.

"Where is she," he asked Tank as his friend led him down the hall. "Where the hell is Olivia?"

"I don't know, man. Right now, we need to get you away from the cameras, *capice*?"

"No, damn it. Where is she? I need to see if she's all right." He pushed past Tank and tried to make his way back to the main hall. "I need to know what that asshole said to her."

Tank took his arm and turned him, pushing him away from the main space where the cameras were running.

"No, Jerome. What you need to do now is to calm the fuck down and do so in private. You dig me?" He shoved Hatch into a side conference room and pushed him into a chair. "What did I tell you about Daniel Forrest? Huh? Didn't I say that while beating him into a pulp would do the world a favor, it was ill-advised? Didn't I?"

Hatch turned his head away from Tank's badgering. "Leave me alone."

Tank snorted and didn't budge. "You wish," he said, handing Hatch a bottle of water.

"Find Olivia for me? Please? Make sure she's all right?"

"Man, if I didn't know she were already spoken for, I'd scoop her up and carry her off. Did you see? She took a hunk out of that shithead's tongue." He slapped Hatch on the shoulder. "His tongue. What a woman."

Hatch glared up at him. "Back off."

"Don't worry. I don't poach. You know that."

"Is she all right?"

Hatch sat across from him and downed half a bottle of water before answering. "She bolted. I tried to follow her, but she told me to help you. To get your sorry ass out from in front of the prying eyes of our buddies, 'the media,'" he said, hooking his fingers around the words.

"Yeah." Hatch stared at his water, suddenly exhausted in a way he'd never experienced, and he was fairly experienced when it came to exhaustion. "Jesus," he muttered before putting his head on his arms on the table in front of him.

Tank patted his shoulder. "Yeah, might call on that guy right now. I don't know how this is gonna play out for you. Regardless of how much that twat-waffle deserved the beating you gave him."

Hatch jerked his head up. "Did I... Is he...okay?"

Tank shrugged. "He's gonna be sore for a while. That much is for certain. Not bad for a lame-ass QB." He held up his water bottle. "Cheers to you, my friend."

"Kiss my ass," Hatch muttered, realizing that he'd dug himself yet another hole. One that his winning season and guaranteed bowl game might not be able to overcome. "Oh…shit."

"Yeah. That about sums it up."

Tank sat with him for the next half hour while Scott managed the situation and put the best spin on it. They waited until the entire building had cleared out before they headed out into the cold night air.

"I need a drink," Hatch said.

Tank glanced at him. "Let's get you home. The last thing you need right now is more bad PR."

Hatch waved a hand at him. He no longer cared. All he wanted to know was that Olivia was okay. And what Daniel had said to her those few seconds before she bit off a hunk of his tongue as Tank had claimed. But no matter how many times he texted or called her, he got no response.

"Fine," he said. "Here are my keys. Take me home." He tossed them. Tank caught them in mid-air. "And order a pizza. I haven't eaten since breakfast."

He pressed his aching forehead against the cool glass of the passenger's side window and wondered if anything would ever matter as much as today had. When he realized that Tank hadn't driven him to his house but they were parked in front of Olivia's townhouse instead, he grinned at his friend, waiting him out.

"Go on, lover boy. Do your romance thing. Your lady awaits you."

"Thanks. For everything, Tank."

"You're welcome. But you're gonna want to clean up that hand first." He pointed to Hatch's bloody knuckles.

"Yeah, right." He frowned. "Are you sure she's…"

Tank waved a hand. "You'd better get used to her

trusting me to get you where you need to be, Duncan, my friend. We worked it out. She's expecting you. So beat it, already." He revved the engine.

"All right, I'm going." Hatch jumped down to the street, reached into his pocket again, and put the ring back into the passenger's seat. "Saving this for later."

"Whatever," Tank said, rolling his eyes. "Begone. Make up. Make out. See you later."

Chapter Nineteen

I never thought we'd get back to this place, but damn, I'm glad we did.

Their reconciliation had been everything she could have hoped for. When she opened her door after all that chaos with Daniel, to see Hatch standing there, her heart nearly stopped beating. She tried to read the expression on his face, but he gave nothing away. Until he cupped her cheeks in his hands and brushed the skin with his thumbs. "I want it all. With you."

Tears welled in her eyes, and she threw her arms around him. "I do, too. With you. I'm so sorry that—"

He skated a kiss over her lips. "Not your fault. I made a bad mistake in my life, took too long to try and correct it, and then got scared because I saw my life falling apart again."

"Oh, Hatch." She took a step back. "Come in, Please. Right now. I don't need the neighbors watching while I get naked with you."

She captured his hand and led him inside, closing the door and locking it. Locking out the world.

"I want you, Liv." He pulled her against his body, the hard swollen length of his cock pressing against her.

She melted into him. "I want you, too."

"Are we good now?"

"We're good. Very good."

"Then let's get even better." He led her into her

bedroom, and they made love. After he cleaned up his hand, they'd taken showers, grabbed something to eat, and made love again.

She still relived every single one of those incredible moments, smiling every time.

The furor over his *episode* with Daniel had died as quickly as it blew up. Having a reputation as an asshole didn't make people want to take up for him.

She was sure she'd never forget her conversation with Tank when he spilled everything on her about Hatch. Or how damn happy she'd been when he'd shown up at her place, willing to do whatever it took to get past all the BS between them. He hadn't been the only one at fault. Thank the good lord he wanted them to get past it as much as she did.

And the big news? After a hard look at the pros and cons, he'd agreed to do this television bit about gambling and its effect on his life.

"I'll include it in the documentary," she told him, "but the station manager thinks doing it as a stand-alone piece and releasing it first will have greater impact. Plus, we want to get out in front of anything Bert and Daniel might do."

So now here they were, getting ready to tape. The station was going to air it during the sports news tonight, with an announcement about the upcoming documentary. She brushed an imaginary piece of lint from Hatch's Lakeview University jacket and tried to pretend her fingers weren't shaking. She was sure she was as nervous as Hatch was.

"Are you sure you're okay with doing this?" she asked. "I mean, this specific way? We could have—"

Hatch shook his head. "I met with the university

president, the chairman of the board of trustees, and the athletic director, just as we discussed. And remember, most of them knew this when they hired me." He blew out a sigh. "Thank god for those people. They looked at what I've done since my divorce and what I've done with this football team. I answered all their questions. They were relieved that the gambling never included betting on any football games." A wry laugh escaped his mouth. "Believe me, it was a very intense meeting. Almost as intense as when I spoke to the players."

They had discussed this and decided it would be better for the team to know about everything in advance. He owed it to them to tell them first. Hatch said it had gone better than he could have expected.

"And I know you handled yourself with dignity." She smiled. "I just want you to know how proud of you I am. There aren't a lot of men who'd do this, publicly, and take the heat."

"Yeah, right." He snorted. "The way I blew up when you first asked about this? It nearly finished us, and what a tragedy that would have been."

"Yes," she agreed. "But we would have found our way back to each other. I believe that."

"Yeah. Me, too. I'm just glad it didn't take very long."

"Now, if we can just make sure Daniel doesn't sue our asses for what happened after the game…"

"Oh, yeah. Forgot to tell you something." Hatch grinned. "Alison Opdycke, the trustees chairman, has had her own run-ins with your ex. I thought I ought to mention it in case he follows through with his threats to sue us and files charges of assault."

Olivia caught her bottom lip between her teeth.

God. That's just what they needed, right now, when things were going their way. "I'm thinking I ought to consult an attorney—"

Hatch held up his hand. "Forget it. It's taken care of."

She lifted an eyebrow. "How? Who— What—"

"Apparently, Alison Opdycke is also a woman with the money and resources to make anything go away."

Olivia let out a slow breath. "I hope so."

God, that would be so wonderful. She still had to pinch herself that at their age, she and Hatch, both battling demons, had been given a second chance, an opportunity to put their individual pasts behind them and build a new life together.

"Trust me. When she says it's handled, it's handled."

"Guys?" Drew called out from behind his camera. "I'm ready when you are."

"All set?" Olivia asked Hatch.

He nodded. "Good to go."

"As soon as Drew finishes taping, he's racing the video to the station for the six o'clock news. The general manager worked it out with the network so it will go out nationally. Be prepared to be bombarded when this gets out, especially since they are teasing the documentary."

"But you'll be there with me? To help me? Make sure I don't lose it?"

"Every minute," she promised.

"Then let's do it."

Drew counted down, then pointed to him to begin.

"I'm Coach Duncan Hatcher, head football coach at Lakeview University. A lot of you know me from my days at Lakeview as a player, then in the pros, and finally my recent stint as a college coach. There have been many questions about how I ended up at Lakeview, my alma mater, and why. As we end a spectacular season, of which I am extremely proud, and prepare for a bowl invitation, I want to share something with you. It has to do with addiction.

"There's no such thing as a little bit of addiction, no matter what kind. When you are addicted to something, it controls every aspect of your life and you look for ways to feed it. For me, it was gambling. The first time I won big at the poker table, I was hooked."

He went on to describe in honest detail his struggle with the addiction, how it ruined his marriage, and how he had to walk away from a job he adored. He thanked Lakeview for giving him this opportunity, even when they knew all the details, and for their support. He talked about how he still battled his addiction daily, but how he now had someone who truly understood his problem and helped him every day, just by her presence.

When he broke eye contact with the camera to smile at Olivia, she smiled back. She would always stand by him. They had stripped their relationship down to the honest bare bones and were rebuilding from that. For the first time in her life, she knew what real love was, and she would fight for it every single day.

"So that's the deal." Hatch looked directly into the camera. "The Jaguars have come a long way this year, and so have I. We're all looking forward to the Bowl Selection Show. Whatever invitation we get, I'm hoping the team and I can count on your support."

He looked at the camera for a ten second count

before Drew signaled they were done. Olivia couldn't help herself. She hurried over and give him a big hug.

"You were great," she told him. "I can't wait for the world to see it."

"Let's hope they don't throw rotten tomatoes at me." Ignoring Drew, he pulled her down onto his lap. "But as long as I have you, I can get through it."

"I'm not going anywhere, Coach." She looked at her watch. "Except down to the station to make sure this gets aired on schedule. You know, we could have waited to do this until after the Bowl Selection Show."

He shook his head. "This is the right time to do it. Can you still get back here in time for the selection party?"

"I wouldn't miss it," she assured hm. "Let me get going right now, and I'll see you back here before seven o'clock."

He pulled her close for a quick kiss before letting her go.

Butterflies were doing a jig in her stomach as she drove to the station. The general manager as well as the sports director were in the studio as the tape aired so they could monitor audience response. It went even better than they could have hoped. The phone lines lit up before the piece was even halfway through, and the social media platforms exploded. The response was overwhelmingly positive and included encouragement from people who battled their own demons. They applauded his honesty. In the manager's office, it was all smiles and high fives.

"You've got a winner, Olivia," Don Chesterfield, the head producer, told her. "No doubt about it. And the timing is great."

Andy Rienke, the sports director, nodded. "The team will know tonight which bowl they're going to. I'd love to get a short piece with Hatch, congratulating him on both the team's success and his personal victory."

"I'm sure he'll do it," Olivia told them. "I'll set it up."

"How close are you to finishing the documentary?" Chesterfield asked.

"I'd say after getting video of tonight's event, we're pretty close. I have the narrator all lined up, and with just a few script revisions, he's all set to go. So, um, maybe after the bowl game?"

"Excellent. I was going to surprise you with this, but Andy's itching for you to get the news. We won't be running it first on the station. It's going national right away."

Olivia was sure her jaw dropped to the floor. "Really?"

Andy chuckled. "Yes, indeed. And you've earned it. I sneaked a peek at some of Drew's video and you've got a real winner. By the way, I know you're aware that Hoekstra has been sniffing around looking for dirt to throw on Hatch."

Olivia nodded. "He's been a pain in my rear end."

"Well, forget about him," Don Chesterfield told her. "With all that's happened, we're extremely grateful that Hatch chose us to be the instrument of baring his soul, so Andy and I have been putting out the word that Hoekstra is poison. So far he's been banned by his podcast host, and he's lost over twenty thousand twitter followers."

Olivia blinked back the tears that suddenly formed

in her eyes. "I don't—I'm not sure how to thank you."

"No thanks necessary. Just getting rid of some scum. Anyway, we'll talk tomorrow. Meanwhile, get the hell out of here and go to the bowl selection party."

She grinned. "Yes, sir. On my way."

Olivia could hardly contain herself on the drive to campus. She badly wanted to share the news with Hatch but would save it until the end of the evening. This was his night, and she wouldn't do one thing to take that away from him.

The guard who let her into the building on campus recognized her and smiled.

"Big night," he commented.

"It is indeed. Get ready for a lot of screaming."

She hurried down the hallway to the room where they watched game film. It was jam packed, as she expected, with team members, coaches, and some of the university executives. Hatch stood off to one side of the big screen that hung on the wall. He'd obviously been watching the door, because as soon as she walked in he hurried over to her.

"So glad you made it back." He pulled her into a tight hug, ignoring the wolf whistles from the team.

"Told you I wouldn't miss it."

"Yeah, but I was afraid you'd get caught up in business at the television station."

"Not a chance."

He led her to an empty chair in the front row, between the two team members who'd taken competition for a girl too far. They'd come a long way since then.

"We've been saving this place for you," Josh DeLong said.

"Thanks." She accepted the cold water bottle Hatch brought her and settled into the seat, just as the opening of the Bowl Selection Show appeared on the big screen.

Everyone was quiet as the sportscasters talked about the process and how things had shaken out this year. Olivia thought the group around her controlled themselves very well as they waited through one announcement after another, applauding for the teams selected.

"This next one will please a lot of people," one of the hosts began. "It's a great example of what happens when you never give up and how good things happen to good people with the right motivation and support. The Maritime Bowl in San Francisco has chosen Boulder University, winner of their conference for the fifth year in a row. And facing them will be this year's Cinderella team, the Lakeview Jaguars, and their new coach, the legendary Duncan Hatcher."

Everything else was lost as the room erupted in yells and screams and the players high fived and pounded each other in the back. Then they hugged Hatch and the other coaches, then Hatch again, who was grinning from ear to ear. Scott Durbin, the athletic director, who had been leaning against one wall, came forward to shake hands with all the coaches and to give Hatch a huge bear hug.

"I just have a few words," he said, holding up his hand to achieve some sort of quiet. "On behalf of the university, I just want to say how proud we are of all of you, every single one of you, for the effort you made this year. This team will become a legend in Lakeview sports history. Credit goes to you and your coaches." He turned to Hatch. "And to you, Hatch, I say well done. You created nothing less than a miracle here, resurrecting the team while you created a new beginning for yourself. Both things took a lot of guts and courage, and I want to tell you that Lakeview University is both proud and one hundred percent supportive of you."

Olivia was afraid Hatch would break down in tears, as moved as he was.

"Thanks," he managed.

Scott turned back to the team. "You've seen Olivia Grant here with a videographer all season, shooting video for a documentary she's doing on both the school and Hatch. When it airs we'll have a huge viewing party, because it deserves no less." He raised a fist. "Go Jags!"

"Go Jags," everyone roared back.

Hatch held up his hand for quiet. "I have something I want to say to finish off this evening. It's a bit personal, but I couldn't think of anyone else I'd rather share it with. It involves Olivia Grant, the woman who helped me redeem myself."

Olivia watched him walk toward her, wondering what the hell was happening. When he reached into his pocket to take something out and then got down on one knee, she was sure her heart would stop. The entire room went silent.

"Olivia Grant." He cleared his throat. "You came into my life and brought joy and happiness, even if I was too blind to see it a first. You made me believe in myself again and have the courage to go forward, despite my crappy past choices. Our success is due as much to the support you gave me as it is to our own efforts."

275

He stopped to clear his throat again. Olivia was afraid she'd faint before he finished.

"I can't imagine going forward in my life without you, so I ask you, in front of all these people who've been so much a part of both our lives this season, if you will do me the honor of becoming my wife."

Olivia felt the tears tracking down her cheeks and couldn't seem to stop them. Her heart was so full she was sure she'd stopped breathing, and all she could do was nod.

"Is that a yes?" he prodded.

"Yes!"

"Say yes!" someone yelled.

"Yes, yes, yes."

The team erupted in shouts all around them.

Olivia nodded again, but this time managed to say, "Yes, Duncan Jerome. I'll marry you."

Hatch blew out a sigh of relief and eased the ring onto her finger. There was more clapping and yelling, and she didn't protest when Hatch hauled her out of her chair into his arms and gave her a scorching kiss. For those few moments, the room faded away.

Then they were surrounded by people wanting to congratulate them, players and coaches, and not the least of which was Scott Durbin.

"I wish you both the best of luck. And Hatch? On behalf of Lakeview University let me reiterate that we hope both of you will be around here for a long time."

"I look forward to it," Hatch said, his arm firmly around Olivia's waist.

The next hour was a blur as students and staff crowded around to congratulate them. Finally, Hatch hollered that he had five minutes to remind them of the prep schedule to get them ready for the Maritime Bowl. At last, however, everyone was gone and they were alone.

"Congratulations, Coach." Olivia grinned at him. "You done good."

"We did good. If not for you..." He shrugged. "I'm not sure I would have made it through the season."

"It wasn't always smooth sailing," she reminded him. "As much my fault as yours."

"But that doesn't matter anymore. What matters is how we go forward from here." He looked at her, a serious expression on his face. "I just hope when the documentary airs, things won't change."

"Of course they won't. You set a good example for these kids, Hatch. And it will be a great way to show them how to own up to their mistakes."

"How about going back to my place and doing a little celebrating?" He wiggled his eyebrows at her. "And talk about our wedding."

"Sounds good to me." She nibbled her lip. "But I think we should get past the bowl game before we worry about a wedding. I don't want anything fancy, anyway."

"Me, either. All I really need is you." He pulled her against his chest and lowered his mouth to hers.

The taste of him was just as intoxicating as it had been the first time he kissed her. She let herself fall into the headiness of it, enjoying it even more because she knew this man would now be a part of her life forever.

He broke the kiss and pressed his forehead to hers. "I love you, Olivia."

"Get a room!" Josh and Tony said in unison as they walked by the open door.

"You'd better get an A in that class, DeLong. I'm not kidding," Hatch hollered after them. Tony turned, a huge smile on his face. He dragged his friend close, his arm in a lock around the other player's neck.

"Thanks to this nagging ass—um, guy—sorry ma'am," he said to Olivia who did her best not to burst out laughing. "Anyway, thanks to Josh, I will."

"Good," Hatch said. "Go on, get some rest. You're gonna need it."

He took Olivia's hand, and they said goodbye to the remaining players and staff. Finally, they headed out into the cold night, bundled up, their breath making visible puffs in front of them. She unlocked her car, and he held her door open for her. She put her hand to his face, loving him so much at that moment it hurt, but in a really good way.

"Okay, Coach. This has been quite a day. I say let's go home and put together the game plan for the rest of our lives."

He grinned. "Best game plan yet." He kissed her nose. "Race you to the bedroom?" He raised one eyebrow.

"I'll take that challenge," she said. "Gladly."

He grinned, shut her door once she was settled behind the wheel, then motioned for her to roll the window down.

"This feels like a dream," he said, leaning on her window. "I never in a million years thought I'd find someone like you. I wanted to tell you that."

She smiled, her heart so full she honestly thought it might burst. "Same here, Coach. Now get to your car. We have some private celebrating to do."

Chapter Twenty

Hatch stared at himself in the mirror, adjusted his tie for the millionth time, straightened the small red rose in his lapel, then started the process all over again.

"Lord, you're worse than a woman in there, Jerome. Come on out, and have a drink with us."

He grinned at his reflection but stayed put, seemingly frozen in place. He was so damn nervous he could barely see straight. Having a drink of anything would be a mistake. He'd probably throw up all over the place if he tried to put anything in his stomach.

Get a grip, man. You're a famous football player, rich as hell, successful in a new job, beloved by many, including the woman you're a few minutes from marrying. Why are you nervous?

He shook his head and fiddled with his tie some more. They'd chosen and discarded more wedding venues and reception ideas than he could remember in the past few weeks since Lakeview's decisive bowl victory in California. He was game for whatever, whenever, and would have gladly paid for a wedding as big, obnoxious, and destination as his first one. But that was not Olivia's style. When she'd made her final suggestion, he kissed her, declared her perfect once more, and made a few calls.

And here he was now, about to walk down a newly constructed, temporary aisle between rows and rows of white chairs to take a step he never imagined he would toward a future that, for the first time in years, was one he looked forward to.

His knees started shaking so hard he had to sit. He looked up when a hand landed on his shoulder and a glass of bourbon appeared in front of his face. "I can't."

"You can and you should," Tank insisted. "Come on in, guys." He motioned to the door and his coaching staff, Scott Durbin, and a few other football buddies filled the room around him, all of them clutching glasses like his. "You wouldn't let me throw you the epic bachelor party I wanted—"

"We did that once already, remember? It didn't work out," Hatch insisted, his throat scratchy and his chest tight with emotion.

"Yeah, yeah, whatever. So, in lieu of limos, strip clubs, Cristal, and cigars, we have this." Tank held up his glass. "My gift to you—twenty-year-old overpriced bourbon for all! To Hatch!"

"To Hatch," the men around him repeated.

"But more importantly," Tank continued, "to the woman he was lucky enough to snatch out of thin air and convince to marry him. Because she is fine, my friend, in more ways than one."

"To Olivia," the men hollered.

Hatch held up his glass and took a sip, then another, relieved that he could keep it down and that the expensive brown liquor was actually soothing his frayed nerve endings.

"All right, you assholes, everybody out. Our blushing groom needs a few moments to himself," Tank insisted as he shooed the group through the door.

Hatch watched them go, his head still spinning and

his heart racing. He'd never felt more certain about anything in his life. At the same time, he was worried she'd change her mind, that he'd be a disappointment as a husband, that he'd slip and start gambling again. He leaned forward, elbows on his knees, empty glass gripped in both hands. What if he screwed this up?

He flinched when someone poured him another quarter inch of booze. Figuring it was Tank, he sighed and sipped without looking up.

The man sat next to him, his dark-trousered legs close to Hatch's. "Stop worrying so much."

Hatch almost choked on the sip he'd taken at the sound of the voice. He jumped to his feet and stared at his brother, Jack, dressed in a dark suit with a red rose in his lapel. "What in the hell are you…"

Jack smiled, drained his drink, then set it on the bench where Hatch had been sitting and fretting. "That woman of yours…" Jack let out a low whistle. "She's something else, brother. Not sure you deserve her."

"I…you…she…" Hatch gave up and drained his second pour of bourbon.

Jack held up his glass. "Here's to a family reunion, courtesy of the future Mrs. Hatcher, who called me a week ago and insisted that I come here and stand by you when you married her."

"Insisted, eh?" Hatch leaned back against the sink where he'd been standing earlier.

His brother's eyes were bright with emotion. "I have missed you, Duncan Jerome. So much…I…I don't know how it happened, but we shouldn't let it ever happen again, this whole bullshit estrangement thing."

Hatch blinked, trying to compute everything, on this already stressful day.

Jack cleared his throat and ran his hand around the back of his neck. "Look, I'm not expecting that all our problems are solved just because your super-bossy fiancée finagled this little meeting."

Hatch sensed himself giving way, letting go of old angers and hatreds. What had they last fought about anyway? What in the hell did it matter? He took two steps forward and put his arms around his brother. The man hugged him back, then let go.

"You sure you want to marry this one, Hatch? I mean, I'd take her off your hands, you know—"

"Fat chance, brother. Let's go out there and get me hitched."

"You got it."

The men walked through the door, up a tunnel lined with cheerleaders, and out onto the football field. It was a perfect, early May afternoon, and he was going to marry the love of his damn life on the football field—her idea—with a reception afterward in the alumni suite—their mutual idea.

He took a breath, walked down the aisle with his brother, turned and waited for her—his life, his soul, his future, his Olivia—to emerge from the tunnel. When she did, the pep band broke into the school's fight song—not her idea but he hoped she liked it. And his whole universe brightened.

She giggled and cried her way down the aisle on Tank's arm. When she finally made it to Hatch—they'd invited over three hundred people so the walk down the aisle was a longish one—he grabbed her and kissed her, stopping only when the university's chaplain cleared his throat over the sound of the loud, cheering crowd.

About Desiree Holt

USA Today best-selling and award-winning author Desiree Holt writes everything from romantic suspense and contemporary on a variety of heat levels up to erotic, a genre in which she is the oldest living author. She has been referred to by USA Today as the Nora Roberts of erotic romance and is a winner of the EPIC E-Book Award, the Holt Medallion, and a Romantic Times Reviewers Choice nominee. She has been featured on CBS Sunday Morning and in The Village Voice, The Daily Beast, USA Today, The (London) Daily Mail, The New Delhi Times, and numerous other national and international publications.

~*~

Visit Desiree at
www.desireeholt.com

About Liz Crowe

Liz Crowe is a Kentucky native and graduate of the University of Louisville, living in Central Illinois. She's spent her time as a three-continent expat trailing spouse, mom of three, real estate agent, brewery owner and bar manager, and is currently a social media consultant and humane society development director, in addition to being an award-winning author. With stories set in the not-so-common worlds of breweries, on the soccer pitch, inside fictional television stations, successful real estate offices, and even in exotic locales like Istanbul, Turkey, her books are compelling and told with a fresh voice. The Liz Crowe backlist has something for any reader seeking complex storylines with humor and complete casts of characters that will delight, at times frustrate, and always linger in the imagination long after the book is finished.

~*~

Keep up with Liz at:
www.lizcrowe.com

Also Available
from The Wild Rose Press, Inc.
and major retailers.

Moving Target
Guardian Security Book One
By Desiree Holt

They're trying to kill her, and she doesn't know why...

Kathryn Burke knows only that she has to get far away as fast as she can. In a frantic, cross-country odyssey, she transforms from pliable Kathryn to feisty, determined Kate Griffin, staying one step ahead of the killers on her trail. Then Fate delivers her into the hands of a dark knight with a tortured past. The safety he offers is as tempting as he is.

After having his perfect life ripped apart, recluse Quinn sees protecting Kate as his chance for redemption. He never plans on wanting the guarded beauty, never mind falling for her. Denying the explosive chemistry between them is useless, and as danger closes in, he must fight to expose the killer or risk history repeating itself.